SWEET SINNER

Lorinda Hagen

BELMONT TOWER BOOKS ● NEW YORK CITY

A BELMONT TOWER BOOK

Published by

Tower Publications, Inc.
Two Park Avenue
New York, N.Y. 10016

The characters in this book except for figures of historical fame are fictitious.

SEX and SILVER

In 1863 Julia Bernard, a beautiful and high-priced prostitute from San Francisco, arrived in Virginia City, the western boom town that came into being after the famous Comstock Silver Lode was discovered in 1859. She wanted to make a name for herself in Virginia City. But Jug Baily, who owned all the ladies of the night in town, wanted to own Julia, too.

"I take care of my girls," Baily told her. "A girl gets hurt, and I make sure that she sees a good doctor."

"I have no intention of getting hurt, Mr. Baily. I have always operated alone, and I intend to keep it that way."

"You're making a mistake, Julia. You know, it'd be a shame to see that pretty face of yours messed up." He moved toward her.

"Stay where you are." She pulled out a derringer from the pocket of her red robe. "Don't take another step."

"Whore! Put down that toy gun." He went for the pistol.

Without blinking, Julia squeezed the trigger, and the bullet put a hole about the size of a silver dollar in his forehead . . .

Also by Lorinda Hagen

Sister of the Queen
Lacey
Letitia
Mistress of Glory
Corrie
Banners of Desire

dedicated to
Barbara and Vida

PART ONE

I

Madame Bienveillance knocked gently before she entered her daughter's room. Juliette looked up from her needlepoint with a smile. "I almost have it finished, Mamá," she said as she held the work up to the light that streamed in from the window. "Do you think Papá will make a frame for it?"

"I am sure he will, *ma chèrie*," answered Madame Bienveillance, "you are an artist with the needle." After she had settled her crinolines around her in the little bedside rocker, Annette Bienveillance folded her hands on her lap and gave her daughter a solemn look. "But I have come to you to speak of something very serious."

Juliette's dark eyes grew wide. "Oh, Mamá, I do hope I have not caused you to be upset with me."

The mother smiled. "No, *ma chèrie*, you have not. A mother and father could not have wished for a more loving daughter. Your Papá has asked me to convey a message. Monsieur Bruyère has asked for your hand in marriage."

"Oh!" Juliette blushed furiously. "I do not know what to say, my Mamá! He...just recently started coming to our church and I hardly know him, although I will admit that he seemed very much a gentleman and ...." The girl lowered her dark lashes, unable to meet her mother's eyes. Her fingers flew nimbly at her work, which she watched with great care as she spoke. "You will have to tell me, Mamá, how I must conduct myself in this matter. As you know, it is my first proposal of marriage." At last, she turned her great, expressive eyes on her mother. "I want to do what is best for me, Mamá." Tears glistened in her eyes, but she blinked them back. "Tall and awkward as I am, I had designed myself to spinsterhood."

"My child, you are only *eighteen*." Mme. Bienveillance's laugh was genuine. "That's hardly an age to worry about becoming a spinster."

"I have often wished that God could have given me a small frame and a pretty face like either Suzanne's or Emilié's, though," Juliette said wistfully. "And you, Mamá you are small and prettily formed."

Mme. Bienveillance took her daughter's hand. "Juliette," she said. "Of all my three daughters, you are by far the most beautiful. And M. Bruyère is not the first man who has asked for your hand. There have been others, but your papá would not affront you by entertaining the idea of an inappropriate marriage. M. Cartier, whose wife has been dead less than a full year, asked for your hand." The mother raised her own small hands and gestured in the typically French way of expressing the impossible. "M. Cartier was far too old to expect a young bride. Why, his children are older than you, chèrie."

Juliette looked at her mother in amazement. "But

M. Cartier is rich, Mamá! By far the richest man in New Orleans!"

Madame rolled her eyes heavenward. "And no doubt of the opinion that his riches entitle him to a jewel among women. He went so far as to offer your papá a great deal of property along the waterfront. Then there was M. le Clerque, who also wanted you for his bride. But again, your papá felt the match was unsuitable. M. Bruyère is of a suitable age and quite handsome as well as comfortably well-off."

"I know, Mamá! I *know!*" Juliette's young heart thudded. She had been quite taken with the handsome Henri Bruyère when she met him, but she'd never, even in her wildest fantasies, dared to think of him as a suitor.

"Your papá wishes me to speak frankly, chèrie," said M. Bienveillance. "We do not want to force a match upon you. In fact, it would please us greatly if you were to remain at home forever. Still, it is a great and beautiful thing to be a wife and a mother, which is a woman's birthright. You must make up your own mind in this matter. If you choose to become the wife of M. Bruyère, you will, indeed have our blessing." She gestured with her hands to show that the matter was Juliette's decision. "If you choose to wait for a better offer, you will also have our blessing."

Modestly, Juliette kept her eyes averted. "You and Papá were promised to each other when you were very young. Yours is a wonderful marriage, Mamá. Perhaps it is better, after all, to let the parents decide."

"It is true that we were promised to one another as children, Juliette, but even if we had not been betrothed, we would have married each other. In America, it is growing more and more the custom for

9

young people to decide for themselves. Your brother André, your sisters Suzanna and Emilié chose their mates, and they are happy with their respective choices. It is our fondest wish that you will be happy, also." Mme. Bienveillance stood to her full five feet and touched her daughter's glossy black hair. "M. Bruyère was told that you will have the final word, but he asked for an answer within a month, for he is here in New Orleans for only a short time and must soon return to Louisville."

Although Juliette nodded her head decorously and maintained a calm expression as long as her mother was in the room, her attitude changed remarkably as soon as Mme. Bienveillance closed the door. Rising to her extraordinary height, she twirled madly across the carpet, unable to contain her delight a second longer. Henri was the one. The very one she worshiped from a distance. And he was tall! A full six feet, and maybe even more. Ever since she was thirteen years old, she'd been embarrassed because of her height. As the years passed and she measured five feet and eight and a half inches, she'd become even more conscious of feeling like a giantess, especially during the past few years when she'd grown so tall that she was at eye-level with her own father and brother. With flaming cheeks and sparkling eyes, Mademoiselle Juliette Bienveillance stopped moving long enough to examine her face in the pier glass, her mother's words about her looks still ringing in her ears. She told herself her mother was no doubt inclined to look at her, the tall, willowy daughter who stood head and shoulders above the other two, with an eye toward partiality. She resembled her father, and her mother loved her father dearly. But she'd always wondered how it happened that her father was such a handsome man while she, with the identical facial structure and coloring, was not at all pretty. It was like living in a fairy tale. The one she had fallen in love with at first sight found her fetching, otherwise he'd not have wanted her for his bride! Marvelling, she looked at her face and wondered why. Thoughts of her petite blonde sisters made her grow apprehensive. Brown eyes were all right, she supposed, and looked good on her father, but they appeared so bright! So dark that they looked almost indecently black, and the whites were such a contrast that they appeared almost pale blue. Lashes—oh, yes, she had her share of lashes. They were thick and long and black, but *straight*. Suzanne's and Emilié's eyelashes were equally thick and long, but they were adorably curly. With every feature, she found fault by comparison. She'd much preferred to have inherited her mother's softly rounded figure instead of her own, which she considered angular and not at all feminine. Her hair was a mass of glossy black curls instead of well-behaved blonde waves falling softly about her face. Eyes too large, nose too small, mouth rather indecently curved and much too wide. Teeth slightly overlapped in front instead of lined up as straight as a string of pearls. She sighed, wondering if M. Bruyère had an ulterior motive in choosing her for his bride over all the other New Orleans belles who were, she was sure, secretly panting for him.

It was a sobering thought. He was new to the parish and did not plan to remain long in town. Juliette had overheard several people talking about his reason for being there in the first place—to settle an estate. But he was already as rich as Croesus. Drove about in a fancy rig with a matched pair of fine, blooded horses, his family crest on the lacquered doors of his carriage. The very finest of

11

clothes, the most exquisite manners. Breeding and looks and . . . Everything!"

Still staring at her reflection, Juliette's mind seethed with possiblities about the handsome stranger. Because she'd felt inferior to her pretty sisters in her appearance, she'd spent a lot of time reading to improve her mind, studying all manner of things like algebra and Latin so she would have something to fall back on if she became an old maid who had to support herself, pursuits her sisters had teased her about without mercy. "Fool," they'd called her. "If nobody asks you to get married, Papá will take care of you."

In spite of her lack of confidence as far as her looks went, Juliette was proud of her intellect. "Fool yourself," she'd retorted. "Papá won't live forever, much as we'd hope for such a thing, and just because he's a rich man today doesn't mean he'll be rich tomorrow." M. Bienveillance was in the shipping business. Her reading had told Juliette that fortunes can be made and lost overnight. Suzanne and Emilié believed it was unladylike to read. They'd made fun of Juliette's interest in higher learning, in politics and history. When she spoke solemnly of the possibility of Civil strife that could plunge the country into a bloody war of brother against brother, and father against son, her sisters laughed at her.

"They would laugh at me now, too, if they knew my fearful thoughts about M. Bruyère," she whispered aloud as she fell facedown across her bed. "They'd say I'm crazy to look a gift horse in the mouth, but I'm scared. Maybe M. Bruyère is after Papá's money. Oh, dear! He could be an imposter. A doer of foul deeds!" She knew nothing about him except that he was a banker.

12

A week later, Juliette worked up enough courage to ask her father about her suitor's family and learned that M. Bienveillance had thoroughly checked into the background, financial resources, and even the personal habits of the man who wanted to marry his daughter. She trusted her father, and on the third week after her mother spoke to her of M. Bruyère's request for her hand in marriage, she told her mother she would be pleased to become his bride.

The weeks that followed were idyllic. The marriage banns were published and five seamstresses worked on her trousseau. It was a time of whirlwind gaiety, with M. Bienveillance reaching ever deeper into his coffers to supply his one remaining unwed daughter with her every whim. He spent his time on the sidelines, content in the knowledge that his wife knew exactly what she was doing and how to do it. Now and then Juliette and M. Bruyère spent a quiet hour together in the Bienveillance parlor. Sometimes they played backgammon, sometimes Juliette played with exquisite accomplishment on the pianaforte which Henri Bruyère enjoyed tremendously. He had a fine baritone voice that blended beautifully with her own contralto, and the loving bridegroom-to-be was lavish with compliments, which served to give Juliette a sense of her own worth that she had never known before in all of her eighteen years.

"Papá," she confided on the eve of her wedding, "he makes me feel lovely!"

"My dearest daughter," answered M. Bienveillance, "you *are* lovely. Henri will be a good husband for you. He appreciates your mind as well as your outward appearance. And he is as proud of your accomplishments as your dear mamá and I. My only regret is the great distance that will separate you and your beloved from home." His eyes crinkled at the edges as he tried to make light of his words. "But there! Your mamá and I will surprise you one of these fine days with a visit to Louisville."

Juliette and her mother exchanged a secret smile. Her mother had already promised to be with her when she gave birth to her first child, but of course she would not speak of such a delicate subject to her father.

The wedding was the talk of New Orleans for many months to come. Juliette's gown was white silk trimmed with Brussels lace and luminous pearls. When she looked at herself in the full length mirror a shy, rather startled awareness of her own beauty was born in her for the very first time. "Oh, Mamá! I look . . . almost *pretty!*"

As she walked down the aisle with her hand on her father's arm, Juliette appeared to float. The vows were said and suddenly, as if she were awakening from a heavenly dream, she understood that she was married to the handsome man who looked down at her with utter adoration. He spoke to her in French, which was his first language as it had been hers, and his words were inaudible to anyone but the radiantly beautiful bride: "My adored one. I will cherish you always. As long as there is breath in me, I will love, you, love you, love you."

Immediately after the wedding reception, the bride and groom began the long journey from New Orleans to Louisville. Their first stop was at a luxurious hotel just a few miles outside of New Orleans, but the exact location was a carefully guarded secret.

They dined in the lavishly decorated, flower-bedecked bridal suite. The girl was apprehensive as she contemplated the consummation of her marriage. Henri was loving and kind. "You are my light and my love. You have made me the happiest man in the world by consenting to be my wife and I feel your fearfulness. We will continue as we have been, my heart, until you've grown accustomed to living with me, until you trust me. Tonight we will sleep in the same bed and I will adore the privilege of holding you in my arms as you sleep. But never, my darling, will I force myself upon you. You will let me know when you trust me enough for us to take the final step."

"You are kindness itself," she answered as a great wave of relief filled her. "I cannot find the words to express how I feel." She wanted to tell him how grateful she was, but she was too shy. But he was true to his word, and it was not until they were wed a full week that she turned to him and wordlessly offered herself to him.

He was gentle. Later, after several years had passed, Juliette would look back on the night she gave herself to her husband in love and realize that he was experienced in the art of making love. By then, she would have grown to appreciate the difference between animal lust and true physical love between a man and a woman. But when she experienced the great surge of delight in giving herself to him and having him give himself to her, she was not worldly enough to know the difference, although she realized she was lucky. She also knew a certain sense of shame when she realized that in the heat of her passion she forgot about ladylike behavior and rose with her husband on the crest of desire until she reached the apex of delight.

Afterward, she buried her head in her hands and cried. Henri misunderstood her tears. "I am so sorry,

15

my little dove," he said as he covered her face with kisses. "I wanted it to be so lovely for you. As wonderful for you as it was for me. I will stay away from you from now on if you find being intimate distasteful."

"Oh, no!" She propped herself up on one elbow so she could look down at him. "I was weeping because I was ashamed of myself. It was heavenly! I expected it to be a duty I must suffer. I cried because I was afraid I would lose your respect. I . . . behaved like such a low-born creature. A harlot! Oh, dear." She looked at him out of shining, misty eyes. "Please tell me you did not find my behavior too wanton! If you leave me, I shall die."

"Oh, my angel of angels!" Henri Bruyère was blessed with a rare gift in his ability to express himself. He explained to Juliette that he felt honored, even humbled, to be fortunate enough to marry a woman who was not only the most beautiful creature on earth but was also capable of experiencing physical love. He was a man of education who had spent many years in the study of human nature. "I deplore the circumstances of a young girl's bringing up that cause her to be afraid of love. Such fear is a most crippling emotion, my dear, and I'm sure many a husband and wife reap nothing but sorrow from marriage because of the misunderstanding about sex. I only hope the time will come when men and women will enter marriage with the knowledge that making love is not sinful. It is right and good, and certainly a God-given gift to humanity."

Little by little, Juliette grew to accept her own passionate nature. As the months passed and she was settled as a matron in the stately home in Louisville, she grew more sure of herself as a person.

16

When she received compliments, she accepted them graciously. Henri obviously adored her. He gave her even greater confidence in herself and her own worth by speaking to her about the banking business in which he was engaged.

"Such a brilliant mind you have, my dear," he would say after he'd asked for her opinion and she had given it in joy. She basked in the glow of his obvious admiration and respect. The letters she wrote to her parents and her sisters reflected her growing status as a woman who loved and was loved:

> I am altogether happy, Mamá. Henri is unbelievably good to me and he values my mind, which I take as a compliment. We will soon be married one year, but to me, it seems like only yesterday that I wavered, sick at heart for fear I would never be able to hold a man so handsome and brilliant.

She went on to speak of certain alterations she was having made on her home, of new draperies she'd purchased for the library, an oriental carpet for the music room, and added that Henri had encouraged her to take harp lessons, that he'd surprised her by bringing one of those delightful instruments home for her birthday. She spoke of attending the opera and, as always, sent her love to her sisters and brother. It was the last letter M. and Mme. Bienveillance were to receive from their daughter in Louisville, but of course Juliette didn't know it when she posted it.

Juliette was in the music room playing the piano when Henri came home unexpectedly in the middle of the afternoon. She arose, a happy smile on her face, but the smile faded when she saw his tragic expression. Holding out her hands to him, she said, "What has happened, my love?"

He embraced her, then led her to the love seat, where he made sure she was seated before he broke the news. "Your sister Suzanne sent a telegram to my office, darling. Your parents have met with a tragic accident."

Juliette shook her head, and the world became topsy-turvy for a second. Through pale lips, she said, "Tell me all of it, please. Do not string it out. I want to know the worst."

He nodded. "I am so sorry, my dearest. They're dead—both of them. An accident when driving in town. The carriage." Taking the telegram out of his pocket, he read it to her. *Mama and Papa died in carriage accident while on way to theater. Funeral Friday.* He rang for a servant and ordered brandy. When the maid came with it, he held it to Juliette's lips, alarmed at her pale face, her frozen appearance. He rubbed her cold hands and tried to warm them, and even though the day was quite warm, he ordered a fire built in the fireplace and moved her close to it, where he held her in his arms and spoke of the necessity of taking the first train out to New Orleans. She moved away from him, got to her feet, and drew a long trembling breath.

"You are right, my dear. We must go immediately to New Orleans. I can be ready in an hour. If we could take the night train—"

They left at five o'clock in the morning and arrived in New Orleans just barely in time for the funeral.

Henri remained with his wife for several days, but the press of his business made it necessary for him to return to Louisville, and she understood, just as he

18

realized it was necessary for her to remain in New Orleans to consult with lawyers and join her sisters and brother in the first steps toward the sad duty of settling their parents' estate.

The will was clear and none of the grown children were inclined toward greediness. As the oldest child and only son, André was named administrator. Still, there were certain personal items that none of the survivers wanted to sell with the house. Family portraits, their mother's Bible, the diary she had kept since she was eight years old, inexpensive jewelry that had sentimental value, and their father's and mother's clothing were only a few of the more unimportant items that had to be sorted through.

The Bienveillance slaves presented the only problem, and it was a real problem. Unfortunately, disposition of the slaves had apparently been overlooked in preparation of the will, for no mention was made of them. Seven were too old to work. M. and Mme. Bienveillance owned the small house where the old, grey-haired slaves lived, and they'd seen to their needs. André suggested that he and the sisters give a substantial sum of money to the seven slaves who had long been retired from their work in the house, but Suzanne said she doubted that the blacks could handle their own finances. Juliette agreed with her sister and said she thought it would be a good idea to put the funds in the hands of an attorney who could dole the money out on a weekly basis. Emilé, whose home was not far from the family estate, offered to go on a weekly basis to the little houses where the old slaves lived and make sure the attorney took care of *all* of their needs, not merely those that he deemed necessary. Once that problem was solved, they discussed the slaves who were there in the house. ⁓

André wanted to give them their freedom. Juliette objected on the grounds that they couldn't obtain gainful employment in New Orleans. Suzanne referred to their parents' wealth and said there was no reason why the slaves couldn't be given their manumission along with funds with which to purchase land. Emilié shook her head.

"No," she said angrily. "I disagree most emphatically. I want Mamá and Papá's slaves kept in the family. We have inherited them, and it is our duty to keep them with us. There are ten, and they must not be set free to go about the countryside to further this dreadful uprising." Emilié grew agitated as she referred to the savage nature of the blacks, and her words were frightening. "I'm willing to bend over backwards to take care of those who have been put out to pasture by our parents. They've been good and never gave Mamá or Papá a bit of trouble. But the household slaves have been getting very uppity lately. Poor Mamá was halfway afraid of Big Jimpson, he was so bold. I'll take that black ape and give him forty lashes with the cat. I'll do it myself, too! It's the only way to put any sense in their heads, take my word for it. They're nothing but animals, and they'll turn on you the minute you take your eyes off of them. I'll take Big Jimpson and three others. That'll leave the remaining six to divide among yourselves anyway you see fit."

Juliette stared at her sister, astounded at her vitriolic words. "But Emilié, we're talking about *people!* Men and women who have worked for Mamá and Papá all their lives and you want to divide them up as if they had no feelings at all."

Emilié stared right back and her next words were even sharper. "It's all very well for you to speak of niggers as people, Juliette. Your letters have made it quite clear that your husband doesn't hold with slavery, and nincompoop that you are, you no doubt go along with his beliefs. While you were lolling around up North in the lap of luxury, terrible things were happening down here in the South. My husband's brother was killed in the raid on Harper's Ferry. The niggers are turning on their masters and killing them as they sleep in their beds at night. No indeed! I'll not be a party to giving Mamá and Papá's household slaves their freedom. Slaves are slaves, and they're certainly not *people*."

"I do not live in the North, Emilié, and you know it," answered Juliette. "Louisville is in Kentucky. I will take three of the household slaves back home with me, but I will not promise you that I will keep them in bondage. My husband pays our household help. M. Bruyère has never owned a slave."

Emilié sprang to her feet and leaped at Juliette with her fingernails curbed into talons. André intervened, and Juliette was relieved at the calm way in which her brother handled the matter. Suzanne would find a place in her household for two of them, André for two more. That would leave two for Juliette to take back to Louisville with her, and André made it quite clear that he wouldn't put up with any more dissension.

"I am sorry your husband's brother lost his life, Emilié," Juliette said. But Emilié turned her face away and would not speak another word. She gathered her *porte-monnaie,* her fan, and her smelling salts and left the library without saying another word.

"Come home with me tonight, Juliette," offered Suzanne. "Our sister is overwrought because she's expecting again, with her youngest less than six months old. She'll be all right tomorrow."

21

Juliette hesitated. She didn't want to offend Suzanne, but she'd never been comfortable in the presence of her husband, not even when he came to the house as Suzanne's suitor. "I'll stay here tonight," she said.

"Alone?" André disapproved.

"I won't be alone," Juliette pointed out. "After all, the house is well staffed. This was our childhood home. There is nothing to be afraid of, I'm sure."

Suzanne hovered and André spoke of all manner of dire things that might upset his baby sister if she spent the night in their parents' home, but Juliette remained adamant, even when André offered to send a message to his wife to tell her he would remain at the home place.

"You're being silly," Juliette protested. She spoke quietly, but with assurance of her determination to remain on the place overnight.

"You've changed," remarked André as he bowed to her decision. "Once you were so timid that you would agree to anything in order to keep the peace. Now you seem almost a different person, little sister." He smiled. "I do believe your marriage has given you a fine sense of your own value, Juliette. Henri has been good for you."

Juliette smiled. "Thank you, André. I take your words as a sincere compliment. And yes...being married to a man who adores me has done much for my self esteem."

André and Suzanne left, and within the hour Juliette retired for the night in the room where she'd slept all her life until she became the bride of Henri Bruyère. She missed him desperately, even though he had left New Orleans less than five days earlier. As she tossed and turned, trying to find a more comfortable position, she made up her mind to go back to Louisville the very next day. Emilié's angry words kept coming back to her. She'd been more upset by the incident than she'd thought. She wanted the comfort of her husband's arms, longed for the warmth of his love, his tenderness. At last, she slept, but awakened early and was unable to go back to sleep. She left the bed, washed in cold water, and dressed hurriedly, intent on sending one of the slaves to the railroad station with a note asking for the time of departures for Memphis.

Big Jimpson was pulling the heavy draperies away from the windows at the front of the house when Juliette went down. From the kitchen drifted the tempting smell of good strong Creole coffee, but before Juliette would allow herself to go in quest of a cup, she asked the house boy to go to the railroad station.

His smile was sympathetic, his words polite. "Indeed, Mistress Juliette, I'll go right now. It isn't pleasant for you to be away from your husband. Mistress Juliette, my heart is heavy with grief. I would like to speak to you of an important matter. I . . . I am feeling a great distress in my heart." He wiped away the tears in his eyes and his voice trembled with emotion as he continued. "I'm sorry, Mistress Juliette. I should have waited until later to ask you, but if a train is due to leave right away, you might not have time to give my plea consideration. Mistress, will you please take me back to Louisville with you? Your papa taught me to read and write and cipher. Your mama taught me how to be a good houseboy and made sure I spoke well, I will work hard for you, Mistress, I swear it. Your parents were the only people I had in this world. As you know, they bought me when I was a little boy. I am lost without them."

"Oh, Jimpson," said Juliette impulsively, "Of course I will take you back to Louisville with me." She wondered if he'd overheard the conversation of the night before and Emilié's vicious threats. Putting a detaining hand on his brown wrist, she looked up at him and smiled. "My husband will have no slaves in his household, Jimpson, but he will give you a home and pay you fair wages in exchange for your work. But Jimpson, we must find a better life for you than that of houseboy. With your intellect and learning, perhaps we could start a little school in Louisville for young Negro children. You could be their teacher. And...there's Vivian. You care for her, do you not?"

The black man thanked her profusely, then hurried away. Out of breath from running all the way from the station, he returned to say the next train was due to leave at three o'clock that afternoon. Juliette moved quickly but efficiently. She sent a polite note to Emilié, in which she stated her regrets for going against her wishes and taking Big Jimpson with her, as well as Vivian and two other slaves. She'd decided to take Tillie and her daughter Effie Lukie as well, to keep them from being separated. Then she dispatched a similar message to Suzanne and André. At precisely two thirty in the afternoon, she paid for four tickets for the black people to Louisville. The slaves were restricted by law to ride in the Colored car. For herself, Juliette reserved a private car, since Henri's last words to her before he left were instructions to do so.

On such short notice, she could only be assured of connections as far as Memphis, but she preferred spending a few hours in the Memphis station to prolonging her stay in New Orleans. She gave Big

Jimpson the four tickets and instructed him about what to do when they reached Memphis. "Sit quietly and wait for me. Jimpson, you're in charge. We might have to wait a few hours before we can make a connection, but we won't worry about it." She gave Jimpson money with which to purchase food from the peddlers who would get on the train at some of the smaller stations, and told him she would telegraph her husband to tell him she was coming and bringing servants.

After she had taken care of her responsibilities, Juliette made her way through the crowded depot to the telegraph office, where she sent her husband a wire:

LEAVING NEW ORLEANS THREE THIRTY THURSDAY, CONNECTIONS TO MEMPHIS. BRINGING FOUR SERVANTS. WILL WIRE ARRIVAL TIME AS SOON AS I FIND OUT. ALL LOVE, YOUR DEVOTED WIFE.

From the telegraph office, she went to the waiting room for white people, her anxious eye upon the big clock on the wall. The train was five minutes late, but she was relieved to see Jimpson helping the black women she had placed in his care on a coach just as she stepped aboard. At five o'clock she made her way to the dining car where she ate sparingly, aware of a great lethargy, due to her troubled sleep of the night before. As soon as she came back to her car, she retired and drifted into sleep almost immediately.

When she awakened, she lay quite still for a moment, listening to the creaking of the train, the monotonous sound of the wheels, and wondered uneasily what had startled her into wakefulness. A dream, perhaps, although she couldn't recall it. For a while, she watched the flicker of lights come and go against the ceiling, and realized the train was nearing a town, which explained the lights. There would be street lamps. Buildings were illuminated with gaslights as the train passed by in the night. She doubted if it was late. Possibly nine or ten o'clock. The greater length of time it took for the wheels to make the clicking sound told her the train was slowing, getting ready to stop. She would look out her window and try to see where she was. Then she smiled at her childishness, telling herself it didn't really matter where she was. It would be a long time before she reached home, so she might as well go back to sleep.

Just as she felt herself begin to drift off again, the train screeched to a stop, and she couldn't resist the temptation to look out the window. She sat up, put her face close to the pane, and peered curiously toward the depot, where dark forms moved about in the night, their shadows long and thin because of the gaslights that blazed from near the building. Although she couldn't be sure, she had a pretty good idea the train had stopped in Jackson. She moved away from the window and prepared to stretch out again when a sound, a motion, something she couldn't identify alerted her to danger. Rigidly, she stared blankly into the darkness, convinced that she was not alone. She had locked the door. She was positive she had. She went back over the time she'd returned from the dining car, step by step, as she tried to reassure herself that it was only her imagination that had brought her to a state of mindless terror. Yes. She *had* locked the door. Shot the bolt.

Holding her breath, she strained her ears for the slightest sound and heard nothing but the thumping of her own heart. But then she heard the unmistakable sound of someone else drawing breath. It was an ominous sound. Dry, with a slight wheeze. As if the breather had a cold and found it difficult to fill his lungs with air. Her voice was shrill when she spoke. "Who's there?"

The alien sound of someone breathing ended abruptly. She fumbled against the pillow where she'd put her reticule, remembering the long hatpin, which would be better than nothing. Then she thought she heard an explosion, but she'd been hit on the head.

II

Big Jimpson waited patiently in the Colored section of the Memphis depot. When Effie Lukie, who was only sixteen and inclined to flightiness, asked him for the hundreth time if he thought Mistress Juliette had forgotten all about them and gone on to Louisville without them, his patience broke. "Damn your black hide, girl, if you ask me that question one more time I'm going to give you a split lip. Miss Juliette is an angel on earth. She wouldn't *do* anything like that."

Vivian, who was more white than black, gave him the evil eye. "Don't you threaten that young wench, Jimp. She's scared and so are you. I can smell it on you. You're musky as any field hand, and there's no sense in you actin' like you're not ever' bit as worried as me and Effie Lukie and Tillie. We been here in this depot so long folks are beginnin' to look at us like they wonder if we intend to *live* here! Now, I'm not sayin' Miss Juliette would forget about us and go on to Louisville by herself, but I'm sayin' *this* to you and you better listen. I'm sayin' she might have took sick and had to get off the train somewhere back there. I'm sayin' me and you and Tillie and Effie Lukie is in a mighty precarious position. Niggers travelin' around on trains as nice as white folks! Niggers takin' up settin' room in the train station. We's *niggers*, Jimpson, ever' last one of us, and if we don't do somethin pretty quick, we goin' to be in a heap of *trouble*. Them *po*-lice has been in here two times already. They goin' to come up to us and ask us questions nex' time, and you better have an answer on your big ole ugly mouth."

Big Jimpson scowled. "One thing I can't stand, woman, is a high female who thinks she knows it all. I'll tell you what I'm going to do. I'm going to go find a policeman and ask some questions of my own. That'll show 'em we're not up to anything we shouldn't be."

Vivian threw back her head and gave him a sullen look. "Well, now, Jimpson, honey," she said sarcastically, "you be sure and talk like white folks. Maybe them *po*-lice will think you're gettin' ready to go to a costume party and you painted your face brown, just to make the other white folks laugh."

"You had an opportunity to learn how to use good English, Vivian. Master and Mistress offered. But you wanted to lay around with the bucks and go down to the voodoo woman's house in your spare time. Now you're mad at me because I applied myself." But Jimpson gave her a sickly smile and added, "Don't you worry, honey. I'll take care of you." Mistress Juliette put me in charge. I'll do what's right." Squaring his shoulders, he left the Colored waiting room and walked among the porters and hurrying patrons while he tried to bolster his drooping spirits. It was the fifth time he'd walked up to the doorway of the waiting room reserved for white people to look for his mistress. When he turned away, his shoulders sagged for a moment, but only for a moment. He had done no wrong, he lectured himself. As a slave, he had no status, no rights. All he could do was carry out orders, which was exactly what he had done. He would not tell the white policeman that he had begged Mistress Juliette to take him back to Louisville with her. No, he would leave that part out. He would say she sent him to the depot in New Orleans to find out when she could get on a train heading for Memphis, that when he came back to the house she told him he, along with Tillie, Effie Lukie and Vivian, were coming with her, and he'd not argued. The tickets she'd purchased for all four of them were reassuring, as he took them out of his pocket and ran his finger up and down the little punched-out places. He'd show the policeman the tickets and the money Mistress Juliette had given him, and ask him kindly to go into the Colored section and speak to the women folks, who would verify his statement. But he was worried in his mind, even as he forced himself to step up to the policeman who stood just inside the big doors that led outside. Hat in hand, he explained his predicament, growing more and more humble as he spoke.

The policeman listened politely. "Five hours? You've been waiting for your mistress for five *hours,* boy?"

"Yessir." Big Jimpson looked at the clock on the wall. "Five hours, sir. The women folks are worried."

"Well, I'd reckon so." The policeman scratched his beard thoughtfully. "You step over here with me, boy."

Big Jimpson stepped. They went to the ticket window where the agent looked at the tickets Jimpson held in his big, sweaty hand and said they were valid, that they were paid all the way to Louisville, but no connection had been made from Memphis. "Train due in about an hour and a half from now, boy," he said to Jimpson. "You can get on it and get to Louisville if that's what you want." To the policeman, the ticket agent said, "No problem here. The tickets are for four niggers, plain as the nose on your face."

At the telegraph office, the officer asked if there was a way to find out if a Mrs. Henri Bruyère had sent a telegram to her husband in Louisville after Jimpson remembered that his mistress told him she was going to. It look almost an hour, but the wait was well worth it to the frightened slave when the officer came sauntering into the Colored waiting room to say everything had checked out. "I'll tell you what I'd do if I was you, boy," he said. "I'd just get on that next train and skedaddle on up to Louisville. I don't know what might have happened to your owner, but you done right by comin' to the Law and speakin' right up. It could be that the lady took sick and had to get off the train. But I sent a telegram to her husband, so he'll be meetin' your train when it pulls into the Louisville station. It's the best I could do for you, boy, and good luck."

With his faith in himself restored, Big Jimpson turned to the women and smiled. "Now, you see? We never had a thing to worry about, just like I told you." But he continued to have a worried mind all the way to Kentucky, and even the warm and friendly handshake of Mr. Bruyère didn't ease it, because he could see that Mr. Bruyère was out of his mind with worry, too.

Over and over, Big Jimpson repeated everything that had taken place after Henri Bruyère left New Orleans, being completely truthful with Mistress Juliette's husband. "When Mistress said she was going to go home, I begged her to take me with her because I was going to go to Mistress Emilié and she was going to whip me, sir. I heard them talking the night before. Mistress Emilié and Mistress Juliette had a falling-out, some way. I didn't get the straight of it, but Mistesss Emilié is powerfully against the folks who want to do away with slavery, and she didn't speak the truth when she said Mistress Bienveillance was afraid of me. I *loved* Mistress Bienveillance, sir. She was good to everyone, and so was Master. Your missus said she would take four of us with her when she came home, sir, and named their names. We packed up, she took us down to the railroad station house, and she bought us these tickets and told us just exactly what to do when we got to Memphis."

The long, heartbreaking search of Henri Bruyère for his beloved wife began.

III

Waves of nausea and dizziness vied with the crashing pain in her head as Juliette strained against the bonds at her wrists. For long periods, she lay immobile, disoriented when awake, and sunk in the throes of a nightmare state of half memory, half dream. Lucidity descended on her for a shattering space of time and she panicked, struggling against the ropes that fettered her. At times she wondered if the blow on her head had blinded her. But now and then she came to herself long enough to sense motion, and wondered if she were on a boat, a ship. When dawn came, she recognized it and knew that she was not, after all, blind. Little by little, she grew stronger, more aware. She was on her back, her arms cruelly tied behind her, her ankles crossed and tied.

Fog and dampness hung about the place where she was confined. Feeling with her fingertips, she recognized the grooves between boards and envisioned ship planking. A rough, stinking blanket covered her, but the cold and damp penetrated it and she shivered uncontrollably. After considerable struggling, she jerked and rolled until she was lying on her side. Darts of needle-like pain in her arms after relieving them of the weight of her body caused her to cry out.

The sun grew brighter, but the fog was so heavy that she could barely make out the outlines of what appeared to be wooden crates, casks, and a coil of thick hempen rope. Nonetheless, she took what comfort she could in the awakening of her senses as she smelled turpentine, heard the shuffle of laggard footsteps somewhere above her, and recognized the slip and lap of waves against what she was now certain was a ship of some kind. With an almost clear mind, she went back over the events that had brought her here. Her memory was startlingly clear, but only for small spaces. First had come her terror at realizing she was not alone. Then the blow that had knocked her senseless. She remembered walking on her own two feet when she was taken off the train. Not walking well, but stumbling along in a dazed condition, arms and hands supporting her, whiskey breath an offense in her nostrils. She'd pitched forward often and almost fallen on her face. There had been voices in the darkness, laughter, and the station sounds. Some people were scurrying about, and she'd tried to cry out for help, but the person who led her along spoke authoritatively to the faces that appeared in the night. "Stand back. Clear the way. The lady has taken sick. I'm a doctor, so she's in good hands. Get away, folks, give the lady air!" And the men whose faces returned to her in memory as concerned and compassionate, faded away. She'd tried so hard to protest. To scream. But she'd been unable to do anything but whine, her head falling forward as she was dragged along a rocky road. The man was not as tall as she, but he was wiry and strong.

Something else took place, but she couldn't recall it for sure, since she was unable to separate reality from dreams. Next came a conveyance into which she was thrown. Her memory was blurred because she had no remembrance of being taken from the conveyance, although the agony of being driven over bumpy roads was clear. Blinking against the blinding rays of the sun as it settled for a moment on her face, she recalled a shadowy scene that came back to her like a segment of a play. She'd been on the floor, probably the same floor where she was at the moment. Two men spoke to one another, their voices subdued, their words unintelligible. After a while, footsteps vibrated hollowly under her head, and the men came closer, which enabled her to hear them clearly.

"She's a tall one, all right, mighty tall for a woman. How'd you take her offa that-there train, Banty, and her that big of a female? I seen you comin' and I marveled at the sight, seein' that you ain't much bigger'n a banty rooster. She drunked up some?" The man's voice was soft, but cruel.

The other one, the one who had hit her on the head and pretended to be a doctor, spoke in loud, slightly nasal tones: "I had to hit her on the head. She knowed I was in there with her, I could tell. Called out, she did, bold as brass, asked who was there. So I never had no choice in the matter. Kind of knocked her for a loop, but she wasn't too hard to handle. Ever'time she'd start to fall, I'd just pull her back up. She throwed up a time or two in the trap, goddam bitch."

"How'd you get her through them crowds, Banty?"

"Told folks I was a doctor." Juliette opened her eyes and saw two shadowy forms, one tall and fat, the other much shorter and thin. The one who had taken her from the train laughed mockingly. "Folks is goddam fools, Clint. Right away, jist as nice as you please, they moved on back when I said she was sick, and I was a doctor."

One of the men had lit a lantern. Even though she'd kept her eyes closed, she was aware of brightness. Either the sun was screened by trees or the boat had shifted slightly, for the place was again murky with shadow. The light was painful as it was brought closer. She could feel the warmth of it on her face and knew she was being looked at closely. The one with the pleasant voice drew in his breath and swore with increasing anger. The lantern was taken away from Juliette's face, and the fat man turned his wrath on the short one. "You scabby son of a whore, this woman ain't no redhead. She's got hair as black as Coaly's ass. You done went and grabbed the wrong woman, Banty, you little bastard!"

Scuffling sounds filled the darkness. The one who was called Banty screamed and swore. Juliette had no trouble identifying his voice, because the nasal quality was much stronger as he begged for mercy. She broke out in a cold sweat as she realized she was overhearing a fight that sounded as if it could end by snuffing out the life of one of the men, and she doubted very much if it would be the short one who survived.

He panted, his voice rising to a shriek as he babbled crazily. "Take a care, for the love of God, man, it was a ordinary mistake. I seen her—the redheaded one. Went to the dinin' car, she did. I waited! Please, Clint! Don't *do* it to me, man! You *know* I cain't swim a stroke!" The sound of feet beating against what Juliette believed to be the side of the boat was loud. "I got into her car when she went to eat. Waited for her! Goddammit, me and you has been *friends*, ain't we?" His voice rose to a harsh bleat as he spoke of the way all the cars had looked alike. Again, the sound of boots scrabbling against wood came to her and in the darkness, a lost, terrified cry cut through the night. The cry was cut off abruptly and as she lay on the hard, wooden floor, Juliette stiffened as she heard a loud splash.

"Rotten bastard." The other one spoke with satisfaction, his breath rasping for a while. Later, she heard footsteps falling against floor boards, and was relieved when they went away, the sound finally tapering off into nothing.

A great thirst consumed her as she looked again into the streak of sunlight against the misty shrouds of fog. The sun was now burning the fog away, enough for her to make out the barrels, the wooden crates, and the coil of rope. When she licked her lips, it was difficult for her to bring her swollen tongue back inside her mouth. She sighed, then sobbed, because of the pain in her head and because she was terrified. There was no doubt in her mind that the man called Clint would kill her. Tears were hot in her eyes as she thought of Henri, whom she would never see again. He would be worried about her, expecting her to send another telegram from Memphis. God alone knew what had become of them, stranded as they no doubt were in the Memphis station! Tears ran down her face as she attempted to make some sense out of the exchange of words between the two men during the scuffle. The one who was called Banty had lain in wait for a red-haired woman, believing he was in her private car when he'd been in

Juliette's. Strange that he'd not noticed his mistake, for her hair was not red. But of course it was very dark, and he'd probably never thought to look closely at her, believing he had the woman he'd come for. Besides, he'd been drinking. With distaste, she removed her thoughts from the dreadful stench of his breath.

Big Jimpson! Jolted again, she wept harder as she considered the fate of the four slaves. She moaned, remorse mingling with regret as she wished she'd not acted so impulsively. If she'd only done what was right—mended the disagreement between herself and Emilié—she would not be facing death at the hands of a desperado who, for reasons unknown to her, had been in cahoots with the drowned Banty to kidnap a red-haired woman from the train. For a moment, she wondered who the red-haired woman was, and why the two men had conspired with another to commit such an awful crime, but her miseries were too great, her fears were too overwhelming for her to concentrate on the unknown.

"My dearest," she cried out as she strained against the ropes at her wrists. "Oh, my beloved! My husband, my Henri." If only he could hear her. If there was some way she could send a message to him. But of course there was not, and he would never know what had happened to her. Her body convulsed as she considered meeting her death by drowning. The big man had to qualms about overpowering the smaller one and throwing him into the water, so it was reasonable for her to believe she'd meet the same fate. Whimpering, she again struggled frantically against her bonds, but to no avail. Exhausted from thrashing about, the pain in her head worsened by her wild motions, she closed her eyes again and prayed for a quick and merciful death.

"You're a looker, all right." The voice was loud and smacked of amusement. "Old Banty done hisself proud, even if he did get the wrong wench, the drunked-up bastard. I reckon you'd be wantin' out of them ropes and a chance to answer the call of nature. A bit of ale and a bite to eat might not go down too hard, either, would it, lassie?"

She was lifted into a sitting position and the man cut the ropes from her wrists and ankles, then helped her to her feet. "Yes, ma'am!" He whistled long and loud. "A real looker! And all decked out in silks and satins, a regular gentlewoman, or I miss my guess." He lifted her hand and she cried out as the blood circulated again in arms and legs after so long a time in bondage. "Jools, too! A rich lady with a weddin' band on her finger and a emerald big enough to knock a man's eyes out. Well, don't just stand there, woman! I'm givin' you a chance to walk, so walk. What the hell! You're teeterin' like you're tipsy!" He grabbed her before she toppled over, unable to feel a thing except the agony of millions of pin-prickles in her feet.

"My legs are numb," she cried. "My feet! I can't feel them."

"My stars, I should of thought of that. My apologies, ma'am." The man chortled as he lifted her skirts and boldly rubbed her legs. "Right shapely gams you've got, and that's a fact, me bein' a fair judge of what's nice in the line of legs. Yessir. As purty a piece as I ever seen in my life, even if you are tall as many a man." He straightened and grinned at her, then placed his big dirty paws under her bosom as if he mentally weighed each breast.

"Please," she begged as her face turned crimson.

39

"No jade, either. Well, well!" He put an arm around her waist and guided her across the deck. "Shy as a little chickadee, that's what you are, a rare jool among women and you'll fetch a fair price even though you be married and no virgin, more is the pity, for then you'd bring twice as much. This way." He led her around a corner where she contemplated a narrow set of steps. Glancing backward over his shoulder, she saw the wide expanse of what she took to be the open sea. "Go on down below, lady. You got your legs back under you steady-like, and you'll be right as rain. Just follow them steps and you'll find my quarters, chamber pot and all, fresh water so you can wash your handsome face, a pitcher of ale close at hand. When you've made yourself all pretty you can come back, and mind, I'll be waitin' for you."

"Thank you," she murmured automatically.

He roared his approval. "Manners and all the finer signs of a lady-like bringin' up. Even says thank you. But don't think I'm so soft I'm lettin' you go free, sweetheart. You get yourself back up those steps as soon as you've done what you got to do, and I won't harm a hair on your pretty head. You try to make a jackass out of ole Clint, and I'll throw you overboard."

Juliette nodded and descended the ladder-like steps.

The little cabin was just large enough to accommodate the narrow bunk, a plain wooden commode with pitcher and the bowl on top and a round table for instruments of navigation. The walls were spartan-plain, the floor was of well-scrubbed planks, but above the commode was a mirror with an ornate silver frame where she gazed without recognition for a moment at the dirty, tear-streaked

40

face that stared back at her. She was grateful for the chamber pot, for the water in the pitcher, which she poured into the china bowl and looked at suspiciously, wondering if it was fit to drink. A smaller pitcher rested inside a wooden frame that was fastened to the top of the instrument table. Before she bathed, she sniffed the ale in the small pitcher, found it pleasant enough, and immediately poured some into the tin cup and drank thirstily. While she lathered to the waist with a square of yellow soap her eyes fell on a straight razor. The monstrous man's statement that he'd tossed off so carelessly about the price she would bring had not fallen on deaf ears. During the year of her marriage to Henri Bruyère she had spent many hours at her favorite pursuit, which was reading. Her husband's extensive library contained books that were far more enlightening than that of her parents, and she'd discussed the fascinating subjects with her husband as well as the more sordid ones. She fully understood the seaman's words when he'd referred to the price she would bring. When a white woman was sold by an abductor, it meant that she would be used as a harlot.

Shuddering, Juliette drew the top half of her clothing up over her body as she looked at the straight razor. Then she turned her hands over so they were palm up, and contemplated the blue veins at her wrists. A quick slash on both wrists, then another at the pulse on her throat, would be quick and almost painless. It was preferable to the loathsome thought of bedding one man after another, of submitting to their lusts, with the hopeless knowledge that another day would bring nothing but more of it. But she wanted to be clean when she died. Tentatively, she picked up the razor,

41

unfolded it, and ran her thumb over the sharp edge, a part of her mind recoiling from the deadly weapon. Her Calvinistic faith had taught her suicide was the unpardonable sin, which meant she would never be delivered from hell. She dropped the razor and jumped at the rattle of sound, wondering if God in all of His infinite mercy would not find death at her own hands more acceptable than becoming a slave to the merchants of flesh.

"What was that noise I just heard?" The thunder of the fat man's voice was a threat.

"Nothing," she cried. "I dropped the soap."

"The hell you did!" His feet pounded down the steps and he was there, big and smelly and outraged as he grabbed the unfolded razor. "I try to be good to you, and you meddle with my razor. I got sharp ears, Miss Lady Hoity-toity. You was thinkin' about cuttin' your pretty throat or my name ain't Clint Babcock. I got a good notion to put you in chains."

"No, please!" She faced him in fear. "I was merely looking for a comb and happened to touch your razor and dropped it! I swear I wasn't planning to—to take my own life, I swear it!" She forced a smile and put one hand to her matted hair. "I have no comb, no brush. Could you—that is, if you have one, I can make myself much more presentable."

He grinned at her and she had to close her eyes for a second at the sight of his teeth, which were encrusted with greenish slime at the roots and gave off a foul odor. "Who for? Who you want to make yourself all prettied up for, anyway? Ain't nobody but me on this here ship."

"For you, of course," she said, amazed at her ability to face up to him and find words she instinctively felt would placate him. But at his next words, fear of drowning again filled her mind. The

42

ship was very small, it was big enough to require a crew. The idea of being on the open seas in a frail craft made her feel faint. She forced herself to smile again, and hoped she had a convincing expression of admiration in her eyes as she fawned on him and said, "You are a man of great courage, Mister Clint, to go to sea in a craft small enough to be manned by only one. But of course you are obviously a man of great intellect."

He belched, then laughed in her face. "You're as crazy as a bedbug. We ain't on no sea. We're on the Mississippi River, headin' down to New Orleans. And don't you try to silky me with fine words, lady. I ain't the brightest bastard in the world, but I ain't no fool. You take care that you don't get too spunky on me, or like I said before, I'll throw you overboard. I'll take them rings you're wearin' and that-there ornament in your hair. That way, if I have to give you the pitch, I'll have made myself a bit of extry draw. Seein' that Banty made off with the wrong woman ain't goin' to do my case much good, so I'll get no money from that quarter. But I ain't goin' to be done out of my expenses, and your jools will just cover them nicely. Anything else I get off of you will be profit."

She nodded, removed her rings, and gave them to him without a word. When he snatched the pearl and diamond ornament from her hair, she didn't wince. He opened a drawer in the commode and gave her a tortoise-shell brush. She removed the pins from her hair and tried to ignore him as she brushed out the tangles.

"You got pretty hair, honey. What's your name, anyway?"

"Julia," she answered on the spur of the moment, because she didn't like the crafty look in his eye. She was thinking of Henri, who would give up all of his wordly goods if he was asked to pay ransom for her. But it would all go for nothing, because men who lived without honor did not keep their word. Henri would reduce himself to a pauper, and she would still be sold into the white-slavery market.

"Julia What?" He snatched the mirror from her and whirled her around to face him. "Damn your high falutin' ass, you answer me decent-like when I ask you a question."

"Bernard," she said levelly. "My maiden name was Veil. My husband was Hercule Bernard. I am a widow."

"Any little Bernards?"

"No. I was married for only a short time when my husband died of smallpox." Tears flooded her eyes and she made no attempt to hide them.

"I reckon you got a mother and a daddy, though." His voice was soft with an unspoken threat, and his eyes shone with greed. "I reckon your ole mother and daddy would pay pretty penny for your safe return."

Her tears flowed harder as she was reminded of her recent sorrow, and in her mind's eye, she saw the two vaults as they had looked on the day of her parents' funeral. "My mama and papa are..." she sobbed, bending her head and wiping her tears with her hands. "I was on my way to their funeral in Memphis," she lied. "They were killed in an accident with the carriage. Oh, please, can't you see that I am grief-stricken?"

"Ain't that too bad. All alone in the world. So I guess you'll just have to use that little old coozey of yours to make eatin' money. Here." He gave her a square of linen. "You got a snotty nose. Wash your face again and I'll take you to the galley. I reckon you know how to cook. My guts is as empty as a poor box in a whore house."

While she was frying salty bacon, Juliette's hopes rose. He'd said he was expected in New Orleans. The man who hired him to steal away the red-haired woman was to meet them there and pay them for the crime of abducting her. She would make a break for it. Her head still hurt when she bent over, but the partial bath and the cup of ale had rivived her. The smell of food made her mouth water, and she looked forward to the strength it would give. Hope was high in her heart as she nibbled a crust of hard tack while she beat up half a dozen eggs for an omelette.

"Not bad atall," said Clint as he eyed the heaping plates. "I had you figured for a rich lady. Pampered and spoiled, and too good to soil dainty fingers at cooking." He sampled the food and nodded, smacking his lips. "Ain't nothin' delicate about the way you eat, either."

"My folks were farmers," she said. Then she asked, "What's a coozey?"

"It's that thing you got between your legs, sweetheart."

"Oh." She'd had an idea that was what he meant, but wasn't sure. "Why did the man who is going to meet you in New Orleans want you to take the woman from the train?"

"You ain't too bright. What's most men want a woman for?"

She swallowed the bacon she'd been chewing. "Why didn't he ask her?"

Clint guffawed and slapped his knee. "She's a married lady. You know, Julia, you ain't so bad, for a woman. Aww, well, hell, you had to have your little cry, but when you seen tears wasn't goin' to get you anyplace, you settled right down and behaved

45

yourself. Me, I'd much rather of had things work out the way they was supposed to. I ain't a bad guy, but I got a livin' to make. Maybe this rich gentleman will take a shine to you, seein' that he didn't get the one he wanted. I'll try to proposition him for you real slick-like. He'll treat you good and he's got plenty of all it takes to make a woman happy."

She shoved aside the plate that contained half of her omelette, and fixed him with a horrified expression. Too late, she realized that she'd allowed him to see her revulsion, and wished she hadn't.

"It'd be better than goin' to work in a joy house. You think on it, girl. You'd have just one man to please, not a whole slew of 'em."

In a low voice, she said, "Of course you're right."

"That's more like it. If you ain't gonna eat that fancy mess of eggs, I'll feel right pleased if you'd hand it over."

"Have it and welcome."

He ate in silence, shoveling in the food as if he were throwing wood into a furnace. When he looked at her again, she shivered, believing he was looking at her with lust. His next words surprised her. "Men, at least some of 'em, are horses' asses. Break their necks over a woman." He stood and she cringed. "What the hell is the matter with you now? I'm not goin' to hurt you." His big laugh boomed again as he put his hand on her shoulder. "Son of a bitch! You think I'm goin' to sample the goods? Not me, lady. I like pretty young boys for my bed."

"You *what?*" She gawped at him in amazement and disbelief. "I'm sure I misunderstood you," she finally said.

"No you never, either. I guess you just never heard tell of a man and a man havin' fun between the bed covers."

46

"Oh, my God!" Her hand went instinctively to her throat, where she wore a slender chain with a small golden cross. He reached out his fat hand.

"Gimme that."

But before she could make a move toward unlocking the clasp, he snatched it from her, breaking the gold chain. Squinting, he read the inscription Henri had put on the back of the cross. "J.B., most beloved, from H.B.," he read. "Well, I reckon you spoke the truth when you said your name was Julia Bernard." Surprisingly, he gave the cross back to her, but he sneered when she kissed it.

Full darkness was on the Mississippi when Clint dropped anchor in the harbor at New Orleans, which was a disappointment to Juliette, since she'd been eagerly looking forward to a crowded wharf and broad light of day. Clint crept up on her from behind and slipped a lasso over her head, drew it tightly around her to bind her arms to her sides, then shoved her into the galley. "Just in case you try to make a dumb move," he said. He forced her to the galley floor and secured the ends of the rope to a piece of hardware, then forced a handkerchief into her mouth, which he kept in place by tying another square of linen around her head. "Women are cunning creatures. Any man that trusts one to keep her mouth shut is a damned fool," he explained.

After a long while, she heard the rise and fall of voices, but was able only to recognize Clint's louder, sometimes belligerent tones above the other one, and could make out no words. Other noises interfered, such as the hustle and bustle of people who walked along the wooden docks, bursts of laughter, and the forlorn horn of a tug boat as it neared the shore. At last, footsteps sounded just outside the tiny galley along with Clint's voice speaking jovially. "She's as pretty as a picture, healthy as a horse. Got good, sound teeth, and she's a virgin. Or at least she said she was."

"I wouldn't dare take a woman aboard the Golden Hawk, Clint," answered the other voice. "You were to put her aboard my ship at the appointed place. The harbor is crawling with acquaintances. Anyway, a deal is a deal. You didn't hold up your end of it, and I'm not interested in another woman. I want Martha, and I mean to have her."

"Aww, Christ, a woman is a woman," wheedled Clint. "Wait until you see her. She's young and fair. Tall and slender as a wand. Almost made *me* sit up and take notice. None of your big tits and broad hip. Built trim as a fine ship, I say." He carried a lantern, and once he was inside the galley the wheedling tone left his voice. "You there, Julia. Strip down." He removed the rope that bound her arms to her sides.

"No."

He snarled. "You do as I say, you filthy tart. I got a right to show my wares to the gentleman."

The lantern was bright as he shone it next to her face. She could see nothing but darkness in back of it, but she'd heard the other man's voice before and tried to place it with his name and face.

"Let her alone, Clint," the other man said crisply. "She's a beauty for fair, but she's the looks of a she-devil. I'd take her and have a high time with her, but she'd never come willingly. Now Martha . . . damn!"

She sensed that the other man turned away. Clint followed, and the light of the lantern grew dimmer. He came back immediately and removed the gag, then freed her from all her bonds. "Cain't blame a man for tryin'. You should of done what I told you. I bet you got a pretty body. I bet it's plumb milky

48

white and just as firm—Get on up off of that floor. Well, you had your chance." He shone the lantern around until he found two glasses. "I reckon I got off easy. He could of been real mad, seein' that he already give me a bit of earnest money and I spent it. But he was real tickled to get your emerald ring, sweetie. Said that'd even things up. He splashed liquid into the glasses and gave her one after he had her on her feet. "That's real fine wine. Drink up, Julia. Be glad he never took back the wine he brought me as a gift. It's a pleasure to drink the good grape."

She drank because she was thirsty and because she planned to use the glass as a weapon. It would break more easily if empty, and she would take great delight in plunging the jagged edges into his fat belly. She'd conceived the plan while Clint tried to bargain with the other man, realizing it was her only chance to escape. She tossed the wine down and found it smooth and mellow on her tongue. Then she saw the bottle, the neck an open invitation to grasp it in her hand. A far better weapon, too. She grabbed it, sent it crashing against the edge of a cabinet, and lunged to the galley floor.

"You goddam tiger-bitch!" Clint raised his hands to protect his face, but in her fury she didn't care where she cut him. The bottle glinted green under the lantern light. It had broken off in several great, knife-like shards, and each time she pierced his skin with it a flower of sheer delight bloomed inside her head. The spilled wine was slippery underfoot. She went down, but righted herself as she continued to slash at him. The lamp overturned as he flailed out at her, swearing and screaming like a stuck hog each time she made contact with his arms, his belly, and his chest. The feeble flame of the lamp was

49

extinguished in the sloshed wine, and the room was plunged in darkness. The battle continued, and Juliette tasted the sweet triumph of victory as she felt him slump to his knees.

"I'll kill you!" She was panting, screaming those words at the top of her lungs as she fumbled for him in the darkness. She found his hair and pulled hard, snapping his head back so she could get at his throat. "I'll kill you!" She raged against the sudden weakness that sent her sprawling on top of him. She was vaguely aware of her lifeless fingers as they relinquished their clutch on the neck of the bottle. A sweet, sickening taste was in her mouth, and before she blacked out completely she realized that she'd lost. "In the wine. You put something in it. The wine."

IV

When she regained consciousness, Juliette was naked under filthy rags. She drifted in and out of consciousness, not knowing whether days, weeks, months, or mere minutes had passed during her periods of awareness. Nor did she know the difference between dreams and reality. She might have been bathed, but she wasn't sure whether it really happened. And she might have been lifted, moved about, forced to walk out somewhere amidst strange, colorful birds and tropical flowers of vibrant hues. She was sure she'd been on a ship, but then she knew for a fact that right then she was not, because when full recognition of her surroundings at last returned, she knew no ship would present the elegance and luxury of the bedroom in which she found herself.

Clean, cool sheets were under her and over her. Downy soft pillows cradled her head. When she lifted the silken sheet to glance down at her body, she blinked in amazement at the gossamer gown that covered her nakedness. Clean. She *had* been bathed, and when she moved she was treated to the scent of hyacinth.

Filtered light streamed in from two windows, but she couldn't see out because of silk draperies, embroidered with beautiful birds. She sat up, looked at her hands, and found them thin. She'd lost weight, but at the moment she felt very well—until the memory of the night she had tried to kill Clint Babcock came back in all its bloody horror.

A very small woman entered the bedroom and spoke to her in a language she didn't understand. Juliette shook her head, feeling helpless. *"Parlez-yous francais?"*

The woman laughed. "No, no," she said as she cocked her head on one side. *"Inglese?"*

"Yes, yes! English. Where am I?"

"San Francisco," the girl answered. Then she corrected herself and said prettily, "In your language, it is pronounced so. In mine, it is Sahn Frahn-see-sco."

"Then I *was* on a ship."

"Yes, my lady. And now you are here. You will eat, now, please? I have brought you broth and fruit, believing you would be awake when next I came to administer to you."

"I am very hungry."

The little maid put covered bowls on a night table, placed a spotless white cloth under Juliette's chin, and began to spoon delicious broth into her mouth, but she wanted to feed herself. "I feel quite strong. Tell me the name of your mistress."

The tiny woman giggled. "Mistress is called Sweet Bird of China. She paid many, many American dollars for you and will be pleased to know you are gaining strength. Soon you will be able to dress

52

yourself in the lovely clothes she has selected for you and be a lark of happiness. It is a great privilege, lady, to be one of the larks in the house of Sweet Bird. Already, you have been spoken for by a fine gentleman. Mistress Sweet Bird allowed him just a tiny glimpse of you as you slept."

As she separated the segments of an orange, the meaning of the girl's prattle sank in. "I am in a brothel, then? Your mistress paid for me? How much? And to whom? And tell me your name, please."

"Already I have spoken too much. My tongue waggles and I forget my place, but you know, lady, it is so wonderful to work in a place of such beauty and happiness. Young girls like yourself come in as sparrows and soon they make the transformation to larks. After that, it is no time at all until they, too, are beautiful birds of paradise. I am Evita, from Mexico."

Evita rambled on and on. Thoughtfully, Juliette ate her orange. As a child she'd gone to a private school where the instructress referred to all the little girls as flowers. Those who first came to school were dear and charming, but since they were unlearned, they were known as the wild roses. After they learned to read and write, they became lilies. Each term, the children were elevated higher into the realm of flowerdom until they had completed the schooling. Then they were *Les Fleurs les plus Belles de New Orleans*. Apparently, she thought with an unexpected giggle, the levels of harlotry were much like levels of learning. From sparrows to birds of paradise!

"Mistress Julia laughs," said Evita. "Is good."

"A lark," said Julia. "Already, I am a lark!" And she laughed again.

Sweet Bird entered her room with a welcoming smile. Like Evita, the Chinese woman was tiny, but she was exquisitely beautiful, with a flawless ivory-colored complexion and dark, mysterious eyes. She walked in a cloud of heavenly perfume and spoke perfect English. "It is wonderful to see you in such good health, Julia. Evita tells me you have laughed. Laughter is a better treatment than that which is given by the finest physician, for it heals a wounded soul."

"Once I was very timid," said Juliette for no reason at all.

"For a timid person, you showed a remarkable courage. You came very close to killing Mr. Babcock," remarked Sweet Bird. "Perhaps your timidity left you upon your marriage?"

"Not right away. For a long while, I was terrified of my shadow, afraid to speak because I might say the wrong thing, but the love of a good man changed all that." She chose her words carefully, wondering what the man named Clint had told the proprietress about her.

"Your husband is dead, then?"

"Yes." Her lips trembled, but she held back her tears. At least she'd learned that Clint had relayed that particular lie to the one who had purchased her from him.

Sweet Bird's lips curled. "Clint lied. He said you were a virgin. But you were very sick. Sick unto death. My own physician learned that you are not a virgin, and I guessed you had a husband."

"How kind of you. And clever," retorted Juliette.

Sweet Bird shook her finger, but she smiled. "Let us not be naughty and show our temper. You will be a valuable asset to my establishment, Julia. Many men ask for a tall lark, with dark hair and flashing

54

eyes such as yours. You have been here for two months, and every day my physician has done all he could to make you well. He is highly skilled. I saved your life, Julia."

"I do not doubt it. I didn't know a sleeping draught would bring one so near to death, though." He held up her hands. "I am very thin."

"You were unwell in another area, Julia. A sleeping potion is always dangerous, but you were with child. You lost it." Sweet Bird stood and put a cool hand on Juliette's forehead. "Do not allow yourself to become distressed. It is good in some cases to lose a child. It is nature's way of disposing of the weak. What did your husband die of?"

"Smallpox." At the moment, it seemed best to stick to her earlier story.

Sweet Bird's expression was sympathetic. "And it is true that you have no family, or was that another one of Clint Babcock's fabrications?"

"I was an only child. My parents recently lost their lives in a carriage accident."

"Ah. Poor dear. Julia, you must not look upon your circumstances as a lowly state. It is a great privilege to serve men in love. You will soon recover your strength and you will be desired by many. If you wish to be released from my house after you have repaid me the funds I have lavished upon you out of the tenderness of my heart as well as the price I paid the Clint Babcock for you, I will not hold you here. Do you understand me?"

"Yes." Juliette forced a smile. She would soon find a way to escape. Once she was back in the arms of her beloved Henri, he would reimburse Sweet Bird. But she was to weak to do anything but lie there and pretend to be agreeable.

"Now I will soothe you further, Julia." Sweet Bird

clapped her hands to summon a servant. "My lute," she said. "Please bring it to me at once, and a small bit of ice cream for our lovely sick one."

Juliette ate the ice cream with enjoyment, determined to regain her strength by eating nourishing foods. For perhaps a half hour, Sweet Bird played the lute with wondrous skill. She sant a love ballad, first in English, then in French.

"You are accomplished," Juliette said. "I can play the pianoforte and . . . before my husband died, I was learning to play the harp."

"That is good. We shall buy you a harp. Music lulls the savage beast in the breasts of men. Do you sing?"

"My voice is not as pleasing as yours, but I am somewhat talented."

Sweet Bird smiled. "Thank you. Very few have my special gift." Again, she strummed on the strings of the lute and sang the love ballad in Chinese, then Spanish.

Within a week, Juliette was able to get out of bed and walk around the room, but she did so in secrecy. She stood in front of the windows and took the fresh air for long minutes, stretching her legs and arms, sometimes daring to wirl around on her toes, exulting in her sense of well-being. Very soon, she would pull back the embroidered draperies, open the windows as wide as she could and step out on the lush green lawn. She would do it under cover of darkness, when Sweet Bird was entertaining her many admirers, and seeing after the other girls who dallied with the men who were able to pay the price for their expert attentions. By then, Juliette had learned all about the operations of the House of the Sweet Bird of China from talkative Evita.

Day by day, she grew stronger. Her cheeks glowed

with color, and her eyes sparkled with health. She was no longer thin. On a Saturday evening as she ate her solitary meal of roast duckling, wild rice, and asparagus with an exotic sauce, she continued to feign a lethargy she didn't feel as long as Evita's watchful eye was upon her, while she worked out the details of her escape. It must be that very night, she decided. The house would ring with revelry. Each of the five ladies of the evening would be busy with their gentlemen, and Sweet Bird would have no time to look in on her. But she had seen a glint of suspicion in Sweet Bird's fine almond-shaped eyes during the afternoon when she asked, solicitous as ever, if she did not feel well enough to walk out in the garden.

"Not yet," she'd said. "My legs feel wobbly when I stand up for any length of time." Then she'd given Sweet Bird a bright smile, but said her dizzy spells were growing more infrequent. "Another week, and I will be as good as new."

"I think so," was Sweet Bird's quiet answer.

Sometime after she had finished her evening meal, Evita brought her bath water as usual, which she poured into the porcelain tub that slid out of sight into a recess in the wall. She bathed as usual, delighting in the fragrance of the bath oil, the luxurious hyacinth-scented soap that she recognized as imported from France. Her mother had ordered it by the case, a tradition Juliette had kept in her own home in Louisville.

When she had toweled herself dry and dusted her firm body with hyacinth-fragrant powder, she slipped into the fresh nightgown Evita had left at the foot of the bed. It was Evita's habit to check on her at about eight o'clock, and she wanted to appear somewhat weak, ready for sleep. But Evita did not enter her room at the accustomed hour. She waited, forcing herself to remain quiet as she reminded herself it was Saturday night, that the week before Evita had been there later than usual.

At last, the door opened quietly. The shadows of evening had all but faded into darkness, but the windows faced toward the west, which bathed the room with the last rays of the setting sun. She kept her eyes closed.

"You are sleeping, my beauty?"

Startled, Juliette opened her eyes. Instead of Evita, a man stood at the foot of the bed. She stared, her eyes luminous.

"Do not be afraid, my beauty." The strange man lifted her hand and kissed the palm. "I know you have been indisposed, so I will be gentle with you," he said after he replaced her hand. "But I was able to watch you through the shadow-screen. You are well enough to walk about the room, to dance all alone to the tune in your lovely head." He undressed and got into bed with her. "Ah, yes. Skin like silk. A joy to look at, a much greater joy to possess. And my dear, I mean to have you. I paid Sweet Bird one thousand dollars for the privilege." His hands caressed her flesh under the diaphanous gown, even though she struggled mightily against him.

He laughed. "You are being very foolish. I am a strong man. Your little fists cause me even greater desire. I like a woman with spirit. It whets the appetite."

"What shadow-screen?"

"I do not care to hold a conversation while I make love to you, sleeping beauty. I much prefer you to fight me. As I said, it sharpens my desire."

She yelled. "What is a shadow-screen?"

He sighed. "Oh, very well." Sitting up, he pointed

at the wall where an enormous picture of birds in flight hung. "On this side, you see a picture. On the other side, Sweet Bird sees you when she chooses. And I saw you, too, my beauty." He kissed her and fondled her breasts.

"I hate you," she screamed.

"Lovely! Such words are music to my ears. My fat wife tells me she adores me, but I cannot bear to touch her. I grow weary of my mistresses when they become docile. Tell me you hate me again, sleeping beauty."

Some three hours later, he left her bed, flushed with satisfaction. When he was fully dressed, he stood at the edge of the bed and looked down at her, speaking politely. "Julia. A beautiful name for a beautiful lady. I will return tomorrow night, my beauty."

She kicked him violently, which sent him into a fit of new passion, but she was saved from further torment. Sweet Bird had entered the room silently.

"Get out, Roy," said the proprietress. "You've had enough for one night, and so has Julia." The man left and Sweet Bird lit a long, white taper, which she held close to her own face and ordered Julia to look at her when she spoke. "Now. I have been patient. Henceforth, I will tolerate no more deceptions from you. Stand up and walk to the windows."

By candle light, her eyes were almost golden. They were evil and hooded, with a reptilian threat.

"Draw back the draperies," Sweet Bird ordered calmly. "You will see that I am not without resources, in case you planned to repay my kindness by slipping away into the night."

"God in heaven!" On the ground just outside her window stood a dwarfish little old man all dressed up in bright red pantaloons, a matching jacket, and numerous gold buttons. His face and his uniform were illuminated by two torches set into the lawn. But it was not the man who caused her quick exclamation—it was the double brace of four squat dogs that strained against the leashes he held. They were not big dogs, and their legs were short and bowed. It was their massive chests and shoulders, their pushed-in faces that commanded her attention. The dogs' jaws appeared to grin up at her, their long, sharp teeth jutted upwards.

"You are looking at my man, Harley. His four animals would end your life very quickly. Harley has three brothers, all of whom are in my employ." Sweet Bird's musical laughter tinkled, an unreal sound as Juliette looked at the red-eyed, straining dogs. "I might add that Harley's brothers each have a double brace of four magnificent animals identical to those."

Forcing herself to speak calmly, Juliette left the window. "I, too, am not without resources, Sweet Bird. If you will let me go, I shall pay you handsomely. I find I do not care for the life of pleasure."

Sweet Bird laughed again, but the sound of it was cold with fury. "You are a nothing. I have surrounded myself with riches, dress myself in sables, and pick and choose from an array of jewels that would be the envy of any princess. I have not acquired such riches by listening to the lies of frightened women. When you first began to come out of your long sickness you were too sick to pretend. You have no parents, no husband. I will allow you to go when you have repaid me for my investment, and not until then. And of course I will have to make a little something in return for it. That is the way of a good business person, male or female.

Evita will come with fresh bath water. Wash yourself and prepare to entertain a fine gentleman."

"The last one was crazy."

"True." Sweet Bird's shrug said more than any words. "But Roy is not cruel in his madness. If you are cooperative, I shall see to it that you are not hurt by any man. If not—" Again, she shrugged, and Juliette understood.

It was slightly more than six months before she saw her opportunity to leave the House of Sweet Bird. There was a slight chance of being ripped to pieces by the pit bulls, but she took that chance, and made it to freedom, although she walked in fear through the hilly streets of San Francisco for hours, constantly looking over her shoulder and halfway expecting to find one of the red-uniformed dwarfs with dogs in hot pursuit. She had bargained with her body and gained a confederate, but she dared not leave a trail, which was why she strolled aimlessly about. When she was sure she was not being followed, she made her way to the *bistro* where Crazy Roy had agreed to meet her. Mad as he was in some ways, she'd grown to be rather fond of him, and as the months passed, she slowly wormed her way into his heart.

A cold damp rain made the streets slippery and shiny under the street lights as she slipped into the bistro, hoping she'd not gone from the frying pan into the fire. It did not cause her a moment of guilt to use Crazy Roy. She accepted the cold, hard way in which she had endeared herself to him as just one more necessary evil. He had promised her the moon. He would divorce his wife and marry her. Anything her heart desired—he would provide it as long as she did what he asked her to.

Several weeks passed by after her initial experience before Crazy Roy could bring himself to spell out his strange desires. Fighting him, biting, slashing, and kicking were not enough. He wanted her to whip him. She was still too new at the business of love for hire to hide her true feelings. Roy sulked. "First you begged me to tell you what I want. Now you look at me like I'm a criminal. Is it too much to ask of you?"

"I'll do it," she said softly. "For a price."

"Always, there's a price. I thought you were different."

"Go to hell, then," she said nastily.

"All right! *Anything!* What's your price?"

"When I leave here, you must give me shelter. Provide for me. Keep me safe."

"Sweet Bird will cut out your heart and stuff it down your throat if you try to run away. She's cruel. She'll kill me without batting an eyelid, too, if she learns I helped you." But Juliette could read the hot desire in his eyes. She was learning more and more each night she spent in scented elegance under the roof of the beautiful Chinese woman.

"I'll never go out of the house. Whatever you want, I'll do it," she insisted as she gave him a playful cuff across the face. "Just think! You can purchase all manner of fancy whips. Red ones and black ones—I'll even tie you to the bed post. Think of how lovely it would be, Roy, to be tied up in red ribbons while I flail you with a little red whip."

He hemmed and hawed and spoke direly of the fate that would await him if Sweet Bird ever learned of his part in her treachery, and it took him a full five weeks to agree, but Juliette had known all along he couldn't resist her.

He awaited her with his collar turned up, a look of frozen fear on his face. "You're quite sure you were not followed?"

"Absolutely. Take me to the house you've provided for me." She licked her lips and made her eyes sparkle as she whispered sweetly of the tortures she had in mind for him. He rushed her out of the place so quickly that she didn't have time to finish her wine. A closed carriage awaited them in the alley in back of the *bistro*. Juliette entertained her protector all the way to the top of Market Street and had him in such a state of excitement by the time they arrived at the rather pretentious house that he was drooling.

In two months, she was on her way home to Louisville. Crazy Roy had been more than generous, but she had no qualms when she vacated the premises, taking every fabulous jewel he'd given her along with the cash. She had earned it.

It was a long and tiring journey. She went overland, by stagecoach, by train, and the final lap by riverboat. San Francisco and the House of Sweet Bird was a different world. There she'd thought of little except home and her husband. The war that was raging between the North and the South was sometimes mentioned in passing, but it had not seemed real to her, since there was no outward sign in California. The fraternal war became very real, however, as she was frustrated again and again during her journey eastward. A private car was no longer available, she was told. All accomodations were being used for the troops. Trains were being fired upon by both the Union troops and the Confederates. It was dangerous to travel, said kindly men who wanted to be helpful. Runaway slaves had come North and were running in packs, gone wild as any animals, people warned her. They raped and killed and especially preyed upon white women who traveled alone. She heard it all and found most of it hard to believe.

At Vincennes, Indiana, she was told of a hundred or more rebel soldiers who had broken out of a jail where they'd been taken prisoner by the Union. They were cutting across Indiana as they made their way back down South. Her life wouldn't be worth a penny if they took a notion into their heads to attack the coach she was riding in.

Most of the time, Juliette turned her thoughts toward the future. She would be truthful with her husband and throw herself on his mercy. If he loved her as she believed he did, he would forget the past and they would go on together as they had been. Holding fast to her conviction that he loved her truly, she was calm and serene except when she slept. Then she dreamed of the other girls at Sweet Bird's establishment. Of Sweet Bird herself, and the packs of vicious dogs. Of some of the more trying clients who had demanded unspeakably demeaning acts— although she was helpless to do anything but comply.

At last, she stood trembling and misty-eyed in front of the beautiful home she had known as a bride. The hack-driver pulled away. As if in a dream, she climbed the steps, and seemed to float across the brick walk that led to the wide porch. She found herself staring blissfully at the leaded-glass front door. Never before had she rung the doorbell, but it was a pleasure to do so, and an even deeper pleasure to hear the melodious chimes sounding from within. She had been away for a year and three months, almost to the day.

A neatly uniformed maid came to the door. A stranger. "I am Mrs. Bruyère," said Juliette. "Mrs. Henri Bruyère."

The maid gave her a blank smile. "Yes?"

"I live here." Never had she felt so elated.

"I must go for Mistress," said the maid. She closed the door and Juliette heard her run through the spacious hall. She turned the glass knob, but the door was firmly locked.

After an eternity, the door opened again and a gray-haired woman asked her to come in.

"But the furnishings," protested Juliette. "They're not—"

"My dear Mrs. Bruyère, won't you please sit down," said the woman gravely.

"My husband. Mr. Henri Bruyère. Where is he? Are you his housekeeper?"

"My dear Mrs. Bruyère," the woman said again after Juliette was seated in a rocking chair. "There is no way I can soften the blow. Your husband . . . passed away five months ago. Oh, dear!"

Juliette heard her soft voice as the room went black all around her.

The smelling salts revived her into searing grief. She listened, stretched out on a sofa while a gray-haired woman with kind blue eyes said she was the wife of Henri's attorney, that they had moved into the house after their own burned down, and that they were paying the rent into Henri's estate in case the missing Mrs. Bruyère, who had disappeared so mysteriously, should ever come home to claim her late husband's estate.

Vaguely, Julliette remembered the name of Henri's attorney—a Mr. Joseph Ware. "Then you are Mrs. Ware. My husband . . ." She clutched her heart against the dreadful ache. "What caused his death?"

Mrs. Ware shook her head sadly. "The doctors said it was consumption. But my husband and I believe he died of a broken heart."

Juliette wanted to know everything, and M

65

Ware understood. She related the events that followed her disappearance in her soft, gentle voice. "Your husband would not rest until he had combed every inch along the railroad tracks between New Orleans and Memphis. He couldn't sleep, and wouldn't eat properly. His resistance was low, and he fell sick. He passed away with your name on his lips, Mrs. Bruyère. I was with him myself."

"I cannot bear it," she whispered. "I shall follow him to the grave, for I no longer care to live."

"Please, Mrs. Bruyère. If it is God's will, He will call you. It is not for mere mortals to decide when they will leave this earthly coil."

Night fell, but Mrs. Ware did not have her servants light the lamps. She continued to speak quietly, remembering every little detail that Juliette asked about. Big Jimpson had gone to Nevada. Mr. Bruyère had given the big slave his freedom and financed him. He would buy land. He had married Vivian in a ceremony right there in the parlor. The other two slaves wanted to stay on after they were given their manumission. They were living in the house and working for Mr. and Mrs. Ware. "They've never given up hope that you are living, Mrs. Bruyère, and as soon as you feel strong enough, it would be a kindness if you spoke to them."

The reunion was tearful with Tillie and little Effie Lukie falling to their knees and kissing their former mistress's gown. Juliette could not weep. She would have found relief in tears, but the final blow after so many others left her chilled and numb. She stayed on with Mr. and Mrs. Ware for a week, and then she traveled to New Orleans against the advice of the lder couple, but her reasons for wanting to go back New Orleans were compelling. Somewhere, she t be able to find peace. She could not find it in the house where she had known perfect love and contentment. Every room was a painful reminder of her lost love. She visited the cemetery and knelt at Henri's grave for a long time, but she couldn't possibly believe he was there. The gravestone Mr. and Mrs. Ware had selected was an abomination to her, although she appreciated their thoughtfulness and knew it was necessary to erect one. She wanted to tear it down. To topple it over and crush it with her bare hands because she hated the stark, ever-so-final words inscribed in the stone that spoke of his birth and of his death.

When she arrived in New Orleans, she regretted not having sent her sisters and brother a letter or a telegram to say she was coming, but she'd not been able to bring herself to do it. Every mile of the way, she hoped she would come back to herself and be able to feel things again. To smell the flowers, appreciate the pure blue sky, to taste food.

Suzanne was cool and unsmiling, answering questions bluntly with a mere yes or no. Grudgingly, she finally said André was with General Lee's Army fighting for the Confederacy. Juliette had been in her sister's house for less than an hour and felt very uncomfortable. At last, she said, "Why are you so distant, Suzanne? My heart is broken. I've suffered greatly, God knows. You act as if you barely know me."

Suzanne put her teacup down. It was then that Juliette saw the flash of green fire on her finger and recognized her emerald ring, but in her state of agitation she couldn't find the words to ask how Suzanne happened to have it. Instead, she gazed sorrowfully into her sister's eyes.

"You've been here for almost an hour, Juliette," Suzanne said as if the hour had wounded her. "But you've not said one word of explanation about your...whereabouts during the year you've been away. Your impulsive actions caused the death of your husband. Your brother and sisters have died a thousand deaths, wondering what became of you. When we found out, which was four months ago, we were naturally disturbed. You have brought shame to the memory of our parents. Not a one of us have been able to hold our heads up in polite society since the story of your...frightful behavior came to light."

The cold, hard grief that had been like an icicle inside Juliette's heart ever since she learned her husband had died grew icier. Raising her eyebrows, she said, "It would appear that you have already made up your mind about me. I don't know who was kind enough to tell you what you know of my shattering experience, but it's obvious you believe it. In all truth, I found it hard to begin, but I came here with the intention of telling you what happened to me, how my life has been during this past year. I also came home in search of peace, and hoped to find filial love, if not from Emilié, then from you, Suzanne."

The blonde woman's features were unruffled. "My husband's business partner was kind enough to relieve us of our suffering and worry. I do not know how he came by his information, but for many months he was silent. It was only after your husband died that he came and told us that you had taken up with a man named Clint Babcock, a renegade if ever there was one—and that you were on your way to a house of prostitution. Mr. Gordon purchased your ring from the despicable person. He saw you with his own eyes, Juliette. In fact," Suzanne said as she lowered her eyes, "he admitted that you offered your charms to him. He gave me the ring."

Juliette threw back her head and howled with laughter. "And even though you were ready to believe that I am immoral and despicable in all ways, you do not find it contaminating to wear my ring! How strange! But of course if you had known I would appear on your door step, I am sure the ring would be in the box with your other jewelry." She stood, put on her gloves, gave her sister a pitying look, and left. There were many things she could have said to her sister. Later, she would wonder why she had remained silent. For the rest of her life she puzzled over her refusal to attempt to clear her name.

From Suzanne's house, she went to the law firm of Delacorte and Gordon where she waited patiently until Mr. Gordon was free to see her. With blazing eyes and head proudly high, she sailed into the private office of the man who paid to have a red-haired woman named Martha abducted. Until the moment Suzanne spoke Mr. Gordon's name she'd been unable to place the voice she'd heard that dreadful night when Clint had tried to pawn her off on the man who had sent for another.

Mr. Gordon stood, his face the color of chalk. "Mrs. Bruyère," he said shakily as he tried to smile. "What a wonderful surprise!"

"No doubt it is a surprise," Juliette answered. "But I doubt if it is wonderful. I have come to kill you, you lying, thieving, immoral knave! If you recognized me that night, you could have helped me, and it is obvious that you did know me." She moved in on Gordon with her bare hands, her face a mask of murderous intent. A rather short man, he took a step backwards until he was against the wall. All he did to defend himself was try to fend her off with his hands. She grabbed him by the throat and shook him, then raised him into the air and continued to shake him until his glasses fell off. Gurgling and pushing ineffectually against her shoulders with his open hands, he tried to speak coherently, but all he managed to do was sound as if he were being strangled. Those protests reminded Juliette of the screeching of a cat with his tail caught in a door, and she was forever glad that she'd come to her senses enough to laugh, then to drop the squirming, wriggling little man.

He fell in a disjointed heap to the floor where he peered up at her with a twisted look to his head, and abject terror in his eyes. "If my wife knew about Martha she would have me horsewhipped," he whined. "Surely you—" She considered kicking him, but thought better of it. She just left in disgust.

When she got home, she realized that she could no longer live in New Orleans. She had to find a new home, a place to start over again. It had to be far away. Maybe the West. Yes, Nevada Country. Ever since Mrs. Ware told her Big Jimpson had gone there, she'd had the territory on her mind. It was a big, thinly populated land, empty of habitation in some areas, but booming in others because of the silver mining. Passing through, she'd seen strange contrasts in the way of the land. Verdant land dotted with sheep at pasture stretched along the roadside for miles, only to fall away to the desolate bleakness of desert sands. Mountains and plains. Lakes and hot springs. A heavenly blue sky above pine forests in the high country.

At Sweet Bird's she'd heard one of the clients speak of the Nevada Country as a place of silver mines and saloons. The peace and tranquility she'd sought had not awaited her in the state where she was born. The more she considered the idea of going to Nevada, the more she liked the idea. She would not concern herself with the hurly-burly of the silver-booming towns. She'd had enough excitement to last her a lifetime. No, she'd use some of the money she'd inherited from Henri and buy land. Raise sheep, live alone, and allow herself time to heal herself. She wanted to rid herself of the coldness in her heart.

V

For more than a year, Juliette lived quietly in a one-room cabin on the thousand acres she purchased in what would one day become Washoe County. Once each month, she hitched up her horses and drove eleven miles into Sparks, Nevada, where she purchased her supplies. During the first summer, she put out a little garden, which she tended with care. She kept two goats, a number of chickens, and ducks and geese. In time, she planned to put the great expanse of land to a more practical use, but her main objective was to heal herself. It was her state of mind that gave her more concern than anything else. The violence of her nature was new and disturbing. She knew her tendency to lash out at the slightest problem that came along must be quelled. Although she didn't want to return to the too-docile, timid girl she'd been when in the bosom of her family, she longed for the tranquility she had known as Henri's wife. Her mother had often said that time healed all wounds, and she had respected both the memory of her mother and her wisdom. But as the months passed and she became more and more withdrawn, she began to wonder at the wiseness of closing herself away from all contact with others. At twenty, she'd become a recluse. When she went into Sparks to buy seeds for her garden and staples for her kitchen, she had to force herself to step up to the counter of the general store and state her needs. Keeping to herself was doing nothing to throw off the black clouds of despair. Instead of getting better, she realized she was growing more and more morose with each passing day.

Mrs. Miller was the wife of the man who owned the general store. She went out of her way to be cordial, but Juliette froze at any display of kindness.

"There's going to be a church social next Saturday, Mrs. Bernard," said Mrs. Miller on a fine sunny day in early May. "We'd love to have you join us. It seems a shame for a young woman like you to be alone so much, shut away from social life."

"I prefer to keep to myself," Juliette snapped. Immediately she was humiliated at the great, wracking sobs that shook her from head to toe, the flood of tears that came without warning and rained down her face.

Mrs. Miller came from behind the counter. "You've been hurt," she said as she put her arms around Juliette. "You poor little thing, my heart just breaks for you. The first time you came in to do your trading, I knew you'd been through an awful lot of trouble, and when I asked you about your family I sure didn't mean to pry. But when you said you were a widow lady, I knew right away you didn't mean to be so cold and hard. It was just the way you had to be, in order to keep from falling down and dying. So young. So young and pretty."

73

In her motherly way, Mrs. Miller insisted that Juliette come to the back of the store until she'd calmed down. Not wanting to make a public display of herself in the crowded general store, she consented. Over a cup of coffee, she continued to weep uncontrollably. After the better part of an hour, she was able to control herself and apologized to Mrs. Miller, saying she didn't know what had gotten into her.

"A person just never knows what sets them off," said Mrs. Miller as she poured fresh coffee. "I tell you the way I look at it—I think you held all those tears in and they just had to get out, that's what. Maybe you were crying for a lot of things besides the death of Mr. Bernard."

"Oh, yes, I'm sure," Juliette answered. "The baby I lost, my home, my parents—so many things. But I didn't try to keep from crying, Mrs. Miller. I just couldn't." She didn't add that she wished she had not used the name Bernard when she purchased her land. She'd done it because she did not want her sisters to know of her whereabouts. Looking back, she realized it was doubtful if either one of them would have been inclined to try to trace her, anyway, but she'd come to the Territory as Julia Bernard, and she was stuck with it. Smiling, she said, "If your kind offer still stands, I would like very much to come to the church social."

As the following Saturday grew near, her emotions soared. A new life was what she'd wanted. She dressed with care, choosing a beige silk dress that was modestly becoming. Once, she even laughed out loud at the idea of being so excited about mingling with people again. Mrs. Miller had spoken the truth. She was young. No man would ever take the place of Henri, but since the breakdown in the store she'd been able to look at her future in a better light.

Someday she hoped to marry again and have children. Her thoughts flew to the future. Soon Nevada would be taken into the Union. With the Civil War raging, the silver would help the North win the war. Looking out over her land, after she harnessed the horses to her buggy, she stood for a moment and gazed at the distant mountains. It would be good to be a part of a new state, to see her children growing up in a place where there were unlimited opportunities. The land was clean and bountiful, a good place to bring up children. Peace—suddenly she was filled with it, and pleased with herself for having the sense to recognize it.

Two hours later Juliette was sitting under the shade of a piñon tree involved in animated conversation with two women, one of whom had a baby on her lap. They wanted to enlarge the church, which was not nearly big enough to hold the new families who were flooding the area.

"I would be willing to donate one thousand dollars to the church building fund," said Juliette.

Mrs. Miller, who happened to be passing by at that very moment, was ecstatic. "And to think that you're not even of the Presbyterian faith, Mrs. Bernard! My, my, I think that's just the most wonderful thing that could happen to this community. Our little church in the wilderness has been sufficient until just lately, but—"

"We need a school, too," said Juliette. She was happy. Elated. "And it doesn't matter what one's persuasion is, Mrs. Miller. A house of God is a house of God. But we should consider getting together some day soon and talking about the matter of a school."

"And you could be the school ma'am," one of the other ladies said. "Why, anybody in the world can see it as plain as can be that you've had a fine education, Julia." The woman's face was flushed with pleasure. "I'd like to have some more of that delicious ice cream," she said. "Can't I get some for you, Julia?

"Oh, I'll just go along with you and get my own," she answered. The idea of teaching children was appealing, and her voice carried to the men who were grouped around the ice cream freezer. "I've never been a teacher ma'am," she said excitely, "but I think I would like it very much. I *know* I can teach!"

A man's voice, crackling with anger, came forth from the vicinity of the ice cream freezer. "Teach, is it?" The three words were followed by a long, drawn-out horse-laugh. "Julia Bernard, as I live and breathe!"

Stunned, Juliette stood absolutely still as Crazy Roy looked at her with wrathful eyes and yelled with a voice loud enough to be heard for a mile. He placed his hand on her arm and shouted. "You'd teach them to lie and steal. To practice harlotry and all manner of sinful, evil acts!" Turning to face the open-mouthed, startled church folk, he continued his tirade, listing every shameful truth he knew about her.

"Julia Bernard was a San Francisco whore in the infamous bawdy house of Sweet Bird of China. She preyed on innocent men and encouraged their un-Christian lust, stealing along with her whoring, bringing virtuous women down with her into the sinkholes of depravity. She stole over a million dollars, and she's wanted by the Law! There's not an indecent act that this woman hasn't performed.

76

She's unfit to associate with good women, let alone teach little children! *Stone her,* I say!" Purple with rage, he shook her arm as he heaped more and more accusations on her. "I say we must run her out of this place of virtue. A Jezebel has no place on sacred ground!" Waving his arms and shouting ever louder, he attracted the attention of even those who were playing horseshoes, a quarter-mile beyond the church.

It happened so quickly. The blood-lust of the men came to a fever-pitch of excitement so fast that Juliette was helpless to defend herself. Several women joined the men, most of them gathering stones. Out of nowhere, Mrs. Miller ran forward and tried to get Juliette to come inside the church building, but she could only stand there, shaking her head and wondering why she'd not noticed Crazy Roy among the other men.

Suddenly she came to her senses. "You! How would you know of the House you speak of, if you were not a customer yourself?" Apparently, she thought in a strangely detached way, his newfound religion along with his change in his manner of living, was stronger than his titillating memories.

Mrs. Miller and five or six other women did their best to smooth the roiling waters.

"You're just like every other old reprobate who comes to see the ways of the Lord too late," Mrs. Miller screamed defiantly at Crazy Roy. "You came here with a young wife when everybody knew you had an old one in San Francisco! But did we judge you? No siree! You can bet your boots we didn't. A reformed sinner is still a sinner when he goes around calling others bad names."

A few stones flew through the air, but although one grazed Juliette, none hit her. It was Mr. Miller who fired his pistol into the air, his wife reminding everyone there of the words of Jesus Christ that the one who feels himself to be without sin should throw the first stone. "You go ahead and throw stones if any of you feel fit to judge another!" She pointed her finger at first one man, then another. "You've killed, Jeffry Kilpatrick. And you, Lawrence O'Malley, you set fire to an Indian village just to see it burn! For shame! And Mister Grummer there! Rustled horses and laid around drunk when you weren't stealing from poor folks."

Juliette stepped forward. "Never mind, Mrs. Miller. I thank you for your loyalty. Half of what I was accused of is true, although I was never a willing worker in the house in San Francisco. I was shanghaied, then sold into prostitution. I came here to start all over again, but I should have known better. I'll be leaving you now. You and the rest of you good ladies who tried to help me are surely true servants of the Lord."

In June of 1863 Julia Bernard arrived in Virginia City. Within two weeks she purchased a beautiful home at the corner of D and Union Streets in that wild, booming town that came into being after the fabulous Comstock Silver Lode was discovered in 1859. Up the street from her house was the Silver Dollar Hotel, where she stayed until her luxurious furnishings were brought in from San Francisco.

Overnight, Julia Bernard was a sensation. Less than twenty-four hours after her arrival, everyone in the bustling town of some thirty thousand people was aware of the elegant creature who had arrived in their midst. She arrived in a lacquered brougham of crimson and gold that was drawn by two of the most handsome steeds the frontier town had ever seen.

Rumors flew. She was said to be a royal Princess, a descendent of Marie Antoinette who had fled France and was favoring Virginia City with her royal presence until it was safe for her to return to her native land and claim the Crown of France.

The hotel maids spoke with envious admiration of her wardrobe and jewels. One hundred gorgeous gowns were said to have arrived inside of twenty-five trunks, each more expensive and elegant than the other. A selection of capes ranging from ermine to velvet threaded with gold were spoken about among the curious women. She had a different diamond ring for each finger, swore the hotel maids, and two smaller trunks were filled to the brim with other jewelry. Amethysts, emeralds, sapphires, opals, and jade were all represented, but the fabulous and glamorous Julia Bernard was said to be partial to the diamonds she wore.

From the day she arrived in Virginia City, Juliette Bienviellance Bruyère was no more. She thought of herself as Julia Bernard. She did nothing to encourage the rumors that ran rampant about her wealth, attire, and jewels, although she was secretly amused. The instant adoration of the rough, tough miners was another area that provided her with mirth, although she gave her admirers no inclination of her inner feelings. She was warm, friendly, yet regal of bearing. Head and shoulders taller than any other woman in town and capable of level eye contact with most of the men, she reveled in the furor she made when she entered a dining hall or appeared on the street.

During the time she was a paying guest at the Silver Dollar Hotel, she refused to give any of her swains more than a friendly smile, a warm greeting. She took her meals alone, behaved decorously, and allowed the tall tales to grow even wilder. When the red velvet draperies were hung in every window, Julia turned in her key to the hotel room and drove to her house where she went through every room with a critical eye.

The parlor was resplendent with velvet and satin furnishings that contrasted with or complemented the red velvet draperies. Gold, crimson, and blue were her new colors, and each room of her palatial home reflected her good, though lavish, taste. A four-poster bed of rosewood graced her big bedroom. It was draped with crimson and spread with gold. Ornate hand painted lamps provided illumination. Each drawer of her hand-made rosewood dresser was lined with red Moroccan leather. Above it hung a mirror that reflected bed, tables, lamps, and chairs. The frame was gold, and the three little maids who eagerly left their positions as chambermaids in the teeming hotels whispered to their friends that the frame of the mirror was twenty-four carat gold, not gold leaf.

The very first night Julia spent in her new home, she slept alone. At seven o'clock, a drunken artist named Evan Willoughby knocked on her back door and gave her a sketch. "You're sure that's what you want, ma'am?" He was pale, unsteady on his feet, but his hands were not trembling when he held them out to show her he was steady.

"That's exactly what I want," answered Julia. "And when you return with the carriage in the morning, I will pay you one hundred dollars and throw in a bonus of a case of fine champagne if you have pleased me." From behind her heavily draperied windows, she watched the artist climb into her carriage and drive off. At precisely ten o'clock the following morning, Evan Willoughby slowed the horses to a stop, climbed out of Julia's brougham, and again knocked at her back door. He waited patiently over a cup of coffee while she went to inspect his night's work.

"Well done," she said as she counted out the hundred dollars. "I'll have the champagne delivered to your room."

The artist left and for a long time, Julia Bernard stood behind her parlor windows, looking through a small opening to watch the expression on the faces of passers-by when they saw the artist's work. The side-panels of her brougham were emblazoned with the crest she had taken for herself—an escutcheon of four aces, crowned by a lion *couchant*. On that same day, she appeared in town where whe walked boldly into the Sazarac Saloon at exactly five o'clock in the afternoon. Her face was modestly dusted with powder and rouge, but her manner was as regal as ever. A subtle change had taken place in the aura given off by Julia Bernard, however. In case any of the clients of the Sazarac were too inebriated to notice a change in aura of her tastefully applied cosmetics, she knew the traditional way of letting the gentlemen of Virginia City know she was in business. Under her gold-threaded gown she wore red net stockings. Now and then she lifted her skirts just enough to show the color as well as her well-turned ankle.

VI

Three days after Julia Bernard let the residents of Virginia City know why she was there, she returned from a trip to the bonnet shop and her maid, Venita, told her a gentleman had called.

"I suppose you gave him my business hours, Venita?"

"Yes, ma'am. But he's not one of *those* gentlemen. He's another sort of gentleman, Miss Bernard." She handed Julia a calling card.

"Mark Twain," she said aloud. Then she turned her dark eyes on Venita and smiled. "Isn't he the editor of the *Territorial Enterprise?*"

"Yes, ma'am. He said he wanted to interview you, and he'd like you to set the time."

"How very nice." Julia was delighted at a chance to meet the editor, but she did not intend to allow him to write anything important. She sent a reply to Mark Twain by Venita saying the following afternoon would be convenient, between the hours of two and four.

After a night of financially rewarding revelry, Julia awakened at noon and prepared to meet the brilliant editor. She was cordial when she showed him into her parlor, and he was charming and witty.

"You've won the heart of every man in town, Miss Bernard," he said. "I admire your *élan*. I might also add that you are the most beautiful and exciting woman in the country."

"Thank you, Mr. Twain."

"My name is Samuel Clemens. Mark Twain is my pen name. Will you do me the honor of calling me Sam?"

"Certainly, Sam. And you may call me Julia." She rang for Venita and asked for wine for the gentleman, tea for herself.

The reporter leaned forward. "Julia, I want to write an article about you. No sense in beating around the bush. I find you fascinating, and I'm sure everyone else in town feels the same way. However, before I write it, I want your permission. The paper has readers in many states of the Union. I wouldn't want to cause you any embarrassment."

"I'm sure you won't cause me the least bit of embarrassment, Mr. Tw—that is, Sam."

Venita brought the tea and the wine, which Clemens sipped with the true appreciation of a connoisseur. Then he leveled his intelligent eyes at her with an intent gaze. "One of the many intriguing things about you is your obvious knowledge of merchandising." He gestured to take in a vast area. "The majority of the women in your profession are nothing more than peddlers. They hustle and hawk their wares on the streets, from the doorway of their crude little one-room shacks, and in the saloons. They're known to be easily obtainable, and make no bones about being competitive. For instance, if

Loganberry Wine learns that Thelma Moss is available for twenty-five dollars, Loganberry Wine reduces her rate to twenty. Down the street, Clara Walters finds out that her competition has done a little rate-cutting, so she goes down to fifteen dollars. I hope I've not offended you by comparing you with a crib-girl, Julia. Believe me when I say I have nothing but admiration for a lady who asks for and receives a minimum of five hundred dollars for a night of love."

"You don't offend me at all, Sam." Julia smiled over her teacup. "Men are not fools. At least not all of them, and neither are women. It's human nature for all of us to want the best of everything. Putting it simply, I am the best. My price is high, but I am well worth it. If a man can't tell the difference between a five cent cup of watery coffee and a goblet of vintage wine that costs a dollar, he'll take the coffee and save ninety-five cents. Most men appreciate the difference between a bawd who bargains her tail for a sawbuck and one who is capable of giving him several hours of paradise for a hundred times that."

"Where were you born, Julia?"

"I don't care to answer that question, Sam."

"Is Julia Bernard your true, legal name?"

"I don't care to answer that one, either, Sam."

"Do you have a protector?"

"Certainly not. I don't need a protector."

"You're obviously well-bred and educated, Julia. I wonder—"

She laughed. "If you're going to ask me that old, old question about why a nice girl such as I have chosen the oldest profession, I won't offer you more wine, Sam."

"I wasn't going to ask you that ancient question, Julia. You'd tell me you didn't care to answer that

84

question or you'd make up a charming little tale, probably the former. I was wondering how you intend to handle the problem of Jug Baily."

She refilled his wine goblet. "Who the devil is Jug Baily? And in what way will he present me with a problem?"

"Jug Baily is doing a little time over in Carson City. The jail here in Virginia City wouldn't hold him because the jades finagled around and got him out every time they locked him up. Jug thinks of himself as the protector of all the Ladies of the Evening who reside in Virginia City."

"For which the ladies pay him a little something out of their proceeds, I suppose?"

"Exactly." Samuel Clemens asked permission to smoke, and Julia opened her own box of fine, imported Havana cigars. He accepted one, sniffed it with appreciation, and leaned back expansively while she lit it for him.

After some thought, she asked, "For what crime is this Jug Baily being incarcerated?"

"He beat a woman to death. Sally Sweet. She had a cozy little house on the outskirts of town."

"You made a statement when you said he beat a woman to death. I was under the impression that newspaper men speak of 'alleged' crimes."

"There were thirty-two witnesses who saw him drag Sally Sweet out of the Yellow Dog Saloon by the hair of her head. Most of those witnesses followed him out into the street and saw him beat her."

"Did they watch it happen as a kind of attraction?" Julia raised her eyebrows. "No one tried to interfere?"

"A few made half-hearted attempts to help the poor woman, but Jug was armed to the teeth, and the men who were sitting there gambling or minding their own business over a drink were not. At most of the saloons, weapons must be checked at the door. Jug shot one of the men who tried to come to the hapless woman's defense. Didn't kill him, just winged him. But—"

"Do you mean to tell me all those men simply stood there and watched him kill a woman? Even after he shot a man? Why didn't any of them go back inside the saloon and get their pistols?"

Clemens shook his head. "Baily's reputation, like that of a number of Virginia City residents, is notorious. This isn't the first time he's killed. I believe he has five notches on the barrel of his forty-five. He's reputed to have done time before. And besides, Sally didn't die right off the bat. It was two days later when she succumbed. At the trial, Baily swore he'd not meant to kill her. The verdict was manslaughter, with a plea for leniency."

"Verdict. Then there was a trial."

"Well, yes. There was a trial, Julia. But Sally was just a jade." He lifted a hand at her quick gasp of anger. "Wait! Those aren't *my* sentiments! To me, Sally Sweet was a human being who had as much right, if not more, to draw the breath of life than Jug Baily. What I should have said was that the general notion of the jury was that Sally was a woman of the streets and didn't much deserve to live anyway. Besides, she was consumptive, said to be infected with crabs, and suspected of sort of helping to spread certain other diseases each time she bestowed her favors on the fine, upstanding men of Virginia City who found her price right. Most of the men who sat on that jury were afraid to bring in a verdict that wasn't favorable to Baily. He's got about three more months to serve. Been behind bars three months

86

already. That'll be six altogether, and Baily has a lot of power."

"So you're wondering what I'll do when he comes back to Virginia City and confronts me with a choice of paying him a certain percentage of my gross receipts or suddenly becoming... in a state of poor health. Is that it, Sam?"

The editor looked at his long, slender hands. "Exactly." He gave her his lopsided grin. "Besides, I sort of felt like you deserved to be warned in advance."

"Thank you." Again, Julia splashed more wine into the crystal goblet. "You didn't intend to write a newspaper story about the new girl in town at all, did you?"

"I'd like to, but you won't give me any facts. Thing is, there was some talk the other night about maybe Jug Baily might be working on a little jail-break over in Carson. He's going to hear about you as soon as he hits town, Julia, if he hasn't already. Some women find him devilishly attractive. I'm talking about the girls who work out of cribs, little shacks, or toss up their heels on the cold, hard ground, of course, not the wives and mothers."

"I've not seen many respectable women in town since I've arrived."

"Well, there aren't many. Not yet. The others... well, some of them sort of have their noses out of joint since you hit town, Julia. What you said about men who don't know the difference between a cup of weak coffee that costs them five cents and a drink of fine wine that sets them back a dollar is true enough, but there's a streak of curiosity in even the most illiterate of men. Business has fallen off considerably in the other sporting houses. A lot of the girls wonder if their former steady customers are saving up their money for that big, beautiful taste of fine wine." He grinned. "Or spending a hell of a lot more time out in the fields with pick and shovel." Clemens looked at his pocket watch, said he'd taken up too much of her time, and thanked her for her hospitality. "But you never did answer my question, Julia. About how you're going to handle the problem of Jug Baily."

She walked him to the door. "Sam, nobody in this world knows how they'll handle a problem until it comes. I'm afraid I'll just have to wait and see what kind of mood I'm in when I'm confronted with trouble. Jug Baily trouble, or any other kind. Sam, I want you to come again. It's nice to talk to someone on a friendly basis."

"My pleasure, Julia. And I sincerely mean that." A pleased smile lit his face. "I just had an idea, remembering the way your piano looked over there in the corner of your parlor. You play?"

"Well, yes, I do. Why?"

"I was thinking about how nice it would be to come to a place where it's peaceful and quiet and listen to a woman playing the piano once in a while. Not too often. I was born in Missouri and wasn't exposed to a lot of culture, but I like to sing and I'm not the only person in town who'd like to relax and listen to music, maybe sing a few songs. I wouldn't want to interfere with your business, Julia. But how about it?"

Her laughter rang out in clear, musical tones. "You're not a bit shy, Sam. But neither am I. And I meant it when I asked you to come back. How about next Monday night? Come to supper and I'll cook it myself."

"Delighted!" He left, whistling. In that way, a rare and solid friendship began between the most sought-after prostitute in Virginia City and Samuel Clemens, who would eventually become one of the most celebrated humorists of his time. Two Mondays out of each month were reserved for Clemens, who was appreciative of Julia Bernard's beauty, but on a purely platonic basis.

During her first three months of Virginia City residency, Julia made it her business to charm the other prostitutes in town. For the most part, she succeeded in gaining their respect. When she pointed out ways in which they could improve their lot in life and helped them attain a better standard of living, they became friendlier.

In August an epidemic broke out among the miners. During the first two days, there were thirty burials, and the disease was spreading quickly. Julia drove her handsome brougham through the hilly streets and gathered up those who had no homes. At one time she and her three maids gave thirty miners twenty-four-hour-a-day nursing care, as well as two orphaned little girls, an old black man, and a parson's wife.

When the epidemic showed no sign of abating, Julia went to each of the saloon owners to demand that steps be taken to rid the booming town of filth. "People empty their slop jars on the ground in back of their houses if they have no privies," she raged. "Dead dogs lie in the streets until they swell up and burst because nobody buries them. Rats and mice are running rampant, and the only time the garbage is removed from the streets is when it rains. And then it just runs downhill, to draw flies and vermin. Are you gentlemen going to sit on your rear ends and wait until everyone in Virginia City is dead before you take steps to curb this killer disease?"

The saloon owners were not too impressed with

her strange notions that filth and pestilence walk hand in hand, but she talked them into organizing a sanitation committee and swore she would take her place along with everyone else in town if they'd sponsor a cleanup day. If they didn't, well, then—she would not be at home to any of the gentlemen who made it a habit to saunter down to what was rapidly becoming known as Julia's Palace.

Mark Twain wrote fiery articles that backed up Julia's plea for improved sanitary conditions. On a crisp, cool, but sunny day in September, Virginia City was swept from hill to festering hill by an odd assortment of harlots, housewives, panhandlers, miners, and drunks. Once the debris was cleared away, the scrubbing began. The clean-up crew was led by Julia and Polly Stacey, who was the late Parson's widow. Mrs. Stacey championed Julia's cause with zeal, and the newly formed Virginia City Sanitation Department was in full swing.

Not willing to stop with the big clean-up, Julia's next civic effort had to do with enforced building of privies. She harangued businessmen and the law officers until they reinforced the law that fined laggards one hundred dollars for dumping chamber pots on the ground. After that, Julia set her fine, dark eyes on a new goal. Through her efforts and those of middle-aged Polly Stacey, all wells and cisterns were covered with stout planking that fitted tightly. A child had drowned in a well just three days after the town clean-up.

A new minister came to Virginia City in October. Julia was going into the general store when he entered. She was dressed in an old calico dress, and a mob-cap and apron, instead of her usual attire because she was about to go down the street to scrub out the town jail. Leland Lantz introduced himself to her, saying he'd just arrived, that he'd heard the Call of the Lord Who had told him to leave Tombstone and come to Virginia City.

"You've mistaken me for a respectable woman," said Julia. "I don't go to church."

"I didn't either until a year ago. It takes longer for some people to get right with the Lord than it does others. You look respectable enough to me."

She smiled and offered her hand since he stood there looking as if he expected it. "You misunderstand. I'm Julia Bernard and I run a house that's much more than my dwelling. I entertain men friends."

"Ma'am, I didn't come her to judge anybody. The Lord didn't tell me to do that. I came because he called, and I heard. I wonder if you'd direct me to the church house."

"The church has been empty since Reverend Stacey died a few months ago, but I'll walk down the hill with you. The late preacher's widow is going to help me scrub out the jail, and her house is next door to the church." It occurred to her that it could do no harm for her to get the preacher and Polly Stacey together. They were both middle-aged and had much in common. After she asked him if he had a wife and learned he'd never married, she warmed to the idea of matchmaking, especially since she instinctively liked the new man of God.

Preacher Lantz was immediately taken with the Widow Stacey. He joined the two women at the task of scrubbing the jail. Julia went home to find Sam Clemens waiting for her in the parlor. She was in high spirits and pleased to see him. After she'd told him about talking with the Reverend Lantz and her part in what looked very much as if it would turn into a romance, Clemens said he would write a

91

column in the *Enterprise* about the new preacher.

"They hit it off pretty good, you say?"

Julia was sparkling. "They talk the same language. He seemed like a nice sort, and she's lonely. Except—who will we get to marry them?"

Clemens said he would drive the couple over to Carson City if it came to it. Then he said, "They sprung Jug Baily this morning, Julia. He's over at the Golden Canary Saloon catching up on everything of importance that's happened since he was locked up. And working himself up into a mean drunk, I might add."

Julia had momentarily forgotten about Jug Baily. "You said you thought he'd get out earlier. Why did they keep him so long?"

"He got into a fight with another inmate and knifed him, so in order to make things look good for the Territory, they had to sort of detain him, I reckon. Julia, I think it would be a good idea if you sort of—took steps to protect yourself. You've only got Venita, Carrie, and Geraldine to help you out if Baily comes over here with blood in his eye."

"What do you think I ought to do, put bars on my bed?"

"No, I was thinking about Big George Kadduck. He's not as bright as he ought to be, but he idolizes you and he's a better shot, half-baked as he is, than any other man in town. Maybe you ought to hire him as your bodyguard."

"I'll think it over, Sam. Thanks for your concern." She didn't say anything about protection from the Law because there was no Law in Virginia City at that time. Sheriff Tate drew a fraction too late in a street confrontation two weeks earlier, and his body reposed in Boot Hill along with several other law enforcement officers. But Tate was the only one who

92

lost his life during the months Julia had been there in that particular manner. One died from injuries he received when he fell off a horse he was too drunk to ride; the other was shot in the back while he sat in on a card game. Had a full house, too, Sam Clemens said in the obituary.

Jug Baily didn't come knocking on Julia's door that day, or the next. Again, Clemens begged her to let George Kadduck move into one of her bedrooms, but she said she'd thought the matter over and decided against it. "George can't hover over me night and day. He'll need to sleep and visit the outhouse, just like anyone else. So that means I'll have to find another man who knows how to use a gun to fill in the gaps. But in case anything happens to me, Sam, you remember this day, the twenty-ninth of November, 1863, that I made a statement to you. I'm not going to pay a ponce a piece of my action."

Clemens argued for an hour in an attempt to let him send Big George over, at least for a while, but Julia remained firm. "Sam, listen to me. Having a bodyguard is just like locking your doors and windows against a thief. If a man wants to enter a house and rob it, he's not going to let a little lock stand in his way."

A number of nights passed with no trouble from Jug Baily. On the fourth day after he'd been released from jail, Julia's maid, Carrie, awakened her at eleven o'clock in the morning to say she had a visitor.

"Tell whoever it is to go away," she said. "I need another two hours of sleep."

The maid leaned over Julia's bed and whispered, her eyes as big as silver dollars. "It's Jug Baily, ma'am!"

"Oh." Julia thanked Carrie for the coffee she'd brought, then told her to stay in the kitchen with

Venita and Geraldine and keep the door shut. "Show Mr. Baily into the dining room first, Carrie, and tell him I'll be down as soon as I've made myself presentable. And give him a cup of coffee."

The young maid, white and trembling, nodded and scurried from the room. Julia washed, brushed out her hair, tied it at the nape of her neck with a vivid red ribbon, and slipped into a long velvet robe to match and chose satin slippers. She was downstairs ten minutes after Carrie awakened her, glowing with good health and fragrant with a subdued perfume.

"Good morning, Mr. Baily," she said as she seated herself at the head of the table. "I hope you enjoy Creole coffee."

"Not particularly." Baily gave her a long, appraising look. "I'm here to discuss a little matter of my status here in town."

She fluttered her eyelashes and said, "I understand many people practically bow down and kiss your hand when you enter a saloon or gambling hall, Mr. Baily."

He smiled. "You don't want to believe eveything you hear."

"Oh, I *don't*. I do find it quite puzzling as to why anyone finds it necessary to do so. You look like a mere mortal to me. Perhaps you possess some hidden talents." Her voice was silky, her eyes innocent,

"Let's get right down to business, Julia. You've got a nice layout here. The best of everything, just like I was told. Doing all right for yourself, I take it?"

"I have no complaints."

He scratched his chin and continued to grin at her. "The working girls here in town see to it that I get a little slice of the pie. I'm a reasonable man. Don't expect the whole hog or even half of it. Twenty-five percent has always seemed like a fair amount of cash on the line to pay for certain . . . favors."

"How about spelling out those certain favors, Mr. Baily?"

"A girl gets hurt, I see to it that she sees a good doctor. I take care of my girls. A girl gets picked up for indecent behavior, you know, like taking too many drinks and maybe going out on the street without any clothes on, why I see to it that she doesn't have any trouble with the Law. And . . ." Baily cleared his throat, stopped smiling, and spoke in a low, icy voice. "I see to it that none of my girls get themselves beat up."

Her voice matched his for coldness. "How very nice. For your girls. I, however, am no one's girl. I operate alone and intend to stay that way. Will you have more coffee, Mr. Baily?"

"You're making a mistake, Julia. How'd you like to have that pretty face of yours all pushed out of line with maybe your jawbone where your nose ought to be? It'd be a shame to bust out that mess of shiny white teeth you've got, too."

"I have no intention of allowing such a thing to happen, Mr. Baily."

He stood, folded back the cuffs of his slightly soiled shirt, and gazed at the brass that circled both his wrists. Slowly, looking at her with contempt, he took a wicked looking ring from his pocket and slipped it on the knuckle of his index finger. Several pieces of sharp metal protruded from the center of the ring, each one a half inch in length.

She waited quietly until he was standing over her, his arm drawn back menacingly before she stood up. She smiled as she brought up the little derringer she'd hidden in the pocket of her robe, leveling it at his chest. "Stand where you are, Mr. Baily."

"Whore! You put that toy gun down. You hear me?" Ignoring her palm-sized pistol, he brought his fist down in a swift arc. Only a lithe movement to the right saved her left cheek from being mangled by the prongs on the ring. Without blinking, she squeezed the trigger, her motions instinctive, deadly.

A blossom of blood about the size of a half dollar appeared on his shirt, but he didn't go down. Both his hands came up, then swiftly down, his wrists with their brass bands a lethal weapon as he bellowed in fury, obscenities falling from his lips. Again she squeezed off a shot, careless about her aim as she felt the crashing blow to her head. The bullet caught him in the forehead, but didn't stop him. It took two more shots to send him to the floor, one in the throat, the other in the chest. He fell heavily. Her fingers released the little weapon, and it fell to the plush blue carpet while she stood staring down at the remains of Jug Baily.

"Go get Sam Clemens, Carrie—Venita— someone." In her horror, she didn't even see the three maids, nor did she know until much later that they'd disobeyed her instructions. When Baily advanced on her, they'd left the kitchen to stand quietly inside the dining room, which was where they were during the insane seconds that passed before she ended Baily's life.

No charges were brought against Julia Bernard. It was the esteemed opinion of the Carson City Judge who reviewed the case that she had acted in self-defense. When the minions of the Law arrived at the gory scene, Jug Baily's index finger was wrapped around the trigger of his .45, a circumstance that sent Julia into a state of belated shock.

To Sam Clemens, she said, "I didn't see him take his gun out of the holster, I swear it!" The expression that crossed the editor's face was not lost on Julia. He looked at the girls who worked for her, and she understood that he was wondering the same thing that she was—if one of the girls had removed his pistol *after* the fact. Prudently she decided against asking about it.

On the fifteenth of December, Judge Clayton of Carson City pronounced Julia innocent of any wrongdoing in the matter of the death of one Jug Baily. Then the Judge accepted her offer of transportation to Virginia City, where he was to join the Reverend Lantz and the Widow Stacey in holy matrimony.

The new preacher had come to Julia's house immediately after the news swept through Virginia City that Jug Baily had died on Julia's dining room floor. "I didn't come to pray for you, Sister, or to talk to you about much of anything. All I'm here for is to let you know I'm right here at your side, neither as judge nor preacher. I'm just a man who heard the Call of God and listened to what He had to say. That doesn't make me any better or any worse than any other person on this earth, but it appeared to me that right now you might need a friend or two. Mrs. Stacey will be along just as soon as she takes her bread out of the oven."

Sam Clemens, who sat quietly with Julia in her parlor, poured the preacher a glass of wine. Mrs. Stacey arrived within the half hour, and soon Julia's house was overflowing with townspeople, most of whom had come to stand by her in what they feared might be her hour of need. Later that day Preacher Lantz and Mrs. Stacey said they'd be pleased and honored to be married in Julia's parlor when she offered, and it was only by coincidence that they set the day for December 15th.

Sam Clemens gave the bride in marriage and Julia

Bernard was Matron of Honor. Other wedding guests included Fancy LaVonne Skidmore, Pretty Kitty Sullivan, Queenie Dismore, and Lourene Mallot, all of sporting fame in Virginia City. Sixteen more-or-less faithful members of the little church milled around with the Ladies of the Evening and rubbed elbows with Johnny Castanet, Silver Pete, Luckie Elmore, and many other respected businessmen, most of whom owned gambling halls, saloons, meat markets, haberdasheries, or other establishments.

Clemens wrote about the wedding in his usual style of dry humor and warmth. He referred to it as the social event of the year and listed the names of all the members of the wedding party with solemn dignity as well as their social standing.

Julia was listed as the "well-known social leader of Virginia City." Fancy Skidmore and Pretty Kitty were written up as "ladies who are well-known for their good works and many kindnesses." Queenie Dismore and Lourene Mallot were referred to as socialites who were instrumental in bringing a number of cultural events to the fair city. When the newspaper came out, Julia read the account of the wedding and almost choked with laughter. The following Monday she chided the editor gently as she served him dinner. "You write well, Sam. But the tongue-in-cheek was rather heavy."

"Why? I didn't write a word that isn't absolutely true. You're a social leader who led the people into ridding the town of the filth. Who took the sick into her own house and nursed them back to health? Julia Bernard. Social leader, my dear, means one who is concerned about and takes the lead in conducting social affairs and welfare of the community. Fancy Skidmore and Pretty Kitty are certainly well-known for their good works and many kindnesses. Fancy and Pretty both go around taking up donations for the funeral service of everyone who dies without enough funds for a decent Christian burial. Besides that, they gave their profits from one Saturday night out of every month until funds were raised for the church house. That leaves Lourene and Queenie. Both are mighty fine dancers, and Queenie has one of the best singing voices in the West. If that isn't promoting culture, I'll eat every sheet of my newspaper."

"What you're saying, Sam, is that words are only words."

He nodded. "Exactly. A social leader in Virginia City just isn't the same as a social leader in Boston. Speaking of Boston, another killing took place this afternoon at the Sazarac. Broke the good record all to hell and back. It's been seventeen days since the last one, and the big money around town was in favor of twenty days without a victim of sudden lead poisoning."

"Who got killed, Sam? And how much did you lose?"

"The owner of the Sazarac. Boys got kind of juiced up and wanted to have a little fun. Nobody meant to do any harm. Nobody was even mad at anybody. Seven miners came riding into the Sazarac with pistols blazing. Poor old Rufus was standing behind his bar when the ruckus started. Didn't duck, I'd reckon. Probably took him by surprise. Funny thing, though, Julia—I was in there one day last week and Rufus told me he'd been down on his back, his legs hurt, and he had a hard time getting out of bed in the morning. I tried to joke him out of it, but he looked me square in the eye and said he never did want to be old and hurting and feeble, that he hoped he'd check out before he got down and couldn't get up. Well, that's the way it happened. They figure it was probably Boston Curley who fired the shot that got old Rufus."

"How so?"

"Well, Boston Curley lost the sight in one eye a few months back. When he gets likkered up, he tends to forget about it. It was his shooting eye, not his squinting one. When he came riding into the Sazarac with the rest of the boys, he said he bet five hundred dollars he could shoot the whiskey glass out of Rufus' fingers. Bad aim, on account of he squinted with his good eye. Shot blind."

"Oh, dear. Poor old Rufus! ... Sam, you didn't answer my other question. How much did you lose?"

"Me? Only two hundred dollars. But think of it, Julia—if we'd gone twenty whole days without a killing, I'd have made twelve hundred! That's the way it goes. Sazarac's closed up tighter than a drum. Rufus had a nephew over in Deadwood who'll probably inherit the saloon. Name of Tom Spencer."

They went on to talk of other things before Julia and Sam Clemens went into the parlor of Julia's Palace, where they spent a few hours at the piano. The name, Tom Spencer meant nothing to Julia, and all thoughts of the casual slaying of Rufus Elia left her mind when Venita announced a gentleman caller.

"But I'm never open for business on Monday evenings, Venita," said Julia as she looked up from the keyboard.

"This gentleman is an old friend, he said for me to tell you, ma'am. A real old friend from away back, when you were just a little girl. He's awful big, ma'am. And he's a nigra, too. Asked to speak to Mistress Julia. What shall I tell him, ma'am?"

100

VII

Big Jimpson and Vivian lived several miles outside the little village of Reno on a spread of several hundred acres they'd homesteaded after they were married and left Louisville. Together they built a sturdy frame home, erected necessary buildings, and worked their land, raising sheep and goats as well as a truck garden.

It had long been Vivian's dream to someday have a greenhouse, and later a flower shop in a town. The greenhouse was now a reality, but the flower shop was still a dream for the future. Vivian carefully tended and nurtured all growing plants and had taught her husband the art of cultivation. As a child, Jimpson was sickly, which was why he'd been brought into the big house where he became a houseboy. Jimpson taught Vivian to read and write, and they were happy in their freedom, their love, and their prosperity.

The couple enjoyed the respect of most of the citizens of Reno. They were kind and thoughtful citizens who lent a hand to anyone who was in need. In the beginning they'd lived quietly and kept to themselves. By 1863 they were solidly at home in the Territory, although it had taken them a long time to reach that place of acceptance. They'd been there two years when a delegation came out to their isolated farm house to invite them to a tent meeting in Reno. They attended the Baptist services and the majority of the congregation made them welcome. When enough funds were raised to build a church, Big Jimpson was the first man to arrive at the site, his vivacious and lovely wife at his side. Vivian mingled with the other wives who cheered their menfolk on at the church-raising and saw to it that they had unlimited supplies of good food and coffee. When she spoke wistfully of her dream of someday having a flower shop in town, the women encouraged her, although most of them agreed that Virginia City or Sparks would be a better place for a business endeavor. Nobody believed Reno would grow into a town of much consequence, but Big Jimpson and Vivian had already committed themselves to the Washoe lands.

The only grief that marred the contentment of the former slaves was their childless state. Jimpson mourned over his inability to father a child, knowing it was his fault since Vivian had given birth to three children before she was sixteen, all of whom had been sold when very young.

The Jimpsons lived with another grief that was less personal; word had come to them that Juliette had returned home to Louisville and found her husband dead. According to Effie Lukie's letter, she had gone down to New Orleans where whe'd had some kind of a set-to with her sisters. Effie Lukie said she didn't know what the quarrel was about, but it was rumored that Juliette was going to Nevada Country. The young girl added that something dreadul had happened to Mistress Juliette, but she'd never been able to get the straight of it because Mr. and Mrs. Ware wouldn't speak of the matter. She knew Juliette was taken from the train by what she referred to as a "bad white man, worser than a bad nigger;" for one of the other servants in the Ware household had overheard that much. What had happened to her between the time she was taken off the train and came back to Louisville, Effie Lukie didn't know, and since she left New Orleans after the falling-out with her sisters, nobody had ever heard from her since. But Mr. and Mrs. Ware knew she was planning to go to the Nevada Territory.

Hardly a day passed that Big Jimpson didn't speak of Mistress Juliette. She had been his favorite out of all the Bienveillance children. When she was a baby he'd been set to amuse her as she played on the floor. He told his wife again and again that if Mistress Juliette was alive, she'd surely be somewhere around Sparks, Virginia City, Goldfield, or Reno. There wasn't much of anything else in all of the Territory except vast amounts of land, mountains, lakes and nothingness. Just as Mr. Bruyère had done before him, he looked for her. Mr. Bruyère hired a Pinkerton man, but Big Jimpson went regularly to every settled place in Nevada where he looked for her, although he could never leave his name because of his color. There were no slaves in Nevada, but he would die before he would bring his beloved Mistress Juliette any shame by linking her publicly with a man of color.

Vivian faced him one day and spoke compassionately. "Jimp, honey, she must surely be dead. Otherwise, you'd have heard from her by now."

Jimpson could not bring himself to believe she could be dead. He loved her too much to consider such a thing. There were other reasons why he believed with all of his heart that she still lived, but they were too complex for him to totally understand them. "I just feel it in my bones, honey," he would say to his wife. "If she died, I would *know* it. I would feel it, somehow. I can't explain, sweetheart, but you know what I mean."

Vivian knew. Big Jimpson knew Mr. and Mrs. Bienveillance were dead before the report of their accident was delivered to the mansion. He'd felt it, but he'd spoken of it only to Vivian. He had also known the exact moment his old mother died, even though he'd been more than two thousand miles away at the time. Mistress Emilié, who was cruel in some ways, was thoughtful in others. When Big Jimpson's mother died peacefully in her sleep, Mistress Emilié sent him a telegram. It was delivered at eight o'clock in the morning, but Big Jimpson awakened during the night, at exactly three fifteen. He said, "Mammy is gone. I feel it in my heart." The telegram was little more than a verification of a message Big Jimpson had already received in some mysterious way that neither of them understood, but accepted.

Jimpson read in the *Territorial Enterprise* about the death of Jug Baily. Something stirred deep in his mind when he looked at the name of the woman who killed the man in self-defense. "Julia Bernard," he said out loud.

"What's that, Jimp?" Vivian was removing the seeds from dried marigolds, to save them for the spring.

"I said there's an account of a killing over in Virginia City. Man by the name of Jug Baily was shot and killed by a woman named Julia Bernard. Says here she's a local lady who's well known for her many philanthropical acts. Something about that rings a bell, somehow or another. I can't quite figure it out just what . . . Julia Bernard. Hmmmm. Now, you know, if Juliette wanted to hide herself, not that I think she would, but if she *did,* seems to me she'd take a name that . . . Julia . . . B. for Bienveillance, B. for Bruyère. You follow me, honey?"

"No, Jimp, I can't say as I do. Anyway, what would Mistress Juliette want to hide herself for? You know as well as I do that she loved Mr. Bruyère better than anything else on God's earth. I tell you, Jimp, something awfully bad happened to her. Miz Ware wrote and said she'd come home, but she didn't say anything else. Then she said Mistress Juliette went on back to her home place down in New Orleans, but we know she left there. Don't know why, but she left. I tell you, Jimp, there's something going on and we don't know what it *is.*"

Big Jimpson put his arms around his wife and held her close. "Hon, you don't think that woman in Virginia City could be Mistress Juliette, do you? If I thought you did, I'd harness up old Nellie and Maud and drive on up there."

"Baby, no. I don't think so. Mistress Juliette, she just went and took her troubles off somewhere to be by herself. Maybe she went over to France or England or somewhere."

Big Jim was putting extra protection around the greenhouse against the cold weather when the edition of the *Territorial Enterprise* came in, in which the editor had written the news of the wedding of Reverend Lantz and Polly Stacey, He didn't have a chance to read it until two days later, but when he did, he was so convinced that he'd found Juliette that he wanted to shout for joy. He asked Vivian if she'd read the paper. She said she had.

"Honey, didn't you read about the wedding?"

"Yes, Jim. Why? We don't know any of those folks."

"No, baby, but listen to what Miss Julia Bernard served the wedding guests:

"Shrimps creole, Louisiana rice, French fried okra, *salade de melon* and hearts of artichoke. The *pièce de résistance* was the five-tiered wedding cake. Before the sumptuous wedding feast, the bride and groom were toasted with champagne imported from the French wineries of Chateau du Breuil. The bride, resplendent in... well I didn't mean to read that part. But what do you think, honey, about all that French-Creole food? Seems to me that when Mistress Juliette married Master Bruyère her mama served Shrimps creole, Louisiana rice—"

"Oh, now, Jimp, you know very good and well folks have come out here from all over the country. Mr. and Miz de Méritoire who recently moved to Reno because the husband is going to be working as a mechanic for the railroad were born and raised less than a mile from the Bienveillance home. Miz Méritoire serves red Louisiana rice every day of the week and if she could get her hands on some shrimps she would serve them too. Lord Jesus, Jimp, but you—oh, well. If you won't rest until you've found out for yourself that this woman is not our Mistress Juliette, then *go!*"

"Come with me, sugar."

"Honey, I can't. I promised the church ladies I would bake a Bible cake. Then there's the flowers. It's up to me to get those dahlias ready, else there'll not be a single flower for old Miz McNaughten's husband's funeral. It'd be a shame for us to not go to the funeral, Jimp, seeing that we're their nearest neighbors. Now don't look at me so sorry-like. If I thought for one minute you'd find Mistress Juliette over in Virginia City, I wouldn't hesitate a minute. But don't you see, honey? We can't both of us go, but you've got to, just like I've got to stay."

Big Jimpson's shoulders sagged for a moment, but he kissed his woman mightily, gave her a big smile and told her he understood. "Look for me when you see me, baby. Something just keeps calling to me, understand? Something that I don't exactly hear with my ears, but more like a voice inside of me telling me to get on up there to the Comstock."

Vivian said she knew what he meant, and she did, too. He knew she did, and didn't hold it against her because she really was too busy, too committed, to go off on what he was willing to concede might be a wild goose chase. Vivian had not taken to the solitary life as well as Jimpson had. She needed to be with people. As he drove down the lane he turned back to wave at her. She stood in the kitchen doorway looking lonely, and he remembered how fun-loving she'd always been, how she'd come alive in the presence of others. But there'd been no other way for them to make a place for themselves and be accepted in the Territory than to do as they'd done. Keep to themselves and wait for white folks to come to them. If they did, why, that was just fine. If they didn't, they still had each other, their love, and their land. They were liked and Vivian needed to do the things that brought her the warmth of friends.

Three days later, just as the distant hills were beginning to purple, Big Jimpson turned his horses into the lane toward home. In all of the years since he'd first turned sweet on Vivian, Jimpson had never told her an untruth. He loved her from the moment she was brought to the Bienveillance home when she was eighteen and he was twenty-one. His own mother had helped to heal the lashes her previous master put on her back, because she tried to run away when he wanted to breed her again. After she was caught and beaten senseless, she was taken to the market and put on the block. Her old master, known throughout the area for his cruelty, stood up in front of the white men who were there to bid on the shackled slaves and swore he bought Vivian out of pity, that her former owner had put her in the shape she was in. She cowered, half mad with pain, the bloody lash-marks on her back festered and running with pus. M. Bienveillance sickened at the sight and angry beyond words, threw out a bid so high that all the other men who clustered around the slave arena drew back and shook their heads at such foolishness. Vivian came home with him that day riding in the back of the wagon on her belly. It was a week before she could walk straight and three more weeks before Jimpson's mother with the aid of Mme. Bienveillance nursed her back to health. All those years they'd worked together and known one another in New Orleans, Vivian shied away from Jimpson just as she'd moved away like quicksilver from all the other young bucks around the place. She'd flirted, laughed, talked, and danced, but she'd never allowed any man to get close to her. It wasn't until they arrived in Louisville in the midst of poor Mr. Bruyère's crushing grief because of his missing wife that she'd given Jimpson to understand she was willing to be courted.

The long love he'd carried in his heart for her, the long years of waiting for her mind to be healed of whatever that was in her that made her fear men had been worth every hour, he thought as he pondered on the past and the present. It galled him to realize that he was going to break a wedding vow. A silent one, but a promise, just the same, he told himself as he wearily fed and watered the horses. It wasn't right to make up his mind to lie to his wife even if he hadn't vowed out loud to never do it. But he was going to lie to her, just the same. It'd hurt her to hear the truth.

Big Jimpson took off his hat, looked up at the sky, and spoke softly. "Lord, Lord. Help me in my need. One thing Master Bienveillance taught me was to be true to myself. Help me face up to it, Lord. I don't want to tell Vivian because it'd hurt me all over again to say those awful words, for her to know the truth."

"It wasn't Mistress Juliette," he said as he walked into the kitchen. "Just like you said, sugar, lots of folks came West to live. From Tennessee and Kentucky, Alabama and New York. Everywhere. Well, well. Smell that coffee. And I believe to my soul that's a pot of good ragoût you just took out of the oven." He sniffed. "Fresh biscuits! Baby, it's good to be home."

VIII

Tom Spencer sent word to Julia by Evan Willoughby that he wanted to see her. It was in the middle of the afternoon and she was slightly taken aback. "He said it was urgent, Miss Bernard," said the artist who had painted her crest on the sides of her carriage.

"Urgent?" Julia's curiosity grew. "But he's been in town only a week. Carrie told me he'd taken the black crepe from the door of the Sazarac this morning, that he'd re-opened the place. Why does he find it urgent to see me?"

"I don't know, ma'am. But he asked me to bring back your answer."

"Tell him to come right away, then."

Within less than a half hour, the nephew of the late Rufus Elia was shown into Julia's parlor. She looked up at him with a sparkling smile. "Welcome to my house, Mr. Spencer."

He reminded her of a panther. His eyes were dark, his hair as black as her own, and he was so tall that he towered over her. He was taller than Big Jimpson, but where the former slave was built on bulky lines, Tom Spencer was sleek and lean. He smiled. She smiled back. "Mr. Willoughby said your need to see me was urgent," she said as she gestured toward the love seat where a decanter of her fine wine awaited him.

He seated himself easily, then leaned back, nodding with a look of satisfaction. "I had to see you in person. That's all."

She poured his wine, then took a small chair across from him, where she sipped a cup of tea. After she put the cup down, she raised her eyebrows and looked at him questioningly. "In person? I'm afraid I don't understand."

"I'll explain. Out of deference to my uncle's death, I waited a full week after his funeral to open the Sazarac. We were as close as father and son. He brought me up, and I don't mind admitting his death was a shock. He was work-brickle and wouldn't want me to keep it closed any longer. The minute I set foot in the place my attention was attracted by a shadowy movement against the wall, followed by a slight cough. It was almost dark inside because all the shutters were drawn, and at first I wondered if I was hearing the ghost of my poor uncle. Then I heard a voice. 'Mr. Spencer, don't shoot. I was hired by your uncle to do this piece of work and I'm unarmed.' As my eyes adjusted to the dimness, I saw a man on a ladder. He had a paintbrush in his hand and I smelled turpentine. After I lit a lamp, I saw the picture on the wall. A portrait of a woman, and the stranger was working on it."

"He climbed down from the ladder, said he was Evan Willoughby, that my uncle had hired him to paint the picture. At first I was ready to throttle the little bastard. It wouldn't be the first time a person tried to pick up a few dollars by saying a dead man had hired him to do a job of work. But Willoughby assured me the work was all paid for. Said he owed my uncle a considerable amount of money. Said he was a drunk. My uncle fed him, let him sleep in the back of the saloon and kept him in booze. He'd started the portrait a week before my uncle was killed. Had a key, which he showed me. Came and went just like he always had, wanted to get the job done before I took over. Poor bastard. So I lit some more lamps and took a look at what he was doing. He'd already signed it. Evan Willoughby. Underneath he'd printed JULIA BERNARD, QUEEN OF THE COMSTOCK. I said by God if there was a woman who looked like that in Virginia City, I had to see her in person. So I sent the message and came on over as soon as Willoughby came back with your answer. And you're as beautiful as your picture. Even more so."

Julia had known nothing of the portrait. "Thank you, Mr. Spencer. I would very much like to see the painting. I'm honored."

"Then let's go." He finished his wine and stood.

When they arrived at the Sazarac, Evan Willoughby was removing the ladder. For a long moment, Julia stood in front of the bigger-than-life portrait, Tom at her side, the artist anxiously awaiting her comments. She nodded and her eyes misted over as she looked at Willoughby. "Evan, you've captured me to perfection. Expression and all. Why, you've put a touch of my personality in that picture. You're a genius."

"I was a little worried about the ruffles on your gown," Willoughby said. "And there's something about the eyes that doesn't quite suit me. I'll do a

112

little more on it after I've figured out just exactly what it is that doesn't quite do you justice about those eyes. But I'm pleased that you don't fault it, ma'am."

Tom said, "This calls for a toast. A double toast." He stepped behind the bar and took a bottle of champagne from a can of cold water. "I'd prefer it iced, but there's a time to do a thing, and if you let it pass the chance might never come again. To Julia Bernard, Queen of the Comstock," he said. The two men drank and Julia curtsied.

"Now Julia and I will drink to you, Evan," said Spencer. He raised his glass. "To a talented artist who has captured the essence of the most beautiful woman in the world. May he live in health, wealth, and happiness."

Willoughby's shoulders straightened and he spoke firmly. "Here, Mr. Spencer," he said after Julia and Tom had toasted him. "You take the rest of this champagne and pour it in the 'corner' bucket. I've had my last drink."

"Good for you, Evan." Spencer clapped the other man on the shoulder. "It's not going to be easy. If you need any moral support, just call on me."

"And me," added Julia.

Wistfully, Evan Willoughby watched as Spencer emptied the champagne from his glass into the bucket under the bar. "Thank you very much. I'll need all the help I can get. I decided back when I first came out of that last drunk that I wasn't going to get on another one. I'm going to stick around town until I know I'm all right, then I'm going back home where I belong. Going to make something of myself. Can't paint when I'm drunk or hung over."

Spencer told the artist he was welcome to continue sleeping in the back room, that he would

113

also provide him with his meals. "But if I catch you in the booze, Evan, out you go. You just made a promise to three people—yourself, Miss Bernard and me."

"I'll keep it, Mr. Spencer. I swear it."

On the way back to Julia's house, Spencer looked down at her and said, "You're going to be my girl, Julia."

"I'm no man's girl, Tom. And every man's, both at the same time. At least every man who can pay my price, although there are certain other qualifications that any prospective client must have. I'm selective."

Spencer laughed. Then he said, "I'm not going to be a client, Julia. I'm going to be your man. I want you, and by God I mean to have you. Just think about it for a minute or two. I laid eyes on you less than an hour ago, but I'm in love with you. It's the first time in my life I've ever told a woman I was in love with her. You ought to feel complimented."

"I am. But I won't be your girl."

"Yes you will, too. I'm going to charm you into it. Look at us, Julia. There we are, reflected in the window of the Silver Dollar Saloon." He took her arm and held her firmly so she could see their reflections. "You're one hell of a woman, Julia Bernard. Taller than most men, slender as a wand in places where a woman ought to be slender, and all soft and curvy where a woman ought to be all soft and curvy. And your face! Lord, you've got the kind of face men dream about."

"I appeal to you because we're much alike, Tom," she said quietly. "We could have been cut from the same mold. But you might as well get any notions of my being your girl out of your head. I have an idea that once you make up your mind you want something, all of heaven and hell won't stand in your

114

way." She looked up at him and smiled. "But you see, Tom, I'm every bit as strong-willed as you are."

"We'll see," he answered.

For a full week, she heard nothing more from Tom Spencer, although Evan Willoughby came to her house in the dead of night once and asked for her help. He wanted to drink, he said, and Tom was out of town. If he didn't talk to somebody who would tell him he must not drink, he was afraid he would do it. Until dawn, Evan Willoughby talked and Julia listened. He went to sleep on the floor of her parlor and she went back to bed, weary, but hopeful.

Late in the afternoon, she was awakened by a sharp little noise followed by Geraldine's voice, low, wheedling, yet indulgent. She couldn't make out the maid's words, but the tone of Geraldine's voice assured her all was well. When she came down at six o'clock, the door that led from kitchen to dining room was closed. Unusual unless she had a guest for dinner, but seeing it closed brought back the memory of being awakened by a strange sound. When she pushed open the door to the kitchen, she saw Geraldine sitting in a chair, a little black ball of fur in her arms.

"Oh, ma'am, I hope he didn't disturb you," said the girl.

"He's *darling!*" Julia knelt on the floor and brushed her hand across the dog's curly fur. "Why, he's only a puppy. Where did you get him, Geraldine?"

"He's not mine, ma'am. He came in a basket." Geraldine gestured toward a wicker basket with a red satin pillow. "I'll run and get the letter, ma'am."

Julia stood and reached for the puppy. Geraldine was back in a moment with an envelope. "See, ma'am, it had your name on it. The man who brought the little thing asked if he had the right place and I said he did, so he left the puppy, basket, and all!"

While Julia read the note that had come along with the puppy, the maid spoke of how she had tried so hard to keep it quiet, how sweet it was, how intelligent.

"He's a gift from Mr. Spencer," said Julia. "But I'm going to let you have him."

"Oh, but ma'am, you can't give away a gift so fine—and anyway, look at the way the little fellow is lying up against your bosom. He loves you already. Look at his eyes, how he looks at you so adoringly. Oh, he's just the most cunning little puppy I've ever seen. How can you resist anything so sweet and cuddly and precious?"

"I can't. That's why I must give him to you, Geraldine. I can't bear to lose something I cherish, and dogs don't live forever."

"Ma'am, that's a terrible way for you to feel."

Julia shrugged. "That's the way I am, Geraldine." With a final pat on the French poodle's fancily groomed head, she handed him back to Geraldine, who tried her best to hold him. But he jumped out of her arms and went to Julia, where he sat up on his little bottom and held his black paws up in a most beguiling manner.

"Oh, Lord," she said as she stooped down and picked him up. "Trouble. That's what you are. Trouble." He looked up at her, yawned, showed his tiny white teeth and pink tongue, then went to sleep, cradled in her arms.

Geraldine told her roses had been delivered, that she'd put them in the parlor. "And so *many,* ma'am."

In the parlor, Julia broke into her lilting laughter at the sight of a room full of roses. The puppy barked

116

when she put him down, then it went over to sniff one of the fragrant red buds. As if he'd been instructed to do so, he took a rose from the vase and brought it to her, sitting up and looking too comical and cunning for her to resist, the long-stemmed rose in his mouth.

For three weeks after he came back from Arizona, Tom Spencer courted Julia with single-minded purpose. Every day she was gifted with a new and exotic present. Every afternoon at promptly four o'clock, he sent her a love letter by Willoughby, who was staying sober. But he didn't come to see her, although each time she received diamonds, pearls, rubies, and all the other baubles, she sent him a warm letter of thanks and an invitation to dinner. On the fourth week, Willoughby brought her a letter and said, "This one is the last one, ma'am. He told me not to wait for an answer."

Julia sent her reply by Carrie:

If you'd stated your case from the beginning as you did in your latest letter, you could have saved yourself considerable expense, Tom. When you said you wanted me to be your girl I believed you wanted me to be yours and yours alone. My answer is an eager yes! May I have the pleasure of your presence at dinner tonight at eight o'clock?

After she dispatched the letter, Julia dressed with care and drove down to the office of the *Territorial Enterprise*, where she asked to see the editor.

Clemens shook her hand, asked her to be seated across from his desk and said, "To what do I owe this unexpected pleasure, Julia?"

"You've been composing Tom Spencer's letters,

then he copies them in his own handwriting."

"I've done nothing of the sort. I know nothing about any letters you may have received from Tom. I swear it."

She laughed. "I don't believe you."

"So don't believe me. But if you've been getting love letters from Tom, he either wrote them himself or asked for help from another direction. I'll be frank with you, though—I know he's madly in love with you, and it's my opinion you'd make a fine couple. Are you going to marry him?"

"Marry?" Julia's laugh pealed out merrily. "Certainly not. But I like him very much. So . . ." She frowned. "Are you sure you didn't compose those letters, Sam?"

"I'll swear it on the Bible, Julia. You're radiant! That's why I asked if you were going to be wed. Brides have that kind of ethereal glow. Unfortunately, the glow usually fades to a scowl a few months after the wedding."

"Or it fades into grief," she commented. "Sam, I heard you were talking about leaving. I can't bear to think of it."

"It won't be for a while, Julia. A few months from now I do plan to leave. I'll miss you very much."

"When you go, I'm going to wish I'd never met you. I've had enough sorrow to last me a lifetime, and here I've grown to love you when I didn't intend to love anyone ever again. It hurts to think of losing you. You're like a brother. A wonderful friend." She thought of little black Trouble, who had wriggled his way into her heart, of the affection she felt for Tom Spencer, of her warm and sisterly feelings toward Samuel Clemens, and Big Jimpson, who had disturbed her greatly when he came unexpectedly and went back to Vivian with his face all clouded

118

with gloom. "Damn it, Sam, I can't understand myself. Here I am, saddled with a dog I didn't want but can't stand to be away from, a friend I didn't want because I knew it wouldn't last—and a man who says he loves me. I want him to, too. What in the world is the matter with me? Why can't I be the one who controls my own emotions?"

"What you need, Julia, is a new worthy cause. All the outhouses are built, we've got the place pretty well rid of mice and rats and dead animals. Nobody throws their garbage on the streets any more—"

"Ahhhh! Worthy causes don't keep me from forming attachments!"

"No, but they help to keep you from stewing around about it." He gave her the new edition of the paper. "City's going to try to buy a new fire wagon. Tom Spencer is going to be the new fire chief. The two families who were burned out last week put the notion into motion. Read all about it in the newspaper, Julia. Then you can help take up a collection to pay for the new fire fighting equipment."

"I asked you for help, Sam. I don't want to get attached to people."

Clemens gave her his crooked smile. "Neither do I. Nobody does, because it isn't human nature to want to be hurt. But life is full of hurts, honey, and it's more human to form attachments than to not."

"Sam, I would rather die than to go through some of the things I've suffered in the past."

He turned pale. "Don't say that, Julia. It sounds too much like what Rufus Elia said to me a week before he got shot."

She stood. "I'll think about helping to raise the money for the new fire fighting equipment. But don't worry about me, Sam. I'm fated to live out my life

119

running scared—of myself and my big, dumb heart. I'll be an old grey-haired woman someday, still running to beat hell."

"You're beginning to talk like a Westerner, Julia."

"It's catching."

"So is love."

IX

In 1864, *The Julia Bernard* mine was duly recorded at the Bureau of Mines office, an event that was written up in the *Territorial Enterprise* in the fine style of the editor. A month or so later, *The Julia Bernard* club car was christened. It was a plush and extravagantly furnished car on the Virginia and Truckee Railroad, and her name seemed appropriate to put in the place of honor above the door.

The shiny new red fire wagon was purchased six months after the Virginia City residents named Tom Spencer Department Chief. Julia embroidered banners for the fire engine she had helped fund, and on the Fourth of July she was crowned Queen of the Independence Day Parade. Her crown was a red fireman's hat, and as she rode in the parade she proudly held aloft the brass fire trumpet, in which reposed a bouquet of red roses. Her red satin dress billowed in the breeze as the entire crew of Engine Company Number One, resplendent in bright red shirts, knelt on a float of red and white roses as they waved their hats at the adoring, stamping, cheering crowd.

Samuel Clemens left Virginia City that year. The War between the States raged on, the Union gathering strength from the silver that was taken out of the hills surrounding Virginia City. Nevada was admitted into the Union as the thirty-sixth state, and Julia Bernard was in the celebration parade, wearing a silver-blue gown in which was sewn hundreds of pearls. Acclaimed the Queen of Nevada, her crown was of pearls and diamonds, set in sparkling silver. Slippers with solid silver heels adorned her feet, and in her upraised hand she held a silver lamp. The vehicle that carried her through town was covered with a blanket of carnations, the legend worked in silvery blue against a background of white: SILVER WILL HELP BRING THE UNION VICTORY. Twenty women worked all day long at dyeing the white carnations the exact shade of blue before the float was put together.

More than a hundred and fifty million dollars was taken from a single mine that year, and Virginia City grew rapidly. When President Lincoln asked for donations for funds to finance a Sanitation Commission, Julia contributed the gross receipts of six weeks of her thriving business, somewhere around twenty thousand dollars. Tom Spencer matched her, dollar for dollar. Her civic duty took her to the site of the mines during disasters, where she kept the watch along with anxious wives and children as well as supplying hot coffee and soup. Widows of miners who lost their lives received generous stakes from her private coffers, and she harassed the mine owners until a permanent widows' fund was put into being. But Julia Bernard did not spend all of her time doing good works. She went often to the opera house, accompanied by Tom Spencer. In summer she wore a cape and hood of white silk and purple velvet. Winters were severe, and she took great pleasure in the luxurious sable cape with matching muff and hood. Four nights out of every week were reserved for her career. The other three were for herself and Tom Spencer, who told her he loved her at least once each day, to which she replied, "Thank you, Tom. I care deeply for you, too."

Almost immediately after Nevada became a state, the Army Engineers moved into town along with their wives and families. New residents moved in when the need for expanded business places was felt. Bootmakers, seamstresses, tailors, cabinet makers, and other merchants who preferred to mine their wealth from the needs of the miners instead of the ground became established merchants with virtuous wives. The wives soon banded together against the lowly women who ran bawdy houses or walked the streets of Virginia City. They went to the lawyers who abounded on C Street, lawyers who had wives of their own who complained about their environment. They wanted to rid the area of harlots and saloons, the sinful gambling halls, and all the other vices that had survived for too long without the loving guidance of pure-minded Christian women, they said. Stock-brokers came home to find their wives in tears. They were offended at the sight of jades who boldly walked the streets and dared to say a friendly how-do-you-do. They spoke of their children deploring the sad fact that their innocent lambs would grow up in an atmosphere of depravity, and demanded to have the jezebels run out of town—from the gambling halls, the saloons, and and the houses of prostitution.

The gentlemen merchants of Virginia City tried to

make a compromise with their wives. They'd get rid of the tarts, but they couldn't very well make a man who had been in business that was considered legitimate in the new, wild and woolly state close up shop. The women were satisfied for a while. The street walkers and crib-girls moved out of town. Far out of town. But Julia Bernard and Carmen DeLaney owned property. They were women of warmth, and Julia was idolized. Julia agreed to attend the opera, performances of *Hamlet, As You Like It*, and less impressive theatrical productions in her accustomed box, but with the box heavily veiled in order to keep the sight of her face from disturbing the eyes of any pious beholder. When the manager of Maguire's came to her and asked if she'd mind, she laughed so hard that she almost fell to the floor from weakness before she agreed. "Sherrod's wife was once the biggest strumpet in San Francisco," she told him between gales of laughter. "I knew her well. There are others who have joined the long list of reformed whores, but I'll consent to having my box covered with veils. I don't want to look at those hypocritical bitches any more than they want to look at me." Carmen DeLaney wasn't a patron of the arts.

Although she was not offended at the few steps toward reform that concerned her personally, Julia was furious when Polly came down and told her a delegation of church ladies had asked her husband to resign as preacher. "They want hell-fire-and-brimstone, but he doesn't believe in scaring people to death with threats of burning in eternal fire," Polly explained. "And they don't like it because I come to see you, either. They *said* so! Mr. Lantz tried to talk real nice to them, but you know how it is, Julia. A bunch of women bent on having their way are enough to drive a man crazy. You'd have thought he

124

peed on the altar or something." Poor Polly broke down and wept on Julia's shoulder. "I had hoped to stay here until I died, Julia. But we'll have to pick up and move, because Mr. Lantz believes in keeping the peace. The ringleader is a puffy little lady named Florence Sherrod. She said it was sinful for a man of the cloth to take supper with...a fallen woman."

Julia steamed. In high dudgeon, she alighted from her fancy coach in front of the Sherrod house, and when she reached the front door she didn't bother to knock. Instead, she marched right in and stood in the foyer, shrieking at the top of her lungs. "Flossie, you get your much-used butt out here, do you hear me?"

Maids scurried forward and took one look at the tall, whitefaced woman who stood as regally as any queen and demanded to see someone named Flossie. "Madame is not at home," one of them finally told her. "And no one named Flossie lives here."

"*Florence*, then!" Julia spat the name. "And I know she's at home. Her carriage is out there, and she won't walk to her next-door neighbor's, the lazy fat pig!" She turned the full wrath of her blazing dark eyes on the maid who had said Madame wasn't at home. "Now you get yourself into whatever part of the house Madame is hiding, and tell her I'll tear this place apart with my hands if she isn't here within two minutes."

A plump blonde woman came runnining into the foyer, her arms outstretched as if she would protect her precious possessions against a hurricane. "Such a disturbance," she squealed. "Mercy *me*, I am quite beside myself at this display of crass *behavior,* my dear woman."

"You're beside yourself all right," Julia said. "You've grown as fat as an old sow, Flossie. There's two of you standing alongside the little thing I knew back at Sweet Bird's place. Now, are you going to retract your demand that the preacher and his wife leave the church? Or would you rather I march you through the streets of Virginia City with a great big banner flying from your rump that says you used to be a doxie at Sweet Bird's whorehouse?"

The woman's watery blue eyes filled with tears. "You are totally mistaken. I shall have you arrested for this invasion of privacy, this . . . outrageous accusation!"

"You'll have one hell of a hard time having me arrested. The lawmen are my friends, every last man of them. And I'm *not* mistaken. You've got a blue butterfly tattooed on the left cheek of your fat ass, Flossie." Lithe as a cat, Julia bent and lifted the woman's voluminous skirts with one hand and yanked down her drawers with another one. "There it is. Plain for all the world to see. Your hired help already knows it's there, Flossie. Do you want everyone else in town to know it?"

Mrs. Bertram Sherrod fanned her face with her hand as she leaned helplessly over, her arms held in Julia's vise-like grip. "I'll—I'll go down to the Lantz house myself," she whimpered. "Then I'll speak to the other ladies. I'm sure I can get them to . . . change their minds. I'm sure Mr. Lantz is a good preacher; in fact, I wasn't the one who . . . I didn't have a thing to do with the petition." Mrs. Sherrod licked her lips and bobbed her head back and forth, her eyes darting from the hired girls' curious faces to Julia's. All three of her chins quivered.

"You *headed* that delegation, you lying *floozy!*" Julia grabbed the other woman's hair and pulled. She almost lost her footing when the blonde curls came off in her hands. Mrs. Bertram Sherrod screamed, clasped her bald head with both hands, and fled up the stairs. Julia went to the Sazarac to see Tom.

Tom said, "You didn't accomplish a thing, Julia, except the satisfaction of shaming the little walrus. Why in the devil did you go flaxing down there without thinking? Why didn't you come down to the saloon and talk to me about it first? I would have told you to steer clear of the woman. So her past *is* shady. She's not the only woman in town who wants to turn out Preacher Lantz, and they're not all former working girls."

"She instigated the movement to have him ousted."

"Oh, you fiery little darling." He came from behind the bar and took her in his arms in front of at least fifty men and a half dozen bed dolls who'd taken refuge at the saloon when the broom of righteousness swept through town. They were employed as dealers. Those who couldn't remember a diamond from a club were called entertainers. During their hours away from the Sazarac, Tom didn't care if they turned a trick or two, he'd told the gentlemen merchants when their wives learned that not all the jades were gone.

Julia felt small and cherished and protected. He called her his little darling, his baby, his little sweetheart. When she was with him she felt almost helpless. "I really should have talked to you before I went sizzling down there. Darn it. I wish I had." She wanted to tell him she loved him, and it wasn't the first time she'd wanted to, but every time she tried to say the words they stuck in her throat.

Mrs. Bertram Sherrod left town the following day. The elite were told that she had received a message that her old mother was very sick. The majority of Virginia Citians knew the truth of what had taken place in the foyer of the former prostitute's magnificent home within fifteen minutes after the incident occurred. Her hired girls were miffed. She blamed them for her embarrassment and swore at them in three languages for not keeping the front door locked so riff-raff couldn't come bursting in. That was bad enough, they said as they ran through the town to spread the titillating tale of the lady's humiliation. Especially since she'd told them in no uncertain terms to not lock the door, she was expecting the jeweler's wife and wanted to open the front door herself. But even worse than scolding them, swearing at them and blaming them, she'd fired them all and refused to give them the wages they had coming.

In time, the true story behind Mrs. Sherrod's sudden decision to leave town became known to even the virtuous, but Reverend Lantz was again asked to resign. They moved to Las Vegas, New Mexico. Julia hid her face in Tom's chest all the way home from the train station because she didn't want to let him see her cry. He patted her shoulder and tried to comfort her.

"I'll be glad when things settle down and get back to normal," she said against his shoulder.

"Darling little girl, the virtuous are here to stay. It's something we're all going to have to accept."

"If you tell me to join them since I can't lick them, I'll hit you," she sobbed. "I'll *never* join anyone with such cruel hearts and hypocritical notions. I admired the preacher, Tom. He isn't a person to judge the actions of others. I *despise* people who sit around and take it upon themselves to decide how other people ought to behave."

Tom pulled her head away from his shoulder,

looked into her miserable face and said, "Hey, now. Who's judging *this* time?"

"Oh, Tom!" He wiped away her tears and after he'd tied the horses, he helped her down and carried her inside, speaking eloquently of humanity all the while. When he put her down, she looked up at him with a quizzical expression.

"I'm convinced," she said. "Finally convinced. You wrote those letters to me yourself, didn't you?"

"What letters?"

"I always thought you had Sam Clemens write them. But you're a philosopher, too. In a way, you're similar to one another, you and Sam."

"Well, I'll be damned. Of *course* I wrote those letters. And I wouldn't have asked Sam Clemens to have written them for me if I hadn't. I never did like him very well. Oh, sure, I would have liked him fine if it hadn't been for those Monday nights you had with him. But . . . well, I guess I was a little jealous of him."

"You never had any reason to be, Tom. We were friends. That's all. Just friends." Trouble came bounding to greet her, and she picked him up to cuddle him in her arms. "Tom, I just love this dog. I guess you know that, though. I'm so glad you gave him to me." She looked at his face and didn't understand the expression. "Don't tell me you're jealous of Trouble."

"No, Julia. I'm not. But I would give the world if you'd tell me you love me. Just once. And I was thinking about the way you hold that little dog. Like a woman holding a baby. We could leave Virginia City, Julia. Go to Arizona or California, or anywhere you'd like. We could start all over. Settle down, have a family, become good, solid members of society. I could establish myself in a respectable business. You could use all those talents you have to make the world a little bit better. A woman's arms ought to hold a baby. What a fine mother you'd be!"

"Don't, Tom." She turned her back on him and walked to the window where she looked out without seeing. "I lost a baby once. When it happened, I didn't know I was expecting. I was happily married. That baby would have been my crowning joy if things had been different. Strange—I wonder about it now and then—I wonder what it would have looked like, whether it would have been a boy or a girl. I loved my husband very much. Since then, I've lived in terror of having another baby. Sam used to say God watches out over little children and drunks. He must watch out over me, too, because I've never had to face the fear of having a baby. It's not the having of it or the giving birth that scares me. It's the idea of waking up one morning and having a little baby to care for and to love."

She turned and faced him. "Tom, I don't want to ever talk about it again."

He changed the subject.

"It's been six months since Evan Willoughby had a drink. He's getting ready to go on back to his home town in Wyoming. Maybe we ought to give him a little going-away party, Julia."

"That's a good idea."

While all the rest of the members of Willoughby's farewell party drank champagne, the artist sipped black coffee. Before he left town, he gave Julia a present. It was a painting of Trouble, his curly hair shiny black against a white velvet pillow, his bright eyes alight with the adoration he reserved for his mistress. Many years later the portrait of *Julia's Trouble* was sold at auction for ten thousand dollars.

She heard from him now and then as he traveled from New York to London, to Paris, Rome and Spain. He never wrote any more than a few words. *Still sober. Love to you and Tom.*

In September of 1867 Julia rolled over in her Sunday morning bed and said to Tom, "I'm going to take a vacation. I need to get out of here for a while."

"Where do you plan to go, Julia?"

"I don't know yet." She yawned, turned back over, and thought about getting up. "Maybe I'll go to New Orleans. I'd like to know if my sisters are living, if my brother survived the war."

He reached for her hand. "I didn't know you were born in New Orleans. But a little vacation would do you good. It's been months since you've entertained anyone but me. Which is wonderful, and you don't need the money, but I've wondered if you've felt well lately. You seem a little tired at times."

"I'm in a rut. Putting on weight, eating too much because I'm bored—I like to cook and we both like to eat. Since Venita and Geraldine left to get married, I've turned into a housewife. But really, Carrie is all we need to run the house. Yes, I think I'll go on down to New Orleans."

"I've noticed some of your clothes are a little tight. We really don't need all those rich sauces, darling— although I'll admit I never push them away! How long will you be gone? Or, had you planned for me to go along?"

"Tom, I can't go down home with you."

"I didn't think you'd want to. All right, little darling." He sighed. "I suppose you'll take Trouble, though."

"Tom, you know that dog would die of a broken heart if I left him for a couple of months."

"Yeah. Well . . . how about some breakfast? Let's go down to the hotel and eat."

She agreed immediately and dressed as quickly as possible, but her mind was on the next day. If she waited much longer, it would be too late.

On Monday Julia waited until Tom left for work before she packed her trunks. If she let him take her to the station, she would have to travel in the wrong direction. So she left him a note, explaining that she didn't want to tell him goodbye. She'd try to be back before Christmas.

Three days later she registered at a hotel in San Francisco under the name of Mrs. Thomas Spencer. A few days after that, she made arrangements to have her baby at the Mildred Carson Johnson Lying-in Hospital where she told the authorities she was Mrs. Thomas Spencer, a widow, maiden name, Marie Thérèse d'Angelo. From there she went directly to a Mr. and Mrs. F. L. Marsdon, who ran a very discreet adoption agency.

Meeting Mrs. Marsdon's eyes, she said, "I am unmarried and my baby will be born in December. I wish to place him with people of French ancestry, preferably of Calvinistic persuasion. More important than the religion is the way the people live. They need not be affluent, but they must care for one another deeply and be childless."

She answered many questions and asked several. Before she left, Mrs. Marsdon asked her to sign preliminary papers, but said she would have until fifteen days after the birth of the baby to return and sign final papers, which would be notarized to comply with legal requirements.

On the twelfth of December Julia gave birth to an eight pound baby girl. Two weeks after her child was born, she was released from the hospital and went to her hotel room where she had left Trouble with an elderly lady. The poodle sniffed the black-haired, blue-wrapped bundle Julia carried and promptly licked the little pink face. Then he settled himself at the baby's side on the bed and put one little black paw protectively on the blanket.

"Stop fawning over that baby, Trouble," she said severely. "We're not going to keep it."

The poodle moved closer to the blanketed baby and rested his small chin on the softly rising and falling chest.

"I really thought she'd be a boy," Julia said to the dog.

For ten long minutes, she paced the floor and wrung her hands. Then she sat down and penned a letter to Big Jimpson:

> You said to write if I want to see you. I need you, and will be there as soon as I can get there from San Francisco, following the directions on the map you gave me.
>
> Love,
> Juliette.

Addressing her words to Trouble and her sleeping baby daughter, she said, "I wondered why I put that map he gave me in my traveling bag. I guess I knew all along I couldn't give him—I mean her, up." After she'd addressed the letter to Big Jimpson, she sat down at the desk in the hotel room and wrote again.

> Dear Tom,
> Please forgive me for not writing. I'll be home as soon as possible, sometime in January if everything goes according to plans. It's necessary for me to stay here in San Francisco

133

for a little while longer, for business reasons, although I would like very much to be with you over Christmas. You will be pleased when I do get there, for I have something to tell you that will make you very happy. I send you all of my love and I am

Your Julia

Big Jimpson had gone into Reno when Julia drove up to the house in her hired rig, but Vivian was at the farm. With her dark eyes running with tears of joy, Vivian said, "He's been looking for you every day, Mistress. Ever since he got your letter, he's been fit to be tied. Oh, my stars. You're prettier than ever, and that little baby is just the spittin' image of you when you were born!"

Julia looked at the way Vivian was holding her baby, and when she spoke her voice was husky with emotion. "I've come to my people. Come home, Vivian, Oh, God!" She put her hand to her face and moaned. "It's been such a long, long time since I've felt like a real person."

Over coffee and freshly baked bread, Vivian told her that if Big Jimpson hadn't taken sick she'd never have known she was in Virginia City. "But he got down real bad, Mistress Juliette, and thought he was going to die, so he told me he lied to me when he came back from seeing you. Said the lady was someone else. And he said you . . . that you . . . well, it was hard for him to talk about what you'd become, Mistress."

"Don't call me Mistress, Vivian. Just as that part of my life is all over and done with, the Mistress Juliette is finished. You're a woman and I am, too. We're friends and just as I said before, you and Big Jimpson are my people. My only people. Blood and kinship aren't the only things that create binding ties."

After Big Jimpson came back home, the three of them talked into the night. It was long after midnight when they went to bed, Julia and her baby in one spotless bedroom, with Trouble on the foot of the bed, Big Jimpson and Vivian in the other.

It was not until January 18 that mother, child, and dog, together with Jimpson and Vivian, set out for Virginia City. A blizzard dumped two feet of snow on the countryside, which kept them from leaving earlier. The air was crisp and bitingly cold. Big Jimpson had put heated bricks in the carriage and piled on thick rugs, but the wind was raw and so strong that it shook the covered carriage. Julia barely noticed. Her baby girl was in her arms, Vivian and Jimpson were with her, and Tom awaited them in Virginia City. Even Trouble was no trouble. Most of the time when Julia was not engrossed in conversation with Vivian, her thoughts were on the future. Entire dialogues came to mind in which she would tell Tom the truth about what she'd planned to do, where she'd been, why she'd not been able to accept the idea of having a little baby to love. Then he would answer her, proud and happy. They would be married, with Vivian and Jimpson as witnesses. She would ask Tom what he thought about naming the baby Annette, after her mother, and maybe Katherine, after his. Under her breath, she spoke the name she had chosen and found it good. "Annette Katherine Spencer." But of course she was not going to walk into the house with a strange man and woman at her side, show him the baby, and expect that to be that. Her flair for the dramatic was too pronounced in the first place. In the second place, she wasn't sure of how Tom felt about colored people—not that it made any difference. And anyway, she wanted to be alone with him that first night after all those months. To love him and tell him she loved him.

After Jimpson and Vivian were registered at the hotel, she walked home through the snowy streets carrying Trouble. The baby slept through the night. Jimpson and Vivian were to bring her over the first thing in the morning. It seemed fitting to her that she should arrive home on a Saturday night. Tom would be at the Sazarac. She'd be waiting for him in a warm house when he came home. She'd not utter a sound, either. She'd just lie there in bed and wait for him to enter the bedroom, then she'd sit up and say, "Surprise!"

When she entered the house, she appreciated the warmth from the stove and hovered near it for a while before she prepared for bed. It seemed strange that Carrie wasn't there, but since it was Saturday, she supposed Tom had given her the night off. Well, no matter. Judging by the fire in the stove, it hadn't been long since Carrie left. She'd just throw on a few more pieces of wood, put hot ashes in the warming pan, run it across the sheets, and climb in.

Heavenly. She snuggled under the warmed covers and sighed luxuriously as she felt some of the weariness from the long, hard journey drain away. She hoped she'd soon regain her strength after childbirth. At her feet, Trouble echoed her sigh, pushed against her legs as he made himself more comfortable, and slept. Smiling, Julia slept, too.

X

Big Jimpson yelled and flailed around until he awakened Vivian. "Shhhh, Jimp, you'll wake the baby," she said as she shook his shoulder.

He sat up in bed and moaned. "Oh, God, oh, God, oh, God. Something awful has happened to somebody...somewhere...oh, God, I feel so all alone and so heartsick and so hurt."

"You were dreaming, honey. That's why I woke you up," murmured Vivian. "You just had a bad old dream, baby-man." She reached for him in the darkness and held him close. "What'd you dream about that caused you to carry on so? Why, you've made a jumble out of the bed clothes."

"I don't remember all of it, Vivian, honey. Something about a...a...seems like it was a fight of some kind. An awful struggle. Seems like I was watching it and wanting to help, but couldn't get through the wall between me and the two who were fighting. But I could see it and hear it. Only I don't remember who was doing the fighting. There was

blood all over. Splattered on the bedclothes and—"
He shuddered, settled himself in her arms and went back to sleep.

Vivian got out of bed, crept soundlessly across the carpeted floor, and groped for Julia's baby in the darkness. They had removed a dresser drawer for her crib, lined it with a pillow, and placed it a few feet from their bed. When Vivian's sensitive fingertips felt the reassuring heart beat, she went back to bed and watched the darkness outside the window take on the first flush of dawn.

The baby fussed a little at six o'clock. Vivian hurried to change her diaper, then picked her up and held her in her arms, walking the floor until she grew quiet. Jimpson sat up just as she was kneeling on the floor to put the baby back in bed. "Time to get up, honey?"

"No. It's only a little past dawn."

"Baby hungry?"

"She was wet. If she starts to cry again, I'll give her a sugar tit. Juliette didn't mean dawn when she said to come first thing in the morning. I reckon the little tyke won't starve to death until eight."

"Sure would like to have a cup of coffee."

"You stay here, Jimp, honey, and I'll go down to the dining room and see if I can get us a pot to bring up to the room."

He said he could go down just as well as she could, but she insisted. "You didn't sleep too well last night. Be better if you just lie there and rest. Besides, it'll take you longer to dress than it will take me."

"I've been trying to remember some more about that dream that woke me up," he said. "Still can't get the straight of it."

"It wasn't the dream that woke you, honey. I did because you were carrying on so." Vivian stepped into her petticoats, pulled her dress over her head, and buttoned the bodice. After she'd smoothed her hair, she took another loving look at Julia's baby daughter and said she'd be right back and left quietly.

When she returned, her face was ashen. "Jim, oh, Jim," she cried as she fell on her knees at the side of the bed. "Mistress Juliette was murdered in her bed. Killed! A neighbor woke up along toward dawn. Heard somebody screaming. Oh, Jimpson! Our Mistress Juliette, dead!"

Big Jimpson shook his head, his hands caressing her face. "No! What are you saying? You *heard* wrong, that's all. Nothing like that could happen to Mistress Juliette, sweetheart. Not now, not just when she's got herself all straightened out, going to get married and give this baby a name, going to—"

Vivian stood and spoke on a hoarse whisper. "Jimp, we've got to get out of here! Leave this place and quick. She left the buggy for us, remember? Somebody's going to remember she brought us. We'll be accused because we're colored folks and we're in a strange place where nobody knows us. As soon as people stop carrying on about the murder and come to their senses, that night clerk is going to remember she brought us to the hotel and—"

"Nobody is going to accuse us of such a terrible thing, Vivian. You've got to settle down and . . . and stop acting like a scared heifer. I want to know what happened to Juliette."

As she threw the few things they'd brought with them into the carpet bag, Vivian told him all she'd heard. Her movements were quick and decisive, and she'd made up her mind that she knew who had murdered Julia Bernard. "It was the one who fathered this innocent child. The very one she loved

139

and planned to marry. She *said* he was living with her right in the house, Jimp. Said she'd written to say she was coming home. Well, he's not going to get this baby. We'll keep her ourselves. We'll raise her up and— Hurry, Jimpson. Hurry! Don't stand there with your mouth hanging open. We can't help Juliette. She's dead and we've got her baby. She'd want us to get out of here as fast as we can." She went to her husband and shook his shoulder.

When they were several miles out of Virginia City, Big Jimpson said, "Vivian, we can't raise up a white baby. I'm a colored man. You're whiter than a lot of white women, but you're my wife. We wouldn't be doing Juliette's baby any favor if we kept her and raised her as if she were our own."

"We'll work something out, Jimpson. But don't you see? We have to keep this precious little baby girl. What on earth would become of her if we didn't?"

Late Monday afternoon, Tom Spencer returned from San Francisco, where he'd gone in search of Julia. Ever since he'd received her letter he'd thought of nothing but finding her and of bringing her back. The way she'd signed her letter had made him the happiest man in the world. Then he'd thought back to September when she left and remembered that she'd put on some weight—the idea that she was pregnant dawned on him for the first time.

He'd told Carrie it was all right with him if she went to her mother's house every night while he was away as long as she built a good fire in the stove, then closed off all the dampers so the house wouldn't burn down. He was concerned about Julia's house, though, because Carrie had turned flighty and walked around in a half daze since Julia left. He was half of a mind to go to her house first and check things out before he went to his saloon. But he changed his mind and went to the Sazarac instead, half hoping that he'd find Julia there. He'd done nothing but spin his wheels in San Francisco. Desk clerks were notoriously close-mouthed about their guests. He'd gone to the Police and stated his case but had drawn a blank there, too. When the police Chief asked if she was his wife, he said she wasn't. Then when he was asked if the woman he sought was his indentured servant, he'd said no to that, too. "A runaway wife or a runaway woman who's bound for a certain number of years, well, I could help you there," said the officer. "But if she's neither one, we've no reason to look. A woman who doesn't stay with her man, well... when you find her I hope you'll give her a good beatin'. These women, that's what they need lots of times, my boy."

A fleeting smile was on Spencer's face as he neared the Sazarac. The picture of Julia allowing herself to be whipped by anyone was ridiculous. It'd take two strong men to tie her down. Even then, she'd probably get the better of them.

Funeral crepe was on the door of the Sazarac. He looked at it, didn't believe his eyes, and fished in his pocket for his keys, hoping his best bartender wasn't dead from another gunfight. So intense were his thoughts that he didn't notice the people.

They'd seen him walking toward the saloon. Then they'd asked one another who was going to tell him. Nobody wanted to. Everyone knew it had to be done. They came silently, in little groups of twos and threes. Carmen DeLaney was there, with two of the girls who worked at the Sazarac, and they came over closer.

His best bartender took his hand and looked at

141

him sadly. "Tom," he said, "Oh, Tom. Jesus. I thought you'd want me to close down. It's so awful, Tom. We tried to get in touch with you. Sent wires to hotel in San Francisco. But you never got a one, I'll bet."

"What happened?" Tom stared into that sea of faces. Then he looked at the crepe on the door. "Who was it?"

Old Doc Etherton silently handed him the Monday morning edition of the *Territorial Enterprise*. The headlines were big and black and bold. As big as they were when the War Between the States ended. As big as they were when Lincoln was assassinated.

HORRIBLE MURDER—WOMAN STRANGLED TO DEATH IN HER BED BLOODCURDLING TRAGEDY IN HEART OF THE CITY

Tom read the headline three times. Then he looked back into the sea of faces and saw them all sway crazily and felt the earth rise up against his feet and he cried out in horror. "Not Julia."

During that moment of realization he looked down at the snow on the street, up at the blue sky with the sun so bright, yet so cold. He saw little odds and ends that had nothing to do with the insane way the world was jolting, at the darkness that was coming in on him from all sides to swallow him, extinguish him, and maul him. There was the barber pole on the corner. The patent leather boots in the cobbler's window across the street. Carmen's dress was wet around the hem from the snow. Old Doc Etherton's teeth were chattering. Funny he should notice such insignificant trifles at a time like that. "*Not Julia!*" He shouted the denial again, then he swayed, toppled, and pitched forward. Three strong men broke his fall before he hit the snow-covered boardwalk. They turned him over and Carmen's highpitched wail broke the deathly silence. Carmen wasn't the only one who thought he was dead. He looked it, with his ghastly-pale face, the beads of sweat on his forehead, and his bloodless lips.

It was five full minutes before Doc Etherton revived him. The first words he said when he came to was, "Who did it?"

"Nobody knows yet," said the doctor as he forced a bit of brandy between Tom's lips. "Don't try to sit up yet, Tom. Just lay real still-like. We brought you on inside."

"I'll kill the son of a bitch," said Tom.

"You got to wait till we know who it was first," said Carmen through her tears.

He looked at her, swallowed a little more brandy, and looked up at the worried faces that surrounded him. "Tell me about it."

"About dawn," Carmen volunteered, "her neighbor lady heard a commotion at the house. It was Saturday night. Well, Sunday morning, actually. It was Mrs. Holmes. Thought she heard someone scream. Knew Carrie was there by herself 'cause she knew you'd gone to San Francisco, Tom. Then she went over there. But she was too late, 'cause whoever it was had gone. Julia was dead. But Tom, she never gave up without a fight. Julia was a scrapper, Tom."

"The walrus," muttered Tom. "But, no, she couldn't have overpowered my girl."

Bit by bit, he learned the gruesome details. Julia had died slowly, fighting for life all the way to the end. She'd been taken by surprise, no doubt sound asleep in her bed. A bloody cudgel was left in the bedroom, and it was matted with her hair, which led the authorities to believe her assailant had tried to beat her brains in as she slept. But she'd awakened and fought like a demon. Under her fingernails was blood along with particles of flesh. Scratches were all over her hands. Apparently her murderer had tried to kill her by hitting her on the head again and again with the butt of a gun. On her forehead was a bruise that almost uncannily reproduced the image of a gun-butt. But it was obvious that she'd fought to the end. She'd died of strangulation.

And Trouble, the little poodle—Julia's savage killer had snuffed out his life, too. Carmen fell to her knees and spoke. "That little dog tried to protect her. He died with a snarl on his face, and he got in a good bite, too, Tom. There was skin between his teeth." She said she'd asked the undertaker to lay out the dog and put him in the coffin with his mistress. "She'd of wanted him with her, Tom."

Stretched out on the tavern floor, Tom kept saying, "Who would do such a thing to Julia? Why? *Why?*"

Carmen supplied him with the answer. "It was a thief, Tom. A lot of her things are missing. That big diamond pin you gave her last Christmas—well, it's gone. The ruby pendant earrings and matching ring you gave her for her birthday is gone. And other rings, her silver bricks, even the one with her name engraved on it that she kept on her dresser. Lodge emblems, the big diamond she wore on her left hand, that beautiful emerald all gone. And I think he even took some of her clothes, but I can't be sure. The dress with the pearls that she wore in the Admittance Day parade, it's not there—Carrie said it was in her closet yesterday morning."

Tom wanted to hear no more. "Where is she?"

The undertaker had her laid out in his own place, keeping her cold, no difficult task with a fourteen-inch snow on the ground and the temperature hovering near zero. Nobody had wanted to make any plans until Tom was located. Several of his friends went down to the undertaking parlor with him because he was still wobbly and because they didn't want him to be alone. He went into the room by himself, though, because that was the way he wanted it. When he came out, he said quietly, "We'll give her a funeral she'll be proud of."

The doctor said they'd have to wait until the snow melted, until the ground had thawed a little. Tom nodded. "She won't mind," he said. "She looks so beautiful. Maybe if we wait long enough, she'll wake up. Lots of times people just look like . . . I mean, it's a good thing we have to wait. Julia is going to be all right."

It was eleven days before the ground thawed enough for a grave could be dug. Every day Tom went down to the undertaker's parlor and sat in the cold at Julia's side trying to get her to wake up. But he didn't remove the crepe from the door of the Sazarac, so people let him alone, knowing at least a part of him was thinking all right, which was a pretty good indication that the rest of him would get back to normal before long.

George Evashuck told the Sheriff about the colored gentleman and the lady who was with him. "They had a little baby with them, and Julia paid for their rooms. She said something about them being her daddy's servants a long time ago. She looked so pretty and so happy that night. Kind of like a lady looks when she gets religion, or right after she gets a proposition she's wanted for a long time or a proposal of marriage. I heard them talking before the older folks went upstairs. Julia told them to come to her house first thing in the morning. It was

145

late at night when they got in, though. About eleven o'clock. She didn't say their names, just said they were her friends, that they used to be her daddy's servants. I should have told you before, but to tell you the truth, I forget about them because of the shock of her murder, I guess."

Sheriff Lowry said, "They could of killed her, you damn fool. And you let them get plumb to hell and gone!"

"Nope," said George Evashuck stoutly. "There's not but one set of steps in the hotel. People were coming and going until after two o'clock. Just exactly at two, old Mr. Hawthorne came downstairs like he always does when he can't sleep and wanted to talk. Decided he wanted to play checkers. So we played checkers from two o'clock until all hell broke loose when the news of Julia's murder came out."

Mr. Hawthorne, who was only fifty, but very ancient and decrepit to young George Evashuck, verified his story, so nothing was done about trying to trace the couple who had come back to town with the murdered woman.

The day of Julia's funeral dawned bright and rosy, but not nearly as cold as it had been. The fire engine was hung with black crepe and the fireman dressed in their best dress uniforms to take their places in the funeral procession. More than seven hundred people followed the special glass-walled hearse to Flowery Cemetery, and Tom sat at Julia's side, never for one minute appearing to doubt that she would open her eyes and smile that special smile at him before they arrived at the grave side. The hearse was drawn by black horses, their black-plumed heads solemnly nodding in time to the Nevada Militia Brigade's funeral dirge. The cortege of mourners were solemn

146

as they progressed along the half mile of winding road to Julia's final resting place.

But Flowery Cemetery was not sacrosanct ground, and at the last minute Tom refused to allow her coffin to be placed there among the other fallen angels.

"Up here," he shouted as he ran to the ridge that looked down on the cemetery. "Boys, I can't let her go down there with the rest of those women. Let's dig."

The firemen dug. Others fought for a chance to man a shovel for the sake of sweet Julia, beloved by any man who ever basked in the warmth of her smile.

Old Doc Etherton, who had been ordained as a minister of the Presbyterian church before he turned to medicine, spoke a few words over her grave:

"Lord, we loved Julia Bernard. She was one of Your children. Even though You didn't call her home, she's with You now, Lord. Maybe she didn't always do what You might have wanted her to, but as our Heavenly Father, Lord, You know derned good and well children don't always do what their folks want them to do. As earthly fathers forgive their children, we know you'll forgive our Julia, and take her into Your heavenly kingdom. Amen."

A brilliantly plumaged Western tanager settled for a moment on the doctor's shoulder as he dropped the first handful of dirt on her coffin. Tom Spencer looked at the bird, then he looked down into the ground at the coffin with the crumbled earth on it. When he looked up again, the bird took wing. "Julia," whispered Tom as he watched it until it was nothing but a pinpoint of blackness against the dazzling Nevada sky.

On the return trip, the Nevada Militia Brigade

147

marched back to Virginia City ahead of the crepe-draped fire engine and all the other wagons, buggies, traps, and rigs, all those who had walked the half mile. Softly and tenderly, they played *The Girl I Left Behind Me*.

The Sazarac opened for business. Tom Spencer stood behind the bar and poured free drinks, and so did all the other saloon keepers in town. Carmen DeLaney, resplendent in black silk jersey, and a black fur cape drooping from her shoulders, said, "Julia would have appreciated that funeral, Tom. It was just right. Fit for the Queen of Nevada."

PART TWO

XI

During the journey back to the farm house on the outskirts of Reno, Vivian conceived a plan for the future. At first, Jimpson protested, but Vivian argued, and in the end he agreed.

"It's strange," he said as they pulled into the lane. "Before, I was strong. You needed to be taken care of, and I was there for you to lean on. Now you're the strong one and I'm weak. Seems like I just can't think straight since it happened and since we left. And I'm afraid it won't work out. Something bad is bound to happen. But if you think we can do it and get away with it, we'll do what you want."

"Jimp, honey, you're not weak. You're shattered. It's a woman's way to step in and do what has to be done at a time like this, especially if there's a baby to consider. It's the same thing that keeps mothers from falling sick when they've got children to take care of. The good Lord knew what He was doing when he put us together. There's a time when a woman needs to lean and there's a time when a man does—and

Jimpson, I sure have done my share of leaning on you."

Recalling that Julia spoke to her of entering the lying-in hospital under the name of Mrs. Thomas Spencer, maiden name, d'Angelo, Vivian suggested an Italian name for the baby. "It'll fit right in with what we're going to do, Jimpson, honey." She listed several Italian names, and they settled on Teresa.

As soon as she could get everything she would need ready for the trip, Vivian took Teresa and boarded a train headed for Chicago and points east. Jimpson stayed behind to sell the farm. At the station he looked into his wife's face for a long, tragic moment. Then he said, "It grieves me to not even know where you're going."

"I'll let you know as soon as I'm settled, honey." They kissed, then he folded back the coverlet to take one last look at the baby's face. "Philadelphia, probably, since you said a lot of Italians settled there."

Vivian didn't reach Philadelphia, although the last ticket she purchased would have taken her there. Teresa began to grow listless. She spit up the canned milk Vivian gave her from the cumbersome baby bottle, and as the miles passed her eyes glazed over with fever. Frantic with worry, Vivian asked the woman who occupied the seat next to her if she knew where the train would stop next.

"Middletown, Ohio," answered the lady. "The children and I are getting off there." She had remained awake and helpful through the long night while Vivian did everything she could to ease the baby. "There's a good doctor in town, Mrs. Jameson. He brought me into the world, and all my sisters and brothers. If anyone can help your granddaughter, he's the one."

It was eight o'clock at night when the train creaked to a stop at the Middletown station house. Mrs. Charles Powell gathered her three almost-grown sons together and when her father met her with his rig, she asked him to take Mrs. Jameson past the doctor's house. "Her grandchild is real sick, Daddy. Just as sick as she can be, and the poor lady is almost out of her mind."

It was the second time Vivian had used her new name to a person who wasn't just someone who worked for the railroad company. She didn't think they counted, because they paid no attention to her when she'd purchased the tickets. Mrs. Powell's father didn't give her a second glance. He was a dark-complexioned man himself, with dark brown hair that was grey at the temples and eyes much darker than Vivian's own.

Old Doctor Drabing put little Teresa on a table, turned up the jets on the Aladdin lamps, and looked her over from the soles of her feet to the top of her head. "Born when?"

"December 12, 1867."

The doctor shook his head. "She's not doing right." He looked at Vivian over the top of his glasses. "You been feeling all right yourself, Mrs.—"

"Jameson," she said firmly. "Yes. I've been very well."

"No stomach cramps, no dizzy spells, no sign of a rash?"

"No. Nothing." She wondered why he wanted to know how she felt when it was the baby she was concerned about.

"Now, have you eaten anything that might have been spoiled? Tainted fish, something that didn't taste quite right?"

"Doctor, I'm this baby's grandmother. My

daughter died in childbirth." It had finally dawned on her that he believed her to be a nursing mother.

"What have you been giving the little thing?"

"Condensed milk." She took a can from her big handbag to show him, along with a nursing bottle, while she composed a believable reason to explain why she was traveling. "Before that, right after my daughter passed away, we gave Teresa goat's milk. She thrived on it, but I had to leave. To... my mother is at death's door. I was going to Phila—"

"We'll have to get her a wet nurse. She'll never make it to any Philadelphia, Missus. Babies don't always take too well to canned milk. Goat's milk is the next best thing to mother's own, but—. You say your mother is near death?"

Vivian swallowed. "Yes, but I—my sisters are with her. If it's a matter of my grandbaby's life or death, I've no choice. I'll stay right here in Middletown until she's well."

He mixed some powders in water and dropped the liquified concoction in Teresa's mouth with an eye dropper. Then he took a bottle from his shelf and gave it to Vivian. "Paregoric. Don't use it unless she shows distress and cries and draws up her legs. Now I'm going to take you to one of my patients who gave birth three weeks ago. She's got so much milk she'll be relieved to have another baby at her breast, and she's a good, kind woman, too. There's a boarding house down the street, too. You can take a room there and bring this little tyke over to Mrs. Stahley's house when she gets hungry. But Missus, I don't hold out too much hope for this grandchild of yours. I'm sorry."

The Stahley house was on Manchester Street, a two-story frame that was fairly bursting at the seams with children, dogs, cats, and plump, placid Mrs.

152

Stahley, who put Teresa to her breast immediately, but to no avail. She looked at the doctor and Vivian out of troubled blue eyes. "Her little lips just moved once. Looks like the little thing is too weak to nurse."

In the room of the boarding house Vivian paced the floor with Teresa in her arms throughout the night. Except for the feeble beating of her heart, and the barely perceptible breathing, she was lifeless until a little after the first cock crowed, when she began to fret, then rooted against Vivian's breast, her cry growing lustier with each frustrated attempt to nurse. Uttering a glad cry, Vivian ran through the wintery dark morning to the Stahley house. Mr. Stahley had just come home from his night job as watchman at the paper mill. His greeting was kindly, and he seemed to Vivian a merry kind of man as he took off his wooden leg and propped it in the corner while his wife settled shrieking, red-faced Teresa to her breast. "Lost the leg in the war," he told Vivian. "This one serves the purpose, but it gets to hurtin' me along toward morning."

He sat at the big round table in the big, cluttered kitchen and ate his supper of sauerkraut, baked potatoes, and weiners, which he washed down with a modest glass of beer. Vivian's stomach recoiled at the sight of food, but at the same time her mouth watered. It had been more than twenty-four hours since she'd had a bite to eat. In her distraction, she'd forgotten about food for herself.

Mrs. Stahley's own little baby began to howl with hunger, and Vivian brought him from his crib to his mother. She was amazed at the size of him, of his weight.

Mr. Stahley beamed. "He's a whopper, all right. Weighed eleven pounds when he was born. Say, Missus, you look like you could use a good meal.

153

You just take a plate from the cupboard and help yourself. There's coffee on the back of the stove, too."

Before she went back to the boarding house, Vivian had made up her mind to stay in Middletown. Teresa needed mother's milk, and Mrs. Stahley had plenty to spare. The doctor had saved her angel-child, and even though Mrs. Powell didn't live there, she'd already paved a way by striking up an acquaintanceship which had ended in getting Teresa to a good doctor. It was a beginning as Mrs. Vivian Jameson, widow of Stanley Jameson, who had been a jeweler and left her well fixed. Her fabricated background would work where she was as well as it would work in another town—maybe better. Vivian was a firm believer in the powers of the Lord, and she was sure He had led her to the right place.

Carefully sewn between dresses and linings was almost ten thousand dollars Julia had left in Vivian's care when she left them at the hotel that dreadful night she met her death. Jimpson was appalled when Vivian told him about the money, but she'd been firm. "It's the working of the Lord," she'd stated. "We've been frugal, and it's a comfort to have that little strong box with over four thousand in it. You'll get a good piece of money when you sell the farm, too. But right now, I'm going to buy us a house with that money Juliette had with her. After you've sold off our own place, we'll put away ten thousand dollars for our grandbaby. It's the only way we can do it right now, honey. You know yourself that a poor person going to a strange place has to work like a dog before anybody begins to sit up, take notice, or pay them any respect. But an old yellow hound could roll into town in a big, fancy carriage drawn by big, expensive horses and start throwing a little money

154

around, and the first thing you know that old yellow hound is going to be a pillar of the community—tail, fleas, and all."

Mrs. Jameson purchased a beautiful brick home on Main Street and furnished it with quiet good taste. She was not pretentious when she drove down the street in her modest black runabout, and there was nothing flamboyant about the way she handled herself when she made her purchases. Taking a cue from Juliette's mother and adding a dash of everything she'd learned from other women of quality, she was quiet, courteous and ladylike in every respect. From the beginning, she was treated respectfully. Instead of giving Mrs. Stahley money for Teresa's milk, she made it her business to find out exactly what necessities were lacking in the home and quietly purchased them. When Mrs. Stahley protested, Vivian said simply, "You saved my granddaughter's life. Surely you won't deny me the privilege of helping out a little. Your husband is a veteran! Men such as he can never be repaid for the great sacrifices they made for the country."

Negroes were already living in Middletown. Men worked in the paper mill and the smelting works. Vivian, however, was never thought of as anything other than a white lady of Italian ancestry. She placed a discreet advertisement in the newspaper asking for household help. She hired a young girl of sixteen, a middle-aged woman, and a boy who said he was fifteen, but looked twelve. Billy would work in the yard until her old family retainer came, she told the boy. If Big Jimp wanted to keep him on as his helper, she'd be pleased; she'd left all the outside work to him ever since her husband passed away.

In that way, she established herself in the way she and Jimpson had planned. When she'd been there a week, the local priest came to call. He said he'd heard she was of Italian descent, and hoped she would attend mass. Vivian was prepared for his visit.

"I was once a Catholic, Father. But I married into the faith of my late husband, and I am at home with my beliefs. Mr. Jameson was a Presbyterian." That Sunday, Vivian attended services at the Presbyterian Church in Middletown where she was immediately invited to join the Missionary Society and the Sunday School ladies of her own age, many of whom were also widows. Vivian accepted with pleasure and by the time Big Jimp arrived in late May, everyone in town who counted knew her old family retainer would be coming with few of the family heirlooms Mrs. Jameson had not been able to part with from her old family home in Mississippi. Her "Italian" heritage explained her dark hair, her amber colored eyes, her olive complexion. By saying she lived in Mississippi throughout her married life, the southern accent she never lost during her Nevada years was accepted as perfectly natural. Every small detail was attended to. Her old mother in Philadelphia passed away shortly after she'd had to leave the train in Middletown. She spoke regretfully of her sorrow, and of the fact that the baby's illness had kept her from traveling on. Middletown matrons were quick to say that Philadelphia's loss was their again., although they were sympathetic when they referred to the death of Vivian Jameson's mother.

Before Jimp arrived, Vivian provided the funds for a stained-glass window in the Presbyterian Church in memory of her mother. To herself, she added that it didn't matter that she never knew her mother's name, and had just made up one for the window. After Jimp arrived, she would talk to him about buying a stained glass window in memory of her late daughter, Maria Jameson d'Angelo. It was a project the church ladies had begun a year earlier, and she liked the idea of having a stained glass window in memory of Juliette—it didn't matter a whit to Vivian about the name on the window. What was right was right, and she convinced herself she was doing no wrong.

Although Big Jimp was expected in late May (from Mississippi, as Vivian had told the church ladies), it was the third of June when he drove the wagon into Middletown and asked directions to the residence of Mrs. Vivian Jameson. He came into town with a worried mind, but the minute the men in the general store over in Excello gave him the direction, he knew he'd had no cause to worry. With respect in their voices, they gave him the directions, adding that Mrs. Jameson was a fine woman. A real fine lady.

It had taken him until March to sell the farm. Then he'd sold the furniture Vivian told him she didn't want. After that, a man and his wife came along who wanted the farm because of the greenhouse, which the new owner was going to tear down. The second would-be purchasers wanted the place badly enough to pay the new owner an extra thousand dollars, and Big Jimpson's sentimental nature was torn between acting as go-between, which would delay him, or staying longer to help the second folks buy the place. The labor of Vivian's love that had gone into the greenhouse, all the hours he'd worked on it himself, meant a lot to him. So he'd stayed on, and helped the second people get the place. Then he'd begun the long, wearying journey to Ohio, driving a horse-drawn wagon. But Vivian had anticipated him, even though he'd never written her a letter since she'd wanted no connection with Nevada.

"When you *didn't* come," she said after the private

reunion that had nothing to do with the Mistress-Servant greeting she'd given him when he first arrived, "I told Billy he could stay on as yard-boy, that maybe you'd gone off and got yourself married." She laughed. "Acted like I was real put-out with you, too, Jimp, considering that you had all the old family heirlooms from my home in Mississippi."

Wordlessly, Jimpson handed Vivian a copy of *The Territorial Enterprise*.

John Millain was executed for the murder of Julia Bernard on April 27, 1868. Jimpson had left Nevada, but when he came through Indianapolis he'd looked around for a copy of the newspaper and finally found one.

John Millain was apprehended after he'd tried to rob a Miss Martha Camp as she slept. Miss Camp, a former lady of the evening but presently employed at the Sazarac Saloon, had awakened when the intruder broke a window to gain entrance to her house. She'd been able to get a good look at his face before her screams, described by the newspaper as long, loud, and blood-curdling, and apparently frightened the knife-wielding Italian away. Three days later, she swore out a warrant for his arrest, in which she charged attempted murder and robbery.

During Millain's first days in jail, evidence that he must be guilty of Julia Bernard's murder accumulated. Mrs. Cazentre, a resident of Gold Hill, came forward and stated that she had purchased a dress pattern from Millain for which she had paid forty dollars. Although she'd not unwrapped the pattern until Millain's arrest, she made haste to do so when she learned of it and found to her horror that the pattern she'd bought from him had belonged to Julia Bernard—that Julia had bought it from the haberdashery down the block from the Sazarac Saloon.

Mr. Nye, a jeweler, hurried down to the Sheriff's office to show him a pin he had purchased from Millain a month after Julia's murder. It was a square pin that blazed with diamonds and both Tom Spencer and Carrie, who had been Julia's maid, identified it as having belonged to her.

The night before Millain was arrested, he'd tried to sell Carmen DeLaney a gold watch. Carmen was busy at the time and told him to come back. When she confronted the man and demanded to see the watch, he swore he'd never spoken to her about any watch, but Carmen had a witness. The police went to Millain's room at the Switchyard Boarding House where they searched his possessions. They found the gold watch in question, and Julia's initials were on the back. They also uncovered a trunk that contained a silver brick with her name on it, several gold rings, red silk stockings, Masonic emblems, fancy drawers, a black ermine-trimmed cape, and several other personal items that had once belonged to the Nevada Silver Queen.

Millain confessed, then retracted his statement, accusing the police of beating a confession out of him. He named two other men as the perpetrators, swearing he'd done nothing but try to sell the ill-gained goods they obtained from the heinous crime of murdering Julia Bernard. When the case went to court, the jury found him guilty and recommended no mercy.

Teresa was now six months old and growing more beautiful every day. "Looks just like Mist—I mean, like your daughter, ma'am," Jimpson said to his wife. "Yes, ma'am. Favors her a whole lot. Only I do

159

believe she's going to have blue eyes."

Jimpson referred to Teresa as The Little Princess. In time, he shortened it to Princess. By the time she was a year old, Teresa's eyes were undoubtedly blue, and her complexion was fair as a lily. When she was three, her eyes turned a darker yet brighter blue that matched the gentians that grew along the country roads. When she was alone with Jimpson, Vivian reminded him that Juliette's sisters had blue eyes, and so did her mother, Mrs. Bienveillance. Jimpson was enslaved to the breathtakingly beautiful child— far more a slave to Teresa d'Angelo than he'd been when he was owned by a master.

Vivian purchased a second stained-glass window for her church in memory of Juliette, but with the name Maria Jameson d'Angelo on it. Every time Vivian went to church she looked at the light streaming through the beautiful windows and her soul was at peace for the lie she would live until she died.

Jimpson didn't mind, but when they were alone, he said, "Just so you don't get any notions in your head about buying one of those windows in memory of *me!*"

Vivian laughed. "Not until you go on to glory."

"But even then," he said, "you'll have to say it's in loving memory of your husband, Ellis Jameson."

"What difference will it make, hon? It'll be for you, and I'll know it, and *you'll* know it. And besides that, you might out-live me by a hundred years!"

The hired girls didn't live in the big, beautiful brick home on Main Street. Billy lived over the carriage house with his sick old father. Vivian and Jimpson had separate rooms, although Jimpson objected to what he considered an unnatural way of a man and wife sleeping. Behaving as if he were Vivian's servant didn't bother him in the least. He said he'd always been her servant, that part of the lie didn't make an iota of difference. But not sleeping together, well, now! His bed was seldom disturbed, but Vivian knew the ways of hired help too well not to take precautions. She made it a practice to always remove the soiled linen from every bed in the house before she sent them to the laundress on Eighth Street, including those on Jimpson's little room on the first floor. Without his knowledge, she took the sheets and pillow cases from his bed every Wednesday and put them on the ones in her big, airy bedroom on the second floor.

On her fourteenth birthday Teresa was five and a half feet tall and secretly admired by every little boy who attended Miss Mary Ann Frazier's dancing school. She had a dimple at the corner of her lush lips, long, thick hair that lay in glossy, dark brown waves to the middle of her back, and a heart-shaped face that set off her incredibly brilliant blue eyes. To her grandmother, Teresa complained bitterly that she was taller than any of those little pip-squeaks in the dancing class. She wanted to look just like Rosabelle Dawson, who had blonde curls and was as cuddly as a kitten. With a pang in her heart because she remembered Juliette had found fault with her looks as a young girl, she told the child to straighten her shoulders and look the world in the face. "You come from tall stock, Teresa. Your sainted mother was taller than I, and your father was a giant of a man."

By then, Vivian's fertile imagination had provided her darling with ancestors who had been good, solid patriots, whether she referred to the fictitious

161

Norwegian Jameson, the equally fictitious Italian d'Angelo, or those fine Americans who had fought in the American Revolution.

In the summer of 1882, Vivian suffered a massive stroke and was left paralyzed from the waist down and on her entire left side. Teresa was sixteen years old. Ten years later, Vivian died in her sleep. At twenty-six, Teresa was a remarkably beautiful young woman with an education and a great talent. All through the tragic years when Vivian lay helpless in her bed or sat in her wheel chair, she begged the girl to leave her. "Go while you're young," she'd say in the whispery, often unintelligible garble that resulted from the stroke. Her eyes would fill with tears as she spoke of her adored one's future. "Anybody who has a voice like yours owes it to the world, Teresa. It's a gift from God Almighty, given to you for a reason. It's not to keep all bottled up in a dark old house with the shades drawn where nobody can hear it."

Teresa had no difficulty understanding Vivian's words. She was a young woman who had been brought up in a home of unstinting love. She tried to explain to Vivian that she didn't remain at home out of a sense of duty. "It's because I love you, Grandma, can't you understand?"

Three times a week, a voice instructor came down from Dayton to give Teresa lessons. Those were the most glorious hours of Vivian and Jimpson's life. Their darling played the piano with wonderful flair, but it was her voice that soared high, clear, and gloriously rich that sent all the household hearts into ecstasy—a voice that Vivian wanted her to share with the world.

A month after Vivian's death, Teresa went to

Vienna where she studied for two years at the school founded by the great Ernestine Schumann-Heink. When she gave her first concert, the dramatic contralto wept with joy. Teresa's tone quality was superb. Madame Schumann-Heink was said to have remarked that Teresa's delivery was much like that of her own when she appeared at the Dresden Court Opera at the age of sixteen. Teresa was now twenty-eight, but her strong coloratura was young and beautifully clear. After she returned to the United States, her first public appearance was in the auditorium of the Manchester Hotel, and she dedicated to the memory of her grandmother the difficult *De la fille du paria*, the "Bell Song" from the opera *Lakmé*. She was famous, successful, rich, and beautiful. Men adored her, sent her so many flowers that sometimes she felt smothered as she toured the nation. But she saw no man except for business acquaintances—she was not interested in matrimony.

Big Jimpson died suddenly in 1900. She came home for his funeral, and everyone in Middletown was touched by the loving care in which she had her grandmother's faithful old family retainer, a former slave, put to rest. It was not until Teresa's third triumphant appearance at Carnegie Hall that she experienced the first flickering interest in a member of the opposite sex.

XII

Rex Anthony Stevens sent her a single rose and a simple note of appreciation after she accepted his request to sing at a childrens' home in Boston during the holiday season. She went because she loved children. Almost as soon as her fame reached its apex, she became well-known for her generous charity appearances. It was at the children's home Mr. Stevens had founded and supported that she met him for the first time. She shook his hand, said she was happy to come, and immediately stepped on stage, where she sang for more than an hour without a break.

The single rose and the simple note arrived the next day. At odd moments, Teresa found herself recalling Mr. Stevens' face. When she was in Boston again, she went of her own accord and sang for the children. Again, Mr. Stevens sent her a single rose and a dignified note of appreciation, but she didn't see him while she was in Boston.

A few discreet inquiries told her he was unmarried. She wondered why he had not been snared by any one of the women who must surely think of him as the most eligible man in the country. When she was in San Francisco she celebrated her thirty-fourth birthday on the stage of the Opera House. The following morning Teresa d'Angelo wrote to Mr. Rex Anthony Stevens, requesting his fine help in the founding of a home for orphans close to her home town in Ohio.

They were married within the year. Teresa's baby was born in 1906, a little girl with a tuft of light brown hair and a heart-shaped face, a set of powerful lungs, and a temper that manifested itself when she was fifteen minutes old.

Teresa's husband wanted to call his daughter Sarah, after his older sister who had died when she was twelve. Teresa added Vivian, in honor of the woman she believed was her grandmother. The baby was winsome, usually well-behaved, and attractive enough, but almost everyone who knew the beautiful, charming, and talented Mrs. Stevens wondered privately how it happened that a woman as stunning as Teresa Stevens could have produced a child who could not charitably be called more than just a pretty little thing.

As Sarah grew out of the plump baby stage and into a little girl, her appearance remained quite plain. Some of the unkind acquaintances of the Boston socialites referred to the child as downright homely. At the age of seven her second teeth began to grow in and they gave every appearance of being too big for her small face, with a pronounced inclination to protrude. Her first grade teacher referred to Sarah Stevens as a little girl who was all eyes and teeth, a regrettable condition in an era when small, rosebud lips and delicate but ladylike features were ideal. When Sarah was seven, she was the smallest girl in her class. Teresa worried. By then she'd had two more children, both sons, both extremely handsome and of average size. Rex Anthony worried. They spoke of their firstborn in guarded tones, always making sure their conversation couldn't be overheard. Teresa was afraid Sarah would never grow another inch. She was exactly the same height she'd been when she was four years old and she had a mark on the door of her sewing room to prove it. Teresa asked Rex if there were any very short people in his family.

Rex claimed to have come from a long line of strong, healthy English stock, most of whom had made enormous amounts of money and a decided place for their progeny in affairs of importance. He had carried on in the family tradition. He had not been willing to sit back and live well from the hard work his ancestors had done before him. Instead, he had increased the family fortune he inherited by working hard, reserving very little time for outside interests, and always doing what was expected of him.

"My mother has traced our family back to the days of William the Conqueror. Never has there been a Stevens or a Blaithwell—my mother's line—who had a physical deformity. Therefore, if you're looking for someone on whom to cast the blame for the unfortunate appearance of our daughter, you'll have to look elsewhere—your own side of the family. Unless, of course, you've been unfaithful."

"For the moment, I'm going to let your snide remark about Sarah's paternity pass. But I'll remind you that my own family tree is full of noblemen, educators, philosophers, preachers and patriots."

She was miffed much more at his reference to bad blood on her side of the family than she was at his unfounded statement concerning her fidelity, since she considered that particular remark nothing more than one more proof of his stupidity.

"The fact remains," he said "there is no tainted blood on my side of the family. You're the one who began this disgraceful scene, my dear. I'm sure no lady of English or Welsh blood would dream of speaking so uncouthly. But I must keep reminding myself that you're Italian."

"No more and no less Italian that I was when you asked me to marry you." She was proud of the noble and romantic blood she believed coursed through her veins. She also often longed for the years when she'd been the toast of two continents; when newspaper accounts were extravagant in their praise of the American/Italian Beauty whose voice was capable of bringing the strongest man to tears. "Anyway," she added truthfully, "I accused your antecedents of *nothing*. It was my wish to have a quiet discussion about poor little Sarah's small stature. If you didn't have your mind on that *floozy* you're keeping, you would be able to speak calmly of a matter that should be of deep concern to you, you—*renegade!*"

Stevens' face flushed, but his eyes were wide, his expression incredulous. "I have no idea what you are referring to. You can't be serious."

"Oh, but I *am* serious. I've known for over a year, and I'm talking about a 'who' not a 'what.' Her name is Delores, which means *sick!* And I'm sure you're just as sick as she is, Rex. Why on earth did you propose to me and go through the ridiculous farce of pretending to love me when you've lived with that woman most of your adult life?"

"I do not care to discuss it."

Teresa exploded. "Well, you're jolly well going to discuss it. And her. And me. How would you like to have the untainted name you're so proud of dragged through the scandal of a divorce court?"

"You wouldn't dare. You have two sons and a daughter to consider. My mother, my grandmother. There has never been a divorce in my family. I will not hear of it."

"Your woman is divorced. She was all right to sleep with, but little Rex Anthony wasn't allowed to marry her. Am I right?"

He looked disappointed. "You were respectable. A lady. You must admit that you wanted marriage when you sent me that letter. Really, Teresa, it was so transparent it was pitiful."

"Yes. I'll admit that I was fascinated with you. My curiosity was piqued. You were the only man I ever met who didn't shower me with praise and gifts." She laughed. "Every day of my life I received at least one proposal of marriage, but I wasn't interested. Then one night when I was on the West Coast, my birthday was celebrated. It was a surprise. A fête that took place on stage. But afterwards, I was depressed. It had never occured to me to think about aging until that very night. Just then, I realized I would soon be too old to have children, and I thought of you. So I wrote the letter. You were charming and attentive and . . . I thought you were intelligent. Hah! You've been a disappointment, and that's putting it mildly. Not only are you a mama's boy, you're a *clod,* Rex. You're lacking in everything but the ability to parrot the words and ideals of others. You can't even *think* for yourself."

"I can think well enough to tell you I won't give you a divorce."

"You don't need to concern yourself with giving me anything. If I decide to divorce you, I shall do it."

"You are a cold woman, Teresa. Cold and unloving."

"No I'm not. Your mama put those words in your mouth. *She* has never slept with you. I have, and frankly, Rex, I am disgusted with your unnatural disinclination to make love to your own wife. Delores is almost twenty years your senior, but you spend several hours with her every day of your life except Sunday, when we go to church with your mother and your sisters, then on to the family mansion to eat that tasteless, sodden mess they call dinner. I will never go again. Neither to your church nor to dinner with your mother."

He opened his mouth, shut it, and looked away from her, a pleading expression distorting his features. When he spoke his voice was full of shrill anxiety: "But what will I tell Mama?"

Teresa smiled. "Tell her you'll come alone, or you'll bring Delores. That way, she'll have a choice."

Mrs. Fairchild Stevens went into a decline on the following Sunday because of her distress when her son dutifully reported everything that Teresa had said except for the part about Delores. The decline began shortly after the last little portion of her heavy dessert had been consumed, a runny pudding of prunes, brown sugar, and heavy cream. It ended just before the usual Sunday night supper of cold roast beef in congealed grease, potato cakes fried in lard, and another dessert Mrs. Fairchild Stevens referred to as "light." It was peaches floating in honey. Teresa had once caused a profound silence when she remarked that the dessert was sickeningly sweet.

After supper, Mrs. Fairchild Stevens told her only son that she would leave her sick-bed and go to his house to speak to his wife. Rex spoke in a weak voice of Teresa's mulish disposition. "I don't think you can do anything with her, Mama."

Mrs. Stevens glared him into submission and sent him to fetch her own carriage, saying his was not built strong enough to suit her, a statement she made every time he was told to take her anywhere. Once she had consented to step inside his carriage and the bottom fell out, which greatly inconvenienced Mrs. Stevens, since it had taken two men to remove the broken floorboards from her legs, which were so fat that every time she moved, another splinter of wood punctured her considerable flab.

The butler opened the front door for mother and son as they came up the steps to the house. "Begging your pardon, sir," he said in a funereal voice, "Mrs. Stevens asked me to wait for you and give you this, sir."

Rex Anthony Stevens read the letter, cried out, gnashed his teeth, and tore his sparse sandy hair. His mother reached out and snatched the letter from his hand. Unabashedly, she stood in the grand front hall and read her daughter-in-law's letter while her son mumbled about his wife's ingratitude, that his poor little innocent children would grow up in the uncivilized Midwest, that he'd long doubted whether he was the true father of Sarah.

With each word, he took a step backwards toward the front door, against the wrathful fire in his mother's eye. He said, "But you brought me up to be a gentleman, Mama. So I never said anything about my feelings in that matter before. And you would have me marry her after you learned of Delor—now, Mama—Mama, you must remember where you are. The servants, Mama—" Fumbling with nervous, jiggling fingers for the glass doorknob, he found it, opened it, slid himself between door and frame, still facing her with alarm. Then he backed out, slammed the door behind him and ran across the porch, down the steps, and to the street, knowing she couldn't catch him. A couple of blocks away he stopped, looked up at the moon and the stars and asked the silent sky above Boston why Teresa had mentioned Delores in that letter. It was beastly of her! She'd known his mother would come to the house with him. Mama always settled the family disputes. He thought of Delores, who was comforting, never-demanding, so soft and easy-going. Never gave him a cross word. Expected nothing from him in return for all the love in the world. The house he provided for her and her two daughters had not been dear, he thought in righteous indignation. Certainly he'd provided well for Teresa, who was rolling in money of her own and would never turn over her funds to him when everyone knew it was the right of the man of the house to manage the money.

Rex Stevens also thought wistfully of his carriage. It would be weeks before he would dare go back to his mother's house and get his own horses from her stable, his own rig from her carriage house. Even then she wouldn't give them up without a scene, and he hated scenes. The most humiliating thing about the way things were was the way his mother had never allowed him to take over the family business, never turned loose the purse-strings. The house he'd bought after he and Teresa were married was in her name. Not that Teresa knew it, but it wasn't right of his mother to place so little confidence in him. Even the horses and the carriage were legally his mother's. The house he'd provided for Delores had been the result of subterfuge. He didn't like to think about how he'd skimmed the price of Delores' cottage from

171

receipts at a fund-raising concert. His face flamed as the fact came unbidden to mind. His mother was a hard, cold, cruel woman. No wonder she'd wanted him to marry Teresa d'Angelo. They were alike. But then he softened a little, remembering the terrible thing his father had done to his mother. He left her for a chippie when she was pregnant, and with his little sister Sarah barely cold in her grave. It was true that he'd given her everything—factory, property, bank account, savings account, bonds, and all. But he walked out and lived openly with that terrible woman. His conscience began to bother him. He was old enough to remember the scandal, the closed door to his mother's room, the smell of camphor in the house, everyone walking around on tiptoe, her muffled sobs that often raised to unearthly shrieks when she'd ask anyone who happened to be listening—or God, whom she supposed to be *always* listening to *her*—"What did I ever do to deserve such misery?"

"Poor Mama." He said it out loud as he looked up at the sky. Then he brightened. In spite of her terrible experience, she'd come out of the throes of her sorrow and faced life. He smiled. Mama was strong. She was also resourceful, and would go to any lengths to get his wife and children back in Boston where they belonged. As soon as she got over being angry with him, she'd take steps. When his sister Cora's husband wanted to leave the family business and go into the disgraceful business of playing a piano in a saloon, Mama had taken care of that. She'd broken all of his fingers. Slammed the lid of the piano down on them so hard that she'd broken every one of them. Then there was the time when his sister Nancy was seeing another man. Mama had fixed that, too. She'd simply had the other man disposed of.

When it was all taking place, he'd been terrified and sickened. But as he grew older, he realized Mama had been forced to do what she did. It just wouldn't have done at all for one of the daughters of Mrs. Fairchild Stevens to run away with a carpenter. Mama had pointed out to the entire family that the blackguard wasn't fit to live on earth with decent people, that he didn't do anyone a bit of good by living. Nancy had never been the same since, but then . . . that was for the best, too. She was quiet and reserved. The very picture of proper good breeding. And that was certainly much better for all concerned than the flighty, flirtatious little creature she'd been before.

He wondered, as his feet carried him to Delores, how his mama would go about bringing Teresa to her senses.

XIII

Teresa d'Angelo Stevens didn't bother to answer her mother-in-law's letters. Nor did she communicate with her husband, who wrote her little notes in which he said he hoped she was well, that the children were well. He missed her very much and hoped she would soon return from her holiday.

To her lawyer, Teresa said, "It's ridiculous. His mother sends me threats. Her last letter is more vicious than any of the others. On the other hand, my husband treats the divorce as if it doesn't exist. He prefers to pretend that I'm taking a vacation."

Her lawyer read both of the latest communications, then put them in his strong box. "Mrs. Stevens, are you quite sure your husband *and* his sister told you the elder Mrs. Stevens paid to have a man murdered?"

"Absolutely." She smiled ruefully. "But I'm just as sure that neither of them would get on the witness stand and swear to it under oath. They're all terrified of her. They'll commit perjury before they'll admit their mother is a fiend who will stop at nothing to get what she wants."

Mr. McGuire's look was searching. "But you're not afraid of her. How can you *not* be afraid of her?"

"I don't know, exactly."

"Do you think she's in possession of her mental faculties? The letter I've just read speaks of divorce as sinful. How can a woman who has murdered look upon divorce as sinful?"

"Mr. McGuire," answered Teresa, "I don't *know* how she can. But I'm sure she's justified the taking of another life to herself. She's a mistress of the art of rationalization. In answer to your question about her mental faculties, well—I don't think she's insane. She knows right from wrong. But she honestly believes she's right. So maybe she's crazy."

"And dangerous."

"Can't you use any of her threats against me?"

"If it comes to it, I certainly can. Sometimes people say things in the heat of their anger, Mrs. Stevens, that they don't mean. I'm hopeful that your divorce will be uncontested. I'm also praying that your mother-in-law will have relieved herself of all her vitriol by then, that she'll remain at home and sulk instead of coming to Middletown to break your back. As I've said, I've handled very few divorces. Husbands and wives tend to live with their problems instead of getting a divorce, because of the stigma. But I've spoken with several colleagues, and they've assured me that the majority of the angry defendants in a divorce proceeding come to terms with the inevitable. Threats dwindle during the waiting period. The hearing is peaceful, and as a general rule, the defendant doesn't make an appearance."

Teresa nodded. "Yes. I'm sure."

The attorney smiled and squared up a stack of

papers on his desk. "Of course that's just the majority of the cases that go before the Court. There have been instances of gun-toting defendants. One colleague told me of a woman who kept the fires of her rage in full flame for years. She came to court and spoke at length in her own defense, pleading with the judge to have mercy on her and many other things. The longer she talked, the louder she became. When she was asked to step down, she refused, and turned on the judge with vengeance. Reluctantly, His Honor called for the Bailiff. The woman sprang from the witness chair, took the lid from a fruit jar she carried in her handbag and threw acid in the judge's face, then managed to evade the bailiff long enough to throw the remainder at her husband. He was blinded. The judge was scarred dreadfully. So, you see, we just never know."

"I'll take my chances. I'll not live with him. Nor do I fancy living out the rest of my life alone. In the beginning I liked married life, and even though the first flush of happiness was soon a thing of the past, I'm sure I have the qualifications of a good wife. The next time, I'll be more selective."

"You're very outspoken, Mrs. Stevens." The attorney looked at the papers on his desk. "I must tell you for your own protection that you are still a married woman. Therefore, you cannot, under any circumstances, take a chance on being... seen in the company of another man. Even in the most innocent pursuit, you stand a very good chance of losing your children."

Teresa turned her beautiful blue eyes on him. "I am a woman of great patience. As much as I deplore the circumstances under which I lived with my husband, I tried my utmost to have a good marriage. I have kept my vows for nine years, and I will keep them as long as I am legally married, even if I must remain neither married nor divorced for *another* nine years. However, I am also a person with certain rights, one of which is the pursuit of happiness. I have taken steps toward that pursuit."

McGuire sighed. "You're a woman of great beauty, talent, and intellect. Your grandmother was one of the most highly respected women in Middletown, and you've done nothing to cause anyone to have misgivings about your behavior. Yet, I'm troubled. Deeply troubled. Your suit is unusual. It isn't the husband who is presenting the problem, it's the husband's mother. Legally, he's the defendant. Actually, she is." He shook his head. "Mrs. Stevens, in spite of your ability to handle money, run a household, bring up children, and all your other assets, you're still a woman."

"What are you getting at, Mr. McGuire? My husband's mother is also a woman. I'm fighting for my rights, too. Among other little items that have caused my discontent, my husband has kept a mistress during the entire length of time we've been married. We've been over and over my grounds for divorce, all of which you've told me are valid. I'm fighting for my *rights,* for my life as a human being. I have no idea why she's fighting, but she is *not* the legal defendant. So why are you worried?"

"She is a woman of power, a financial genius who took a failing business and did much more than put it back on its feet. Mrs. Stevens made her company an industrial power that is second to few in the nation."

Teresa folded her hands. "I'm hardly a pauper."

"But she could buy and sell everything you own within fifteen minutes. Money talks—great wealth screams. I'm worried because under the law you

177

have no rights. You can't vote, for instance."

Teresa stood, pulled on her gloves, and reached for her handbag. "Are you telling me, Mr. McGuire, without putting it into words, that you no longer want to act on my behalf in this matter?"

He lifted a hand and got quickly to his feet. "Not at all, Mrs. Stevens. You misunderstand me. And I'm sickened at the crass idiocy of men and certain women who refuse to consider women's suffrage. I can forgive men easier than I can women. Men don't know any better, for the most part, and the rest of them fear the idea of a woman going to the polls to vote. That's why they're fighting it. Maybe I'm being too harsh on women. Possibly they're as ignorant as men about this issue of suffrage. I really don't know. But you're living in a State where you actually have no rights. Ohio is progressive in some ways, backwards in others. Mrs. Stevens, as much as I regret the idea of your leaving the town where you grew into young womanhood, where you own property and have friends... I would like to see you move away to Wyoming."

"Wyoming?" Teresa's eyes were wide. "Why on earth...Oh. Because women can vote and own property and—" She laughed. "Probably get a divorce a lot easier there."

"Exactly. Also, it's a long way from Boston. My brother and his wife moved to Wyoming some time ago. He's an attorney also."

"I can see the wisdom in the idea," she said thoughtfully. "And now would be a good time to do it. The family who has been renting my house is reluctant to move. They didn't say so, but they were disappointed, and I knew it. That's why I gave them three months to find something suitable. They'd like to purchase it. Perhaps I should burn all my bridges behind me. What do you think?"

"It would be an excellent idea. You've spent a considerable amount on upkeep, but the house is sound, and right now it's a seller's market. It's a good time to sell, both for financial gains and the safety of distance. Your husband's mother sounds as if she'll stop at nothing to bring you to your knees. I'll be greatly relieved if you put two thousand miles between that woman and you."

Before Teresa left Middletown, she gave in to the wishes of Sarah, Marshall, and Kevin and took them to the Fourth of July Celebration. They ate dinner that night in the dining room of the Manchester Hotel. The night was hot and humid, but it was more than the uncomfortable weather that kept Teresa from sleeping. They would leave on the morning train. Wyoming seemed as far away as London or Paris. She asked herself over and over again if she was doing the right thing. Not the divorce; she was sure she was doing the *only* thing as far as that was concerned. She'd toured California and enjoyed it, but Cheyenne was not San Francisco or Los Angeles. Except for California, it was difficult for her to perceive the West as anything but vast stretches of desert, twisted trees, blowing sand, cowboys, Indians, and cattle. Tossing and turning, she wondered if there would be good schools for her children, a chance for them to hear good music, attend the opera. Sarah would grow up. Her heart raced, then thudded to a stop when she thought about her daughter, about her growing up. Already, Marshall was as tall as Sarah, but her first-born son was only six to Sarah's eight. Even Kevin was growing rapidly, while Sarah seemed destined to be less than normal in height for the rest of her life. And not very pretty. Even the prettiest of girls often went begging for suitors. But a girl who was less than pretty . . . She fell to worrying about the welfare of her children in other directions. She was alone in the world. No sisters, no brothers. If anything happened to her, she had no idea what would become of them. Promising herself to make provisions the very next morning eased her mind. Even though she would write her last will and testament on the train, in addition to directions for how she wanted her children brought up—and where—she felt better, and finally slept a few hours.

As soon as the train was five miles out of Middletown, Teresa took out her writing material and drew up a will, then carefully wrote instructions to put Sarah in a school for girls, and both boys in an academy, in the event that she died before they were grown. It was a depressing task, but she rested easier when she'd finished. When they got off the train in Cincinnati to make connections for St. Louis, she mailed the letter to Mr. McGuire. Making those provisions was disturbing because she wanted her children to grow up in a loving home, as she had. But she would not, under any circumstances, allow them to live under the thumb of her husband's mother, whom she fully expected to live forever.

By November, Teresa was settled in a pleasant home, where she served her family a bountiful Thanksgiving Dinner. The children were delighted. They loved living in Cheyenne, and Teresa didn't mind, either. The people were friendly, there was a theater, a music hall, and a fine school. Her eyes sparkled as she enjoyed the conversation around her bountiful table and the laughter of her happy children. Her house was modest but roomy enough for a mother with three children. Thelma was a perfect jewel, and her only household help. Her funds were ample to see her into old age and beyond. She had enough to send her children to college, but she'd been brought up to respect the value of a dollar. She'd never been impressed with butlers and maids, jewels and furs. The luxuries she'd had as Rex Stevens' wife were nothing compared with the freedom to live and love and laugh.

On Thanksgiving evening two ladies who lived down the street dropped by to have coffee and remind her of the Little Theater production. The cast was to be selected the following night.

"I'm looking forward to it," she said.

Mrs. Treadway and Miss Anderson were excited at the idea of having a celebrity in their midst, a woman who still commanded a great deal of attention in the press, even though she'd retired to be married.

In the beginning Teresa was tempted to lie and say she was a widow when she began meeting people in Cheyenne, but she'd always found it difficult to lie. Anyway, she would get her divorce right there in town, so it was hardly a secret she could keep. But none of her new acquaintances seemed to look upon a divorceé as a scarlet woman. She was accepted and appreciated it deeply. And she was looking forward with growing excitement to the idea of not just singing, but acting.

The play was Oscar Wilde's *The Importance of Being Earnest,* which had recently been embellished with lyrics and music. When the director gave her the leading role, she was surprised and thrilled, but also a little taken aback. "But I've never done any acting, Mr. Gerard," she said.

"You read the lines beautifully, Mrs. Stevens," he answered. "Very professionally." His brown eyes twinkled. "Since you will be a great drawing card, we'd already agreed to give you the leading role if you could read the lines with any feeling at all. You sound very polished, let me assure you, and we're all pleased to have you with us."

Teresa laughed with delight. "If you're pleased, then I'm proud."

"Already, you're speaking like a lady who has lived in the West for at least a year," he answered. Then he looked at her in a different way, and her breath caught in her throat. She remembered the time when she'd felt age creeping up on her on the San Francisco stage. She remembered she'd written to Rex Stevens because he'd been different, because he'd not turned cartwheels, sent her one hundred orchids, a diamond bracelet, or any of the other foolish things men who didn't know her at all sent her just because they were starstruck. Right then she knew she had never loved her husband. With a pang she told herself she was not free to love anyone else, and wouldn't be for a long time. But that night after she prepared for bed, she looked out the window into the dark, velvety blue of the wintry Wyoming sky and found her own, private star. "Dear God," she whispered. "Don't let Mr. Gerard be a married man!"

Teresa and the children took Christmas dinner with the Treadways. Ruth and Herbert Treadway were middle-aged, but their sixth baby was only five months old when Teresa went to the first call for actors and actresses at Cheyenne's Little Theater. He came as a surprise, explained Ruth Treadway, after more than nine years. Their daughter Joanne and little Sarah became "best friends," and it was nine-year-old Joanne who actually did the inviting of the Stevenses for Christmas dinner, which presented a problem. Teresa didn't know whether the child had been asked to extend the invitation or decided to do it on her own, but on the last play practice before Christmas, Ruth Treadway said she'd waited and waited, but since Teresa hadn't said a word about whether they were coming or not, she was going to have to know pretty soon. "A certain person," she said mysteriously, "keeps asking me whether you'll be there."

Teresa blushed. "But I thought perhaps Mr. Gerard and Miss Anderson were...."

Ruth Treadway laughed. "Heavens to Betsy! Hazel Anderson has her cap set for someone else. He'll be there at Christmas, too. Now if I were Hazel, I couldn't see this man she's so crazy about for the dust, but then I'm not Hazel Anderson. No doubt she's often wondered why I'm satisfied with my husband. Herbert isn't the most handsome man on earth, but he's the kindest, the nicest, and the most loving one, I'd be willing to bet anything. On top of that, he's a good father. A person couldn't ask for anyone better."

"I've been wondering why Miss Anderson didn't marry earlier," said Teresa. "She's so pretty and so full of fun, I would have thought she'd have found herself a man a long time ago." As she said the words she realized she'd definitely begun to speak with a Western accent. Not only that, she felt free to discuss a personal aspect of another's life and knew she would not be censured for it. Living in Cheyenne was more like living in the bosom of a big, loving family. Everyone knew everything that was important about others, but it was not the kind of knowing that smacked of gossip and nosiness. No, she reflected, the interest came from caring. Everyone she'd met was interested in the happiness of others.

"Hazel was engaged to marry a fine man," said Ruth that night of the rehearsal. "But he died of consumption, poor soul. After that, she wasn't

183

interested in thinking seriously about another man for, oh, about ten years. She's thirty-five. Lives right there in the house where she grew up as a little girl, all alone since her daddy died a year ago. Her mama passed away on the very day after the youngest boy was married. Been sick a long time, but held out until she saw the last one out of the nest except for Hazel, who was still grieving her heart out for her poor young man who died. Well, well. So I can expect you at our house for Christmas. You can bring the pies, if you don't mind. Hazel is bringing bread and fresh butter. She keeps a cow, you know, and I'll tell you there just isn't any comparison between fresh churned and bought butter. David is going to bring the wine. I told him he didn't have to bring a thing except himself and his appetite, living alone as he does, hardly knowing which end of the stove to put a pot of beans on."

That was Teresa's introduction to the Pitch-In Dinner, a custom Ruth Treadway had brought to Wyoming from Southern Indiana. More important, she had learned for a fact that David Gerard was single. She'd known he lived alone in a narrow, two-story house on Water Street, but she'd been afraid to ask about his marital state. Until that moment she'd wondered if his wife had left him, if she was an invalid and living elsewhere, even if he was a confirmed bachelor. She guessed he must be around forty.

"I thought perhaps Mr. Gerard might not be free," she said carefully.

Ruth Treadway laughed. "Oh, he's free all right. Has been for fifteen years. His wife was a Sullivan, the banker's daughter, and he loved her dearly. It was an awful tragedy when she died in childbirth. They'd been married two years and she wasn't expecting the baby until much later. But it came in the sixth month, poor little angel. Fought to live, and so did poor little Donna, but—we can't question the ways of the Lord. David took it awfully hard. They'd grown up together and been sweethearts before they were old enough to know what the word meant. It was just awful. He went away and stayed for seven years. Lived in a monastery, but not because he wanted to become religious or anything like that. Did it because he couldn't bear to talk to anyone who knew her, knew of their love for one another. And I'll tell you the truth, Teresa, it was a wonderful love. Every day was just like a fairy story and when they found out they were going to get a baby they were just simply in ecstasy!

Then it happened. Terrible, terrible. And poor David came back home after those years he spent without saying one word to anyone. Oh, yes, you can do that if you want to. Don't have to, mind! But you can take the vows of silence in this place. It's like a sanctuary. Well, he came on back here to Cheyenne then and went back to work in his daddy's clock-making business just like always, except his daddy had passed away while he was gone. He did a lot of studying and reading on drama when he was away. Always did have a real big interest in acting. Then we got together and started our Little Theater, and I'll tell you, it just took hold like a house afire. And here we are with one of the most sought-after singers in the whole wide world right in the middle of it all!"

The Treadways were members of the Church of the Latter Day Saints, the first of a long list of friends of that faith. As she widened her circle of acquaintances in her new environment, Teresa always thought of her Mormon friends as good people. In spite of her excellent command of the language, the word "good" always came to mind when she referred to people like the Treadways, Jacobsens, O'Leary's, and so many others.

It was two years before her divorce was final, but Mrs. Fairchild Stevens gave her no further trouble except for a continued flood of threatening letters. Rex didn't communicate with her. Suddenly the mail from her mother-in-law stopped. One day she realized it had been a long time since she'd received a hate-letter from Rex's mother and supposed the older woman had finally become reconciled. A few weeks later, she went to the door to find Nancy O'Brien, her former husband's sister, on her front porch. In spite of Nancy's withdrawn personality, she'd liked her better than any of her other in-laws, but when she saw the blonde girl on her porch and her trunks on the sidewalk, she was frightened.

Nancy reached out her arms and hugged Teresa. "I had to come. Wild horses couldn't have kept me in Boston a moment longer. Mother died. Isn't that wonderful?"

"Oh, Nancy!" Overcome with several separate and distinct emotions, Teresa could barely speak. She was relieved at Nancy's news, ashamed of herself for being relieved at anybody's death, overwhelmed with affection for Nancy, delighted to see her, but vaguely afraid Rex was somewhere close at hand. "Come in! Come in!"

Nancy was the most attractive of all the Stevens daughters. Blonde, brown-eyed, and almost as tall as Teresa, she was reputed to have been outgoing, vivacious, and witty as a young girl. Then she'd married the man her mother chose for her, despised him, and in time became involved with another, who was killed at the hands of a hired assassin. The few

186

acquaintances who were friendly toward Teresa during her marriage had told Teresa that Nancy O'Brien was a very different person after she recovered from her nervous breakdown. No one but the members of the family knew the true reason behind Nancy's period of mental sickness. Family affairs were closely guarded secrets.

"I love your house," said Nancy after Teresa had taken her through each of the comfortable rooms. "Teresa, would it upset you terribly if I moved out here, bought a house, and stayed?"

"Why, no." Teresa was not being entirely truthful. She liked Nancy, but she'd never felt comfortable in the presence of Everett O'Brien. "You'll like Cheyenne, Nancy," she said as she hoped the other woman was not really serious.

"I'm going to get a divorce. Everett won't stand in my way, now that Mother is gone. Poor Everett! He's really a decent sort. Took me back after the trouble, never said a word to me about being unfaithful. Mother had him over a barrel, of course. She caught him tampering with the bookkeeping to cover a few hundred dollars he'd borrowed from the company in order to cover the debts he'd incurred for his mother's funeral. The undertaker was pressing him and he was putting the money back a little at a time. He'd already paid most of it when Mother went over the records with that eagle-eye of hers. That was when she decided he would make me a fine husband and gave him the choice of marrying me or going to jail. Teresa, When I dwell on all the monstrous things mother did, I could go crazy. All those years Everett had to beg and plead for enough money to keep the wolf from our door. He was never on a salary. Each week, he had to bring her a list of household expenses. Then she'd grudgingly dole out about half of what we needed. I'm ashamed to say it, Teresa, but it was almost all I could do to keep from dancing on her grave."

"Don't be ashamed, Nancy. I rather think if I had a chance, I would do more than dance on it," Teresa said. Then, with caution, she asked about her former husband.

"He's going to be all right, I think," Nancy said. "He has Delores. Rex would have been all right if Mother hadn't set out to make him a weakling. But she did, and he let her, long after he knew better. I guess it was easier for him to give in to her than to fight her. But where are the children? I'm dying to see them."

Teresa looked at the clock on the dining room wall. "They'll be home from school in about ten minutes."

Nancy had always loved Teresa's children. Her own little boy died when he was three years old and she'd showered a considerable amount of love and affection on Sarah, Marshall, and Kevin as well as her other nieces and nephews.

The children came in with their usual clatter and bang and request for something to eat. When Teresa explained that their Aunt Nancy had come to Cheyenne to visit, that she was planning to buy a house and settle there, they took the news politely but with no great show of elation. When they were in the kitchen making peanut butter sandwiches and fighting over first dibs on the cookie jar, Teresa said, "I hope you don't think I've turned them against their father's family. I've tried very hard not to. It's just that they're not too impressed with much of anything except for their own little world." She smiled. "I hope it's just a stage they're going through. My friends tell me their children are equally self-centered. I've had to ask, because I was an only child so I had no experience of my own to remember. Then, too, I was brought up by my grandmother."

"Don't worry, Teresa," said Nancy with a shrug of resignation. "They're all like that until they get a little age on them." She lowered her voice and her eyes reflected her delight. "Sarah has turned into a little doll! And she's almost as tall as other little girls of ten. I was... terribly concerned about her when you left, Teresa. She stayed so little for so long and she wasn't a very pretty child. But such a change! I can't get over how different she is, especially when I realize it's been just a little more than two years."

Pleased, Teresa said Sarah was a late bloomer. "She shot up overnight. Suddenly all her dresses were too short. I put flounces on the hems, then within a month I had to add another flounce. After that I gave up and bought material for a new wardrobe. Now I'm worrying in another direction. She's ten and a half, but already has a beau."

"Oh, Teresa! You don't allow her to have a young man!"

"No, of course not. He carries her books home from school, though. Walks to church with us. She says she 'likes' Frank Poindexter and giggles a lot. Frank, according to his mother, speaks of Sarah as 'his girl,' and informed his folks he was going to marry her as soon as she was sixteen. He's twelve." Teresa rolled her eyes. "Can you imagine? I didn't even *think* about boys except as slimy, nasty creatures whose palms were all hot and sweaty at dancing school. Most of them were shorter than I, which added to my contempt."

Nancy was comforting. "She'll probably forget all about this boy when she gets a little older. But what about you, Teresa? Have you found someone who can make you happy?"

"No, I'm already happy." She had no choice but

to tell her sister-in-law the truth. David Gerard had waited two years. He was coming to dinner, and they intended to tell the children they were going to be married on the following month. Her roast was in the oven, and the cake was hidden away on the top shelf of the pantry, so her children wouldn't be tempted to taste the frosting. Looking at Nancy with shining eyes, she said, "I don't think any man can make a woman happy. But a good man can make us *happier*." She told Nancy about David Gerard. "You'll like him. He loves me and the children. They adore him and they've begged me to marry him. Of course I couldn't until now, but they're not interested in the fine points of the law. I love him very, very much. Probably a little more than he loves me, but that's often the case. He worshipped his first wife, but he's older now and loves me—or at least he says he does—in a more mature way."

Nancy said she hoped Teresa would be happy. Then, a little wistfully, she asked, "Does he have a brother?"

"No, but there are several unattached men in Cheyenne, Nancy. If you buy a house here, you'll soon have suitors by the dozen. The ratio is about five men to every woman, so you can pick and choose."

Nancy stood up and whirled around the dining room. "Oh, boy! I want a man who has at least three children. Any widowers with several children?"

"Without even thinking, I can name three. Two are Mormons, though. What would you think about marrying a Mormon?"

"Oh, my! And share a husband? No, thank you." Nancy looked crushed.

"It's been a long time since the Latter Day Saints practiced polygamy." She held up her fingers. "Tom

190

Patterson's wife died two years ago, and he's openly looking for a wife. Joseph Conway has been a widower for ten years. He has five children, but the baby is twelve. Then there's Harry Pendleton. His wife sort of . . . decided she didn't want to be married to him any more. She left about six months ago, taking their three children with him. Then Harry's sister and her husband died within two months of each other, so there's poor Harry, who has twin boys to look after. They're cute little devils, six years old."

"If he's the right age, let's start with Harry Pendleton," said Nancy.

"Harry is about two years younger than you, but that's nothing." Pleased at the idea of match-making, Teresa sent an invitation to Harry Pendleton to come to dinner and to bring the twin boys. Sarah came back to say Mr. Pendleton had a visitor, but thanked her very much for the invitation.

"Oh, fiddle," said Teresa. "Go back and tell him to bring his visitor, darling. My lands, we don't stand on ceremony around here." She threw a few more potatoes in the pot and added an extra jar of her home-canned green beans while Nancy wondered aloud if Mr. Pendleton's guest was a lady.

"Oh, no. We're not too formal in Cheyenne," Teresa answered. "That is, even though you aren't divorced, no one will find fault with you if you sit across the table from a gentleman who is neither your father nor brother—but Harry Pendleton wouldn't have a woman visitor unless it was his mother or sister, and they live here."

David Gerard arrived in time to carve the roast. He took Nancy's hand and said he was pleased to meet her. Nancy fluttered like a school girl. In the kitchen, Teresa explained after a hurried kiss that she'd invited Harry Pendleton and his guest to share

191

their dinner and asked if David knew who was visiting Harry.

"A distant relative," answered David. "You've heard of Evan Willoughby, the artist?"

"Who hasn't? I knew he was from Wyoming, but I didn't know he was related to Harry Pendleton." Her face was rosy from the heat of the oven as she took the baked squash and biscuits out. David kissed the back of her neck. Her face grew pinker. "Thelma will be coming back to this kitchen in a second, David! What on earth will she think if she finds us sneaking kisses?"

"She'll think I'm a very lucky man. Thelma is a good, sensible young woman. Matter of fact, your hired girl told me I would be missing the boat if I didn't snatch you up about two days after you came to town."

The front door banged open, followed by the thump, rattle, and shrieks of two six-year-old boys who had been too long without a mother. Thelma returned to the kitchen to put the roast on the table. Nancy, not wanting to appear overly-anxious to meet an eligible man, had gone to her room, so Teresa sent Marshall to get his aunt. Then she turned, smiled, and extended her hand to Evan Willoughby as Pendleton introduced them. "How do you do, Mr. Willoughby. I'm so happy to know you."

"Lord!" The artist looked as if he were about to faint.

XIV

"I'm so sorry," Willoughby apologized. "You resemble someone I knew many years ago. Except for the color of your hair, your eyes, you could be . . . this beautiful woman I knew once. Her eyes were dark brown instead of blue, and her hair was almost jet-black, where yours is auburn. But your bone structure, the shape of your mouth, your teeth—I'm very sorry I allowed my emotions to overpower my good sense. I cared for her very deeply."

"You sound as if you knew her well," Teresa said.

"I did. I also painted a full-length, larger-than-life portrait of her. She was a woman of great charm as well as a stunning beauty." The artist took his place at the table. His color returned and the corners of his eyes crinkled as he smiled. "I was more than a little in love with her. Every man who was fortunate enough to know her was smitten. She passed away a number of years ago."

"Maybe we're related," Teresa said. "I wish my

hair were brown. This red hair has always been the bane of my existence."

Everyone bowed their heads as David asked the blessing. Instead of listening, Teresa wondered about Evan Willoughby. His shock was so great that he'd turned chalky white when he saw her. According to articles she'd read about him, he was somewhere around seventy, although he didn't look it with his sun-bronzed skin, his thick grey hair, and his strong, athletic build. When the food was being passed, she pursued the supject. "Do you think the lady you spoke of and I could be related, Mr. Willoughby? I'm of Italian descent on my mother's side of the family."

"She was French," he said.

Sarah, who was an avid listener and brought up in a home without a father, had not gone along with the idea that children should be seen and not heard. She asked, "What was the pretty lady's name, Mr. Willoughby?"

"Her name was Desirée," Evan Willoughby answered quickly. "Desirée La Fleur. We met in London. So it's not likely that there's a connection."

He spoke smoothly, his expression friendly, candid, and without guile. Even so, Teresa had a feeling that he was not being truthful. For what reason, she couldn't imagine. It was hard for her to shake that feeling, although she tried to. Finally, she realized why she'd felt he was lying. It was because of the too-smooth, too-quick way he answered her daughter when she asked the question about the woman's name, as if he'd mentally practiced the deception. There had been plenty of time for him to realize he'd spoken of someone he didn't want to discuss when he first was introduced to her. Then, during the time David asked the blessing, he could

194

have conjured up another name, one that would sound convincing enough to go along with the things he'd said already. Finaly, she put the puzzling incident out of her mind. Mr. Willoughby was an internationally known artist, a man who commanded respect in every country. It was unkind of her to suspect him of speaking untruthfully of someone from his past. And even if he did, it was none of her business to wonder why. He was married, with grown children and grandchildren. If he'd been indiscreet in his past, it was no concern of hers, she told herself.

Sarah, Nancy, and Teresa helped Thelma clear the table. Sarah proudly brought in the three-tiered cake, and David uncorked the champagne, tasted it, approved it, then poured. Even the children received a token spill.

David said, "I propose a toast to Teresa, our hostess, the mother of three fine children and—soon to be my wife."

Everyone drank. The twin boys quaffed theirs with manly poise, Sarah giggled and said, "Ohhhh! It tickles!" and Marshall and Kevin, different as two children born of the same mother and father could be, reacted typically.

Marshall said, "I like it." But his eyes, round and blue and unable to hide a secret, showed that he was only pretending because the occasion called for it. Kevin licked his lips, grinned impishly and asked for more. Under the cover of the mingled childish antics, the pleased exclamations of Nancy, Thelma and Harry Pendleton, Teresa's thoughts again turned to Evan Willoughby. During the moment of the lifting of goblets, her lovely eyes met David's. For a shimmering moment, they smiled at one another. Then Teresa felt a sob rising in her throat and looked away. She was overcome with intense happiness and was afraid she would cry in front of her guests if she continued to gaze into David's eyes a moment longer. When she glanced around the table, she noticed that even though Evan Willoughby raised his glass along with the others, he didn't touch the champagne. He held it to his lips, yes. But he didn't drink it, which she took as a sign that he either disapproved of her marriage or had another reason to not wish her happiness. Whatever it was, it troubled her.

She cut the cake and passed each one a plate, all the time trying to put the strange behavior of the artist out of her mind. The conversation concerned her wedding. Mr. Willoughby stated his regrets that he would not be able to stay in Cheyenne long enough to attend. A quick glance at his wine goblet told her that he'd never so much as touched it, but he ate his cake, commented on the flavor and texture, and when the children asked for seconds Evan Willoughby said, he, too, would like a second helping. He was altogether a puzzling man, she decided, as she became involved with him in an animated conversation. Friendly, considerate, and genuinely interested in a wide range of subjects, he added greatly to the festive occasion.

Harry Pendleton sent little interested glances toward Nancy, she noted with pleasure. Under his interested expression and friendly overture, Nancy bloomed. It gave her a sense of satisfaction when she saw her sister-in-law look with adoration at the twin boys, both of whom seemed to sense that her fondness was spontaneous. One of them— Teresa could never tell them apart—climbed up on Nancy's lap and leaned his head against her breast. When she was alone in the kitchen with her hired girl, she laughed when Thelma, who never missed anything of importance, said, "Your sister-in-law has one of those little hellions eating out of her hand. Now if she can win over the other one, I won't be in the least surprised if we hear of another engagement."

Flustered, thinking about Nancy's intention of filing suit for divorce, Teresa said, "I think it's a little too soon to start counting chickens. But Nancy loves children. That's no pretense, Thelma."

"Oh, I could see that right off, Mrs. Stevens," answered Thelma. "But it's no secret that Mr. Pendleton would like to find another missus. Seems kind of sad to think about what his wife did to him. Mr. Pendleton was just as happy as a cricket in a clothes-press. Didn't have the slightest idea that his wife was seeing that no-good, fly-by-night photographer on the sly. Everybody else in town knew, but he didn't. And then for him to lose his sister and take on those two little demons, well, it's just a shame!"

Teresa didn't know it was common knowledge that Mrs. Pendleton was seeing another man before she left. *She'd* known, but only because Mrs. Treadway's hired girl had told Mrs. Treadway. "It's impossible to keep a secret in Cheyenne," Teresa said.

"Not hardly," answered Thelma. "I knew about you and Mr. Gerard before *you* did!" She looked at Teresa with a confident smile. "I'm tickled to death. You'll have a fine life with Mr. Gerard. You deserve the kind of happiness he can give you, ma'am."

"May I add a hearty 'Amen' to that statement?" Mr. Willoughby had entered the kitchen while Thelma spoke. "Mrs. Stevens, I feel I must explain...I made a vow several years ago that I would never taste another drop of spirits. I'm overjoyed for you, and I certainly wish you

197

happiness in your forthcoming marriage. I've been wed for thirty-five years and a day never passes that I don't thank my Maker for helping me find a lovely and lovable wife, and for giving me the good sense to take the gift of love when it was offered to me."

"Thank you, Mr. Willoughby," answered Teresa. "I'm glad you explained about the—well, I noticed that you didn't drink the toast with the others. But I understand. Many people are carrying the temperance banner these days. I sympathize with the idea, but I don't think prohibiting the sale of alcohol will stop people from overindulging."

"Oh, you misunderstand," said the artist. "My wife and I serve wine in our home. I made the vow because I drank too much, and too often, not because I want to stop others from enjoying spirits."

Teresa gave him her hand. "I'm so glad you explained. Uh—Mr. Willoughby, when you said the name of the lady I resemble, I had a feeling that you weren't being absolutely truthful."

His laugh rang out. "My wife and children tell me I haven't much ability in the art of deception. I'm not a good poker player, either. The resemblance *is* uncanny. I made up another name on the spur of the moment because the lady was not married. And I was thinking that—the resemblance is so strong, that I must confess I wondered, after I got over my shock, if you could be her daughter."

"You may set your mind at ease, Mr. Willoughby, but I do thank you for your consideration. My mother was married in San Francisco."

"Ahh. It could not possibly be the same person."

"My mother died when I was born, and my grandmother brought me up."

Harry Pendleton stuck his head in the kitchen door to say they'd have to leave because the twins were about to go to sleep on their feet. Teresa extended her hand. "I'm so very glad you came tonight, Mr. Willoughby."

"So am I, my dear. When I come to see Harry again, you'll be Mrs. David Gerard. I try to get around to see all my relatives at least once a year. We're a small family, but very close."

When all the guests had left the house and Nancy and Teresa's children had gone to bed, David held Teresa in his arms for the first time. He kissed her passionately. She threw all caution to the winds and returned his kisses with urgent delight.

"Do we have to wait?" David spoke softly into her ear. "Can't we be married tomorrow instead of waiting?"

"Not tomorrow," she answered. "But I don't really see why we have to keep a certain date just because it seemed like a good idea to set one. How about next week?"

His smile was so bright that she laughed. Then she remembered something she had to tell him, and the smile left her face. "Dearest, I have no father, and no brother to speak to you about this delicate matter, so I'll have to do it for myself. I'm beyond the age of bearing you a child of your own. Some women retain that privilege until they are much older than I; others end it sooner. I hadn't thought about it until last night, after I realized I had been amiss." She buried her head against his shoulder. "I'm sorry I didn't tell you sooner."

"Look at me, Teresa," he said as he moved away from her and gently tipped her chin up with his fingertips. "I am marrying a woman who has three children. They will be my children, and I already love them because I love you, and they're a part of you. When I was a younger man I wanted babies.

But watching poor old Harry try to cope with those two little boys tonight brought a cold chill of fear to my spine. I found myself worrying about how I would cope with a couple of lively children and was glad yours are old enough to have reached the age of reason. What I'm saying, my love, is that I'm very, very relieved to know I won't be the father of a new baby. At forty-eight, I'm not sure I could handle it.

She silenced his words with her lips.

Teresa's wedding gown was rose-colored velvet, with long, narrow sleeves and a moderately full skirt. The train was in the same fabric and embroidered with silver beads. She carried a bouquet of white roses, with three pink buds in the center to represent her children. Nancy was her matron of honor, and Mrs. Treadway and Mrs. Rudyard Kelley acted as witnesses. Mrs. Kelly was the former Miss June Marie Allison.

Immediately before they went to the church for the wedding, Sarah burst into tears. She was so agitated that it took Teresa several minutes to calm her enough to realize what the little girl was saying. During those moments she silently went to pieces, fearing Sarah resented the idea of having a stepfather. But Sarah was upset because Teresa was not wearing a white wedding gown, because her train was no longer than any other fashionable dress!

Greatly relieved, Teresa explained that only brides who had not been previously married wore white. Sarah dried her tears then, and all went well. Later, after the reception at the Presbyterian Church Fellowship Room, long after the newlyweds had checked into the hotel in Rock Springs where they'd spend their honeymoon, Teresa told David about the incident. Then she said, "I was afraid she was going to ask me to call off the wedding."

He gave her a searching look. "If she had, what would you have done?"

"I'm afraid there would have been no wedding. You see, darling, as much as I love you, my children came first. I couldn't face making her unhappy." She kissed him. "And I can't imagine anything more damaging to a marriage than starting it out with a resentful child."

"You're a wonderful mother, woman, and wife, and your devotion to your children was one of the reasons I fell in love with you."

Being married to David was incredibly different from being married to Rex Stevens. They worked together and shared together in all things, including the children. They didn't always agree, but when they had differences of opinion they were able to talk them out without exploding. Rex had whined when he was confronted with problems. David spoke reasonably, made intelligent suggestions, and gave Teresa moral support. Rex had blustered when he was angry; he ran around slamming doors, turned red in the face, and waved his arms. David's sense of humor helped them through the rough times. However, it was not until Teresa realized she'd stopped making comparisons that she knew she was completely free of her first husband. In time, she forgot for long, long stretches of time that she'd ever been married to anyone but David Gerard.

Nancy married Harold Pendleton two weeks after her divorce was final. A year and a half later, she surprised everyone including herself when she learned she was expecting a baby. Teresa was the first to know after Nancy received the great news. Laughing and crying at the same time, she said, "It was the ride in your new automobile that did it, Teresa."

Round-eyed, Teresa stared at Nancy. "How can

an automobile ride be responsible for—"

"Harry and I had our first quarrel when we came home after that ride in your new car," Nancy explained. "I wanted one, too. Then we made up. Now I'm going to have a baby!" She was so elated that she was giggling as incessantly as Sarah was when she referred to Frank Poindexter. "And the doctor told me I'm exactly four and a half months along, because that was why I went to see him. I felt the quickening of *life!* Isn't it wonderful? And—it was exactly four and a half months ago to the *day* that your husband bought that brand-new Ford!"

When Nancy's little boy was born, Sarah wanted to spend all her time at her Aunt Nancy and Uncle Harry's house. She worshipped the child, and on those rare occasions when she graced the Gerard home with her presence, she talked of nothing but little Robert. She had always been very good with her own little brothers, never fussing when she was asked to take care of them, never referring to them as little nuisances. Other mothers often asked Teresa to give them her magic formula. *Their* older children looked upon the task of looking after their little brothers and sisters as something akin to cruel and unusual punishment. Sarah often said she would have at least a dozen children when she and Frank were married. Teresa didn't doubt it. But when Sarah was fourteen, she began to worry. Never once had her daughter swerved from her dedication to Frank Poindexter, and she insisted that she was going to marry him as soon as she was sixteen.

David agreed with Teresa that sixteen was too young for Sarah to marry. They wanted her to become acquainted with other young men well enough to know for sure it was Frank she wanted to spend the rest of her life with, but Sarah refused to do more than speak politely to the boys who asked to carry her books or walk her home from school.

As a very little child, Sarah had displayed a raging temper at times. As she approached sixteen, the temper she'd learned to control returned in the form of defiance. Teresa worried. David consoled. In May of 1915, David said, "Teresa, darling, I think we'd better give her our permission to marry. If we don't, they'll elope." That night they told Sarah they would give her a wedding and their blessings, and Sarah was ecstatic.

The following day, May 8, Americans learned that the *Lusitania* was sunk and the country was on the brink of war. Frank enlisted immediately and Sarah cried for a full month. All through the war years, Sarah remained steadfast in her devotion to Frank Poindexter.

Frank was wounded in the Battle of the Somme, returned home after a stint in the hospital, and they were married in September of 1918.

Within twelve years, Sarah had given birth to eight sons. Teresa was sixty-four years old when her eighth grandson, Richard, was born. Two years later, she was both surprised and relieved when Sarah didn't give birth to another child. Sarah was not relieved at all. She'd planned to have twelve children and wouldn't be satisfied until she had, she told her mother. But it was not until Sarah was in her thirty-eighth year that she gave birth to her daughter, thirteen years after Richard's birth.

Teresa, seventy-seven, looked at her granddaughter and smiled. "She looks so much like you did when you were born, Sarah. Same tuft of brown hair, same little precious face. She's the most beautiful baby in the world."

It was 1943. Sarah's little girl was born in a

hospital, and Sarah was worn out from the long, hard birth, something she'd never experienced with her sons. "I'll not have twelve children after all, Mother. Rosemary is my last child."

PART THREE

XV

Rosemary was not quite three years old when Sarah first began to worry. It was February of 1945. Frank was working in the shipyards. He would soon be coming home, and Sarah decided if she was going to put in a long distance call to her mother she'd better do it soon. Not that Frank would care about the call—he *never* complained about the calls she made to Cheyenne from Los Angeles. Now and then he said something about regretting that he'd not called his own mother more often. She died the year they moved to California, two months after Rosemary was born. Frank's mother was only fifty when she passed away. Teresa was nearing eighty and still going strong. Sarah wanted to talk to her mother about her problem, and she couldn't talk uninhibitedly if he were there. The thing was, Frank wouldn't pay any attention to Sarah when she worried about Rosemary—he wouldn't even talk about it. He'd heard of other children who'd had strange ideas when they were Rosemary's age and everybody said it was just a *stage* they were going through. For instance, his younger brother Christopher pretended to be a horse for a full week. But his mother took care of that in short order. She'd said, all right, if you're a horse, you can spend the night in the barn. Well, that had taken care of Alan's notions about being a horse. Sarah had tried to get Frank to realize that Rosemary wasn't pretending to be any horse or anything like that. Frank said she was partial to their daughter, had been ever since she was born and that she made mountains out of molehills where Rosemary was concerned. Sarah said she wasn't the only one; Frank worried himself to a frenzy if Rosemary skinned her knees, sneezed, or refused to drink her milk. He wanted to take her to a doctor when she had a splinter in her finger. But . . . Sarah was worried about Rosemary's mind.

As she listened to the distant ringing of her mother's telephone, Sarah pictured Cheyenne, the comfortable home close to the heart of town where they'd moved shortly after her mother and David were married. It seemed to her it was taking her mother an awfully long time to come to the phone, and she grew anxious. Anything could happen to a woman living all alone in a big house. She could fall down the stairs, break a hip, and lie there forever, with nobody knowing the difference. Sighing, she decided to try one more time to talk her mother into coming to California to live, but even as she made the decision she doubted if she could be persuasive enough. Teresa was as contrary as she could be and getting more so as she grew older. Not senile, though. Oh, no! A little smile played at Sarah's lips as she pictured her mother's reaction if she were to use that word.

"Hello?"

"Mother, are you all right?"

"Of course I'm all right. Sarah, is that you?"

Sarah almost doubled up with laughter. "Mother, how many daughters do you have?"

"Well, I've got daughters-in-law. Did you call me long-distance just to ask me smart-ass questions?"

Instantly, Sarah sobered. "No. I have something on my mind I want to talk over with you. Is everyone all right? Heard from the boys lately?"

"Marshall is on his way home from England. Of course they're going to live in Montana with Gail's folks until he decides what he wants to do. I told them there's plenty of room here in this house, but Marshall couldn't wait to leave Cheyenne, and that was long before he married Gail. I guess I should just thank my lucky stars that both of my sons lived through this terrible war. I *am* grateful, but I wish one of you could have stayed in Cheyenne. Kevin is mending nicely. But there he is with Jennifer, in Indianapolis. Three grown children, and every one of you scattered to the winds."

"Mother, Frank and I are coming home as soon as the war is over. You know how badly ship-builders are needed just now, and—"

"Oh, well. I shouldn't complain. And I'm not lonely, either, so don't you start in on that business about me moving to California. I'll stay right here in this house until I die, and then I'll be buried right alongside David. What's wrong?"

"Nothing is exactly wrong, Mother."

"I'm getting ready to go to the Red Cross. That's why it took me so long to answer the phone. I was already out on the porch when I heard it ringing."

Sarah smiled as she visualized her mother all dressed to leave the house. Tall, slender, and straight as a ramrod, she went to work at the Red Cross. She spent three afternoons each week at the hospital where she read to patients, belonged to God knew how many organizations, drove her car hell-bent-for-election all over town, and never had an accident or a traffic violation in her life. "Mother, Rosemary has decided she's not going to be Rosemary any more. She won't answer unless I call her Juliette."

Her mother's voice was clear and full of her usual humor. "Don't let that worry you, Sarah. When you were about that age you said you were a boy named Paul. Because you wanted to be like Paul Martin, the newspaper boy. My lands. Don't tell me *that's* why you called!"

"Mother, you don't understand. I'm telling you I can't do anything with her. She won't answer, won't do anything unless I call her Juliette."

"You mean like in *Romeo and Juliet?*"

"Yes!"

"She's probably heard the name and taken a fancy to it."

Things were not going the way Sarah had planned. "She does other things, too. They're strange and frightening. She said I wasn't her mother. Asked where her sisters were. Said their names too, but I can't remember them. But the nights are even scarier. She dreams, then wakes up disoriented."

Her mother's tone of voice underwent a subtle change. "Honey, I know you're worried. When you were five, you went through a period when you believed you were adopted. I had a hard time of it, let me tell you. You cried as if your little heart would break, sometimes for hours on end. Now Sarah, you're not getting mixed up in one of those radical religious groups out there in California, are you? I would hate to think you were being taken in by those crackpots who believe people die and come back as dogs or cats."

"No, Mother. I'm not involved with any church except the Presbyterian. It's just that—Rosemary frightens me. She described the house where she thinks she should be living and named the street, told all about the furnishings, and *Mother!* people don't have furnishings like that. Not now. It's more like around the turn of the century."

Her mother's voice was comforting. "Sarah, children of today know all about things they'd never heard of when you were little. There's the radio, for instance."

"But they don't learn to speak French by listening to the radio, Mother!"

"French!"

"Yes, French. It's the language Rosemary speaks in her sleep. And after she wakes up, she doesn't know me. I *know* it's French. I had two years of it in high school."

"Oh, dear." For a space of time, Sarah could hear nothing but a distant humming. Then she was overjoyed to hear her mother say, "Maybe I'd better come on out there for a little visit. *French!* My lands."

"When? Mother, I'm tickled to death. Frank will be just as happy as I am."

"I'll call you, dear. I'll have to make some arrangements with someone to look after the house."

Sarah's next door neighbor listened with amusement as she described the telephone conversation with her mother. Then Mary Jane Shay leaned forward and said, "Really, Sarah, you should have been a motion picture star. You're every bit as pretty as Lana Turner. In fact, if your hair was blonde, you'd look very much like her. But then she's not a comedienne. Your mother *couldn't* be the character you make her out to be."

"Oh yes she is. You ought to see her tooling around Cheyenne in her Oldsmobile. Bought a new one every year until the war came along and they stopped making them for the duration." Sarah looked into her coffee cup. "I feel a little foolish, finding it necessary to call my mother about that business with Rosemary. I'm forty-one, after all! But honestly, Mary Jane, it's uncanny."

Rosemary was in the back yard playing in her sand pile. From the kitchen table where she was having coffee with her neighbor and good friend, Sarah could see her clearly. "She doesn't look like a strange child. Look at her. Perfectly normal. Adorable, but normal."

"She's going to be tall."

"Like my mother. You know, Mary Jane, for years Mother was afraid my growth was stunted. Then I started sprouting up, and after a while I was almost average. I've never been tall, but— Mary Jane, sometimes I wonder how people get through this life without going batty."

"Maybe you should take Rosemary to one of those child psychologists."

Sarah nodded miserably. "I've already thought about it, but Frank won't hear of it. He thinks I'm allowing myself to get all worked up over nothing, that this thing with Rosemary is just a phase she's going through like the time his brother Alan said he was a horse. Frank doesn't put too much stock in psychology in the first place. He thinks it's just a fad. Anyway, he's worried about our sons who are in the service and the ones who will soon be going in if this war doesn't end. Damn the Japanese. Damn Hitler.

210

Damn them all. I worry about our boys just as much as Frank does. He ought to know that. But he—Mary Jane, he honest-to-God said he believed I was letting Rosemary get to me because I'm starting to go through the change of life. Now *honestly!*"

Mary Jane was appropriately sympathetic. "Men! If they don't blame all the ills of women on lack of sex drive, they blame it on the change of life. Bill doesn't have a lick of faith in psychology either, but he sure has picked up on the vocabulary. He says I'm frigid, and accuses me of being overly-protective of my boys. Christ." Mary Jane lit a cigarette, crumpled the pack, and looked at it ruefully. "That's my last pack. If Bill doesn't bring a carton home from the shipyard, we'll not have any until tomorrow. I hate to stand in line for meat, for cigarettes, or for sugar. We're almost out of coffee, but Bill swills it down without the slightest worry about getting another pound. He won't drink the substitute, but when we don't have anything else he blames me. What am I supposed to do, snap my fingers and produce it?"

"Frank worries about running out of gasoline stamps more than anything else. When I took that job he had a sulking spell every morning because he had to drive me five blocks out of his way. I really wanted to do something for the war effort, but of course building ships is more important than what I was doing. Still and all, I'm sure we could have gotten some extra gas coupons if we'd gone to the authorities. Frank didn't want me to work outside the home. He's not fooling me a bit."

Mary Jane snapped her fingers. "That's it. Rosemary began to have restless nights when you went to work. That was when she first began to say she was Juliette. You know what I think, Sarah? I think she made up her mind to work you around until you quit your job. Listen, kids are smart, even three-year-olds."

"French," Sarah said flatly. "Kids are smart, sure. But where did she learn to speak French?"

MaryJane shrugged. "It's too deep for me." She stood up and looked out the window toward her house. "I have to run. The kids will be coming home from school and I still have the kitchen to wax. I didn't happen to leave a few cigarettes over here yesterday morning, did I?"

"No. I could get you one of Frank's cigars."

"No thanks! I tried one last week, remember? How was I to know men don't inhale cigars, Oooooooh! Was I sick!"

Frank was pleased to hear that Sarah's mother was coming. Sarah said nothing to him about the actual reason for her visit. As she put dinner on the table her mood brightened. Optimistically, she told herself the worrisome stage Rosemary was going through would fade away.

Richard and Michael were fifteen and seventeen. Sarah looked at the two sons who hadn't gone into the service as they ate their dinner and prayed the war would be over before she saw them leave for active duty. Six sons were more than enough. They had already lost two boys, both at the beginning of the war. Although she and Frank had borne up as well as they could, their grief was still raw. Frank wept silently in the night, trying to not awaken her, but she heard him and suffered with him, for himself and for herself, when they held one another close. Every morning Frank said, "Another day." Sarah nodded and echoed him, taking care to keep the heartbreak out of her voice. He meant they had to face another day of torment, afraid a telegram would come again. Every night, Frank came home and said, "We got through that one." Then all they had to do was face the fears that came in the night. Over there where their sons were in the thick of it, the battles didn't cease and the slaying continued. Sarah felt guilty because she was worried about Rosemary. A minor mystery in a war-torn world that was insignificant compared with the two Gold Stars in their window and the fear of more to come. But she was Rosemary's mother, too.

For several days, Rosemary went back to normal. Sarah's mother called to say when she would arrive in Los Angeles and Sarah went into a flurry of housecleaning. Sometimes it was hard for her to believe that her mother had once been a celebrity who sang in theaters all over the world so packed with admirers that standing-room-only was a nightly occurrence. Her memories of Boston were thin and shadowy. Most of her childhood recollections had to do with Cheyenne, where her mother stayed at home and baked bread, cooked delicious meals, and appeared in Little Theater productions. She'd lavished love on her children, idolized her second husband, and sang when she was working among her numerous house plants or in her flower garden. On Sunday she went to church and was active in church work. Later after the children were grown, she became active in politics and worked for human rights. Sarah often felt she was not nearly the courageous, spirited woman her mother had been before her, but then she always consoled herself by thinking of her nine children and her steadfast dedication to the one cause she championed. Sarah spent three afternoons each week reading to the blind, and largely through her efforts, she'd made it possible for blind persons in several states to obtain meaningful employment. She'd written mountains of letters and handled tons of correspondence. Frank was unstinting with his own time and never complained when she was up half of the night getting out letters to employers who might possibly be persuaded to give a blind person a job.

With her mother coming, she wanted the house spotless. She never let it get dirty, but sometimes it was piled with papers, books, unironed clothing, and toys. Sarah was well aware of her mother's ability to do everything in an orderly, efficient manner. For as long as she'd lived, she couldn't remember a day when she didn't feel slightly overshadowed by her mother.

Frank drove her down to the station to meet Teresa's train. It was an hour and a half late and almost eleven o'clock at night, but Frank put it succinctly when he said. "Look at her. Fresh as a daisy, not a wrinkle in her dress, every hair on her head as neatly combed as if she'd just stepped out of a beauty shop. If she's been inconvenienced, she doesn't show it."

Sarah's eyes filled with tears as she smelled her mother's familiar fragrance. "Oh, Mother, I'm so glad you're here!" Mother and daughter exchanged glances after they embraced and Sarah appreciated the secret little twinkle in her mother's eyes. During their last conversation she'd talked of Frank's reluctance to take the problem of Rosemary seriously, to even talk about it, and the glance told Sarah they would talk about it. There was no use in getting Frank upset.

At home they had coffee and a cake made without sugar, butter or eggs, all of which were impossible to get. "Delicious," said Mrs. Gerard. And she ate every crumb. Sarah took her to her room and showed her the bathroom, the towels she'd laid out, and the extra blankets if they were needed. Then she said she'd let her sleep late in the morning. When she closed the door, she smiled, realizing her mother would probably awaken at dawn.

However, at nine o'clock the next morning Sarah grew apprehensive. Her mother never slept late. Sarah came into her mother's bedroom, but her mother lay still. "Mother!" Sarah screamed, crying. Teresa was pale, but she was lovely in death as she lay on her back, her eyes closed, arms at her side, her white hair in short waves. After Sarah reached the plateau of her shock and grief and began to slide down the hill into living and laughing again, she said to Frank, "Mother looked just as if she were on stage, about to make a bow."

XVI

Rosemary was graduated from high school in 1960. Immediately following Commencement, some seventy or eighty people arrived at the big old house in Cheyenne where the Poindexters had lived since the end of World War II. Looking lovely and fragile and somewhat ethereal in her white graduation dress, Rosemary looked at her mother with dismay when the seventh carload pulled up in front of the house. "But Mother, you promised to invite just a few friends!" They were alone in the music room where Sarah's mother's piano dominated one wall.

"We can't let anyone come in here," Sarah said. "It's a mess. But the rest of the house is spotless." Distractedly, she looked at her dark haired, blue-eyed daughter. "People *expect* to be invited to a celebration when the daughter of the house graduates. Her eyes were nostalgic. "Mother had over a hundred guests for mine."

"Mother, people do things differently now," said Rosemary.

"Oh, baby!" Sarah was crushed. "There's nothing wrong with tradition."

"I'm sorry." Rosemary smiled and held her arms out to her mother. She was taller by eight inches. "It's just that—oh! Things are in such a terrible turmoil. People my age might not have a tomorrow. When you wonder if there's a future, things like graduation parties aren't awfully important."

"You're thinking about your brothers. Rosemary, honey, an hour doesn't pass that I don't grieve for your brothers. Your daddy and I lost three sons in the war. Young, handsome, healthy, intelligent boys. But don't you see, baby, your brothers fought for all the things Americans believe in. Everything from Fourth of July celebrations to graduation parties to hamburgers and apple pie. They'd have wanted the best of everything for you. And they'd be so proud if they could see you in your dress, receiving your diploma, getting all those honors, hearing you give your speech as Valedictorian."

Rosemary was not thinking about her brothers. She had no memory of those three young men who gave their lives for their country, but she knew her mother and father would always cherish their memory with mingled pride and sorrow. It didn't matter how many times she reminded her mother she wasn't born when the Japanese bombed Pearl Harbor, that she was only three years old when the war ended. Sarah's memories were so scarred by her sons' deaths that she was never able to quite believe the ravages of war hadn't left a permanent impression on Rosemary.

It was the bomb and the threat of total annihilation that frightened Rosemary and her peers. They spoke about their shaky heritage when they were together, but only when they were sure no person over the age of thirty could overhear. Two cars in every garage, an immaculate kitchen complete with dishwasher, automatic washers and dryers, television sets, formal gowns and proms were of great importance to parents, but of little interest to the majority of the graduating class of 1960. Life insurance, hospitalization, nicely polished shoes, a big Sunday dinner after church were referred to as trappings of the great army of the middle-class. The gung-ho patriots of an era they knew little about didn't understand and couldn't relate to them. They had come into the world during a national emergency of wartime rationing and young men's blood being spilled on foreign soil. Growing up, Rosemary's classmates had experienced few desires that were not fulfilled. The Second World War was a chapter in the history books, just as the Great Depression of the 1930's was relegated to half a chapter. Parents complained because their children did not speak the same language. *Life-style, relate to, wiped out, wasted, a flower-child, U-2 Reconnaisance plane, apartheid, sit-ins,* were just a few of the thousands of words that high school students spoke glibly while their parents wondered what they were talking about. When she was Rosemary's age, Sarah was interested in marrying Frank, settling down and having a family. The first World War had meant only one thing to her—Frank might get killed. It was hard for her to accept a daughter of seventeen who talked wistfully of helping to make a better world.

Rosemary loved her mother and father dearly. Until eleven o'clock, she smiled, shook hands with the guests who had come to her graduation party, opened her presents, and often found her eyes filled with tears of gratitude, touched by the words on the

218

cards. At seventeen, she felt both ancient and very, very young. She was aware of her intellect and proud of her grades, but even though she sometimes felt wise, she often felt stupid. And she was afraid. Twelve years of schooling were behind her. Most of her life was ahead of her, and she wasn't quite ready to leave the home where she'd been sheltered and loved, even though she was anxious to do so.

At eleven o'clock, when only a few of the very close friends and relatives were sitting around the table, Sarah brought out Rosemary's baby book. Rosemary and Eric had gone steady since she was in her sophomore year and he was a junior. The feelings of ambivalence which plagued her in other respects applied to her feelings about Eric as well. She loved him and disliked him. Wanted him with her all the time but sometimes wished he wasn't there when he was at her side. She looked at the pink leather bound baby book with her name in gold on the front and met Eric's eyes. He had finished his first year at The University of Wymoning. Eric grinned when he saw the baby book.

OUR BABY
Rosemary Teresa Pendleton

"Mother, no!" She didn't want her mother to trot out that baby book. Not with Eric there, bored to tears and wanting her to step outside with him so he could hold her and kiss her and touch her breasts before he went home with an erection.

Sarah opened the book and handed it to Rosemary. "Just fill in the page for your graduation, lovey. That's all I ask."

"Okay." Rosemary bent her shining dark head forward and dutifully filled in the blanks.

219

Sarah took the book, flipped back a few pages, and smiled tenderly. "This was taken when you were one year old, honey. That's your grandmother with us. Three generations."

"Oh, crud," Rosemary said. "Mother, you *promised!*"

"All right." But Sarah continued to flip the pages. "Now here. Just this one more page, Rosemary, and then I'll put it away. *Honestly!* You'd think there was something sinful about cherishing golden moments." She held the book out to her daughter. "This one was taken when you scared me half out of my mind. You were two and a half years old, and had decided your name was Juliette. Wouldn't answer unless your daddy and I called you Juliette instead of Rosemary."

Rosemary had heard the story at least a hundred times. She had no memory of it, but was certain that she'd related to *Romeo and Juliet,* because of the big book she'd loved from the time she could turn a page. There was a section in it that had to do with Shakespeare's works and it was illustrated. At four, her father had taught her to read with the aid of Cowel's *Volume Library.* She'd screamed and kicked and stormed until he gave in and answered her burning questions about letters and the magic that formed them into words.

"That was the year your grandma died," Sarah remarked as she looked around the enormous dining room almost as if she half expected to see her mother. She turned to Eric Langford. "You talk about music, my mother was one of the greatest, most renowned—but you already know about that. I was thinking just the other day about music and how it's changed. Mother sang classical music for the most part, and she could still bring an audience to its feet just a few years before she died. She liked jazz and blues, but never cared too much about swing. I don't know what she'd say about that awful, loud stuff you kids like to listen to today."

Frank shook his head. "I know what she'd say. Turn it off. Your mother was a woman of fine tastes in everything from apples to Ziegfeld."

"She used to sing about a sheep," Sarah said. "Her grandmother taught it to her, so it must be at least two hundred years old." Then she brought a blush of shame to her daughter's cheeks as she broke into song:

> Oh, I went down to Darby's
>   Upon a summer's day
> And there I saw the biggest sheep
>   That was ever feed on hay.
> Now this sheep, it had two horns, sir,
>   That reached up to the moon.
> A man climbed up in May, sir,
>   And he didn't get back till June.
> Oh, didderum, didderum, dandy,
>   Didderum, didderum, day --
> Now Darby's got the biggest sheep
>   That was ever fed on hay.
> Now, the man who owns the sheep, sir,
>   Is liable to get rich,
> But the man who wrote this song, sir,
>   Is a lyin' son of a
>   Which way to the orchard, Molly?
>   Which way to the barn?
>   Which way to the meadow, Molly?
>   Don't sing me another yarn.

Everyone else laughed, but Rosemary was choked with embarrassment. When the laughter and applause died down, she said, "That doesn't sound like a classical song to me."

"Oh, it's just an old, old song," answered Sarah. "I

thought you'd enjoy it. It was supposed to have been George Washington's favorite folk tune. I haven't thought about it for years and years, but all you young people are interested in folk music these days and I—Sarah looked as if she was ready to burst into tears. A glance at Eric's face showed Rosemary why, and she was dismayed when she realized that her own showed the shame she felt because of her mother's unexpected song. Eric was openly laughing at her mother.

Rosemary left her chair and went to fling her arms around her mother. "You have a pretty voice, Mother. If you'd followed Grandma's advice and let her give you lessons you'd probably be as famous as she was." She drew in her breath, and was suddenly shocked senseless. For the first time in her life, she smelled whiskey on her mother's breath. Looking deeply into Sarah's eyes, she said, "Mother, are you all right?"

"Why, of *course* I'm all right. I'm just *fine!* Right as *rain!* Except for the day when you get married, this is probably the happiest day of my *life!*" Sarah's shoulders shook and she hid her face in her hands as she sobbed. "I think I'll just die, I'm so damned happy."

Eric cleared his throat. "I guess I better go," he said as he got to his feet. "It's getting late and all like that."

Torn between walking outside with Eric and staying with her mother, Rosemary compromised by walking him to the door. He kissed her quickly, said he'd see her the next day, and left . When Rosemary returned to the dining room, the other guests were murmuring about the lateness of the hour and gathering handbags, handkerchiefs, and the empty food containers they'd brought to the party.

Frank Poindexter put his big, comforting arms around his wife after everyone left. "Honey, for God's sake, try to pull yourself together."

Rosemary felt frozen as she stood by. Her father usually had a highball before dinner, but although her mother mixed them and served them to him and to guests, she never touched liquor.

"I had a drink, Frank," Sarah blubbered. "Just one little drink of rum. It tasted awful, too. Burned my throat going down and I almost gagged. I just thought I would—you know—sort of—I mean, I needed a pick-me-up."

"Looks more like you got a bring-you-down," said Rosemary.

Sarah cried harder. "And I ruined your wonderful day! *Ruined* my baby's graduation day. Oh, Frank! I didn't know one little drink would make me act silly. Singing that awful song, acting like a nut!"

"That song wasn't awful! You didn't act like a nut!" Rosemary stamped her foot and raised her voice. "You're my mother and you've always been a wonderful mother. Stop acting like you've committed a crime, for God's sake! I'm your last kid, Mother. It's tough seeing the last chick leave the nest and thinking about my brothers who were killed in the damned war and—Mom, I love you so much." She was down on her knees, her head in her Mother's lap. Looking up at her father with shining eyes, she added, "You too, Daddy. I don't want to leave the nest. If it's all the same with you, I'd just as soon turn the clock back to the year I was five years old."

Sarah wiped her eyes, blew her nose on the paper napkin her husband handed her and spoke briskly. "You'll soon get over feeling that way, Rosemary, honey. There's a great, big wonderful world out there and you're just beginning to learn a little bit about it. Let's go to bed and to hell with the dishes."

Except for saying hell," Frank Poindexter said mildly, "you sound just like your mother."

Rosemary watched her mother and father climb the steps. Quietly, she went around the room and picked up the clutter of paper plates, glasses, ashtrays, and gift-wrapping. An hour later after the downstairs part of the house had been straightened and the kitchen made immaculate, she went to bed. Sometimes she wondered if she had a split personality, but she felt more torn than split. She wanted to be everything that was expected of her. A good daughter, an excellent student... oh, she wanted to amount to someone her parents and brothers could be proud of. But she also wanted something else. Something that she couldn't define, yet yearned for desperately. Something that was always hovering in the background of her consciousness but was too obscure for her to grasp.

Rosemary also wanted a career. Maybe she would go into law school. Politics. Or medicine. Be a writer, a scientist, or an airline stewardess. A Pilot! All through her last two years of high school she'd listened solemnly when her counselor at school and her parents at home offered suggestions about what she might do with her life. She listened and said she'd think it over, and yes, she knew she was capable of being anything she wanted to be. No use in pretending she didn't know she was intelligent. From the time she entered the first grade she'd never made anything less than an A in any of her grades. Smiling in the dark as she watched the play of light and shadows on the wall opposite her bed, she remembered the surprised expression on the faces of several teachers who had said, "But you're so beautiful!" As if beauty and brains didn't mix.

She didn't think she was beautiful, but she accepted the face that looked back at her from the mirror as attractive enough. Being tall had never caused her a moment's grief. She played a fine game of basketball. Plenty of boys were as tall as she. Models and motion picture stars and airline stewardesses were more in demand if they had a little height. Through her mind whisked a picture of herself in a white doctor's smock, her long, straight dark hair that caused her mother so much grief because she wouldn't roll it, cut it, or curl it, hanging down her back. She giggled, mentally put her hair in a chignon and found the picture more acceptable, but still not to her liking. No, she would not be a doctor.

"Why not, Rosemary?" Her father was positive she would make a fine doctor. Her mother wasn't so sure. There weren't many women doctors. Maybe she should consider going into nursing...

"Veterinary medicine, that's what you want to get into, Rosie." That was Leland, the brother who'd studied dentistry, and believed in McCarthy, God, Presbyterianism, and the fulfilling of the American Dream. Which made it strange for him to espouse the right of men to go into any career they chose no matter what people thought. Lying there in her bed, Rosemary wondered if her successful dentist brother was also tinged with a little schizophrenia.

Marvin was sure she should go to Hollywood. As far as he was concerned all she had to do was walk down the street and she'd be an instant movie star. Both of those brothers entered her name in every beauty contest they heard of and couldn't wait until she was old enough to be a candidate for Miss America.

Then there was Kenny, who had come home from

the war a different kind of person that he'd been when he went away. Rosemary wondered if he'd become dependent on narcotics during the eighteen months he was in the hospital recovering from his wounds. Her mother was alternately ashamed of him and proud of him. Finally, Kenny became a policeman, and not a very good one, either, but he put in his time, appeared to have no ambition to better himself, and spent a lot of time with a married woman, a fact that Rosemary was carefully shielded from, even though she'd known it long before her parents.

Richard married a girl whose family owned a successful chain of restaurants. That brother was a dynamo when it came to management; he was a walking computer long before computers became a part of the vocabulary. Ambitious, possessed with enormous drive, yet humorous and kind, Richard was Rosemary's favorite brother and wanted her to become an accountant, which irritated her to even think about. The home office of the restaurant chain was in Reno, Nevada. Richard's mother and father-in-law bowed out of the business after he married their daughter, Joy. They were confident that he could make things run better than they could, even though they'd been tremendously affluent for years and years. Richard had made things hum, all right. He'd already added twelve new restaurants to the chain and had been written up as the boy-wonder of the financial world in several magazines. Richard didn't want her to go to Berkeley, where boys wore their hair long, didn't wash, had lice in their beards, and smoked weed. Radicals, Richard called them. Sometimes Rosemary wondered why Richard was her favorite brother.

Despite the advice she'd received, Rosemary

decided to take an aptitude test designed to help students choose a career. She knew all about it long before she took it in her junior year, then again in her senior year. But the test was no help. Miss Grant looked at her and smiled and said, "Rosemary, you've scored higher than anyone else in the history of the school on *everything*. You can do anything you set your mind on, and do it well. Creative writing is the only career-choice that you scored a little higher on—but it's just a point above the rest. How do you feel about writing, Rosemary?"

"I don't think I have enough discipline to be really successful, Miss Grant."

"Oh, now! You've plenty of discipline. I've seen you apply yourself. You're a marvel."

Maybe, she thought with a little grin, she'd just marry Eric, settle down and be a housewife... No, not that! What a drag. She was crazy about him, but she wasn't even sure she wanted to marry him, not right then, maybe never.

She slept and dreamed of performing on a stage while thousands cheered. But then she awakened with a dull headache and felt a little queasy. She lay in bed quietly. What she'd do, she decided, was go up to Canada for a while. She knew nobody in Canada. She'd take long walks and not talk to a soul. Then maybe she'd feel better about going to Berkeley in the fall and taking the liberal arts course she'd already signed for.

As it turned out, Rosemary spent the entire summer at home, where she did very little but help her mother around the house and quarrel with Eric when she wasn't loving him. Loving him meant guiltily sneaking off to the Moonlight Motel with him and hoping the place didn't catch on fire or get raided. Toward the end of August, she drove to

Berkeley, found a small apartment six blocks from the school, and fell head over heels in love with Johnny Davis.

Johnny played a guitar and sang better than Peter, Paul, and Mary combined. He was a journalism major, wore his blond hair rather long, and sported a beard. He lived across the hall from her. The day she moved in, he brought her over a loaf of bread he'd just taken from the oven, a bottle of Chablis, and a hunk of cheese. "Welcome to Aunt Maud's home away from home," he said as he stood outside her door, an endearing smile on his fair face.

Sniffing the bread, eying the wine, and liking the look in his mild blue eyes very much, she invited him in. They shared the food and wine, sitting on the floor of her tiny living room and laughing about everything and nothing. Johnny was from Columbus, Ohio. After they'd finished the last of everything, he padded barefoot across the hall, came back with his guitar, and sat down on the floor to play and sing a song he made up as he went along. Across the room she looked at their reflections in the mirror she'd brought along but hadn't found a place for. They were both long, rangy and lithe, but there the resemblance ended. He was blond and tanned. Her dark, dark hair contrasted nicely with his, and so did her skin, which neither tanned nor burned, but stayed as pale as a gardenia except for the two bright spots of color that grew darker and redder as he sang to her of love and love-making and young girls and boys who live in the flower garden of life.

"Do you smoke, Rosemary?"

"No thanks."

"I don't mean cigarettes." He took a plastic bag out of his pocket, a package of cigarette papers, and shook a little of the dark green crumbly stuff on the paper. Then he rolled it, licked the edge, twisted the end, and lit it.

"What if somebody smells it and calls the police?"

"Aunt Maud can't smell a thing. She's been into booze so long her smeller got all burned out along with at least half her brains. That's why so many people are on the waiting list." He looked around. "For damned sure, it isn't because the apartments are all that great." With his eyes half closed, he looked at her appraisingly and reached for his guitar again. She didn't smoke with him, but the afternoon was suddenly over. It was dark outside the windows, and inside the only spot of light was the little burning-red tip of his Salem cigarette.

A week later she said, "I can't make love to you."

He gave her a teasing, lazy look. "Can't? What's this 'can't' business? Either you will or you won't."

"I have a committment to someone else. His name is Eric, and he's in his second year at The University of Wyoming."

"Learning how to be a big cattle rancher?"

"No. His major is chemistry."

"Ummm. I see. Hmmmm." He twisted the ends of his mustache. "I suppose this Eric is true-blue and all that? Lays around thinking of his lady here in Berkeley, whanging off instead of . . . oh, what the hell. The poor bastard. Forget I said that. So long, Rosemary."

He breezed out, and for three weeks a succession of tall, slender suntanned California girls came and went from Johnny's apartment. When she met Johnny on the stairs or in the hall he was sweet and friendly. "Getting along all right, Rosemary?"

"Oh, yes. Fine, Johnny. Thanks." She wasn't going to let him know she noticed those gorgeous blonde girls who hung out with him until all hours and sometimes didn't go home for three or four days.

In November he came over to borrow a cup of sugar. She gave it to him, spilled another cup on the floor, and felt her insides quiver when she walked on it. Then she said, "I won't because I've never been with another boy. And it wouldn't be right until I've seen him at Thanksgiving and told him I'm not his girl any more."

"Yeah. Well, okay. Let's go to the flick tonight, okay?"

"Sure. I'd love to."

He kissed her goodnight and said, "I'll be your brother for a while. You're a great woman, Rosemary. Different. After we get to know one another better, we'll talk about other things."

At home, she basked in the warmth of home and parents. Eric didn't come when she'd expected him. When she called his house, his mother said he was having car trouble. When he came, he talked to her parents for a while before they went for a drive. The night was splendid. He drove toward the Moonlight Motel, and she tried to remember at least one of the ways she'd planned to tell him it was over.

Eric drove past the motel, pulled into a side road, and turned off the motor. "You're going to hate me. I'm sorry. God knows I didn't want it to happen, but sometimes—"

For a dizzying moment, Rosemary was jolted. Then she was glad she'd not said it to him first, had she done so, it would have spoiled the insanely funny chance to say it with him. In duet, they finished together. "—sometimes these things happen and we get all involved before we realize what's going on. I've been seeing a lot of this—"

Eric said "girl." Rosemary said, "boy."

Then Eric caught on to what she was doing, and

he looked at her angrily and shouted, "What the hell do you think you're doing, Rosemary?"

She laughed. Not hysterically, but almost doubled over with the humor of the situation. "Oh, Eric," she gasped. "I'm—just so—oh, God! It's too *funny!* There you were, trying to figure out how to tell me you've been seeing another girl, and there I was, trying to figure out how to tell you I've been seeing another guy."

"It's not funny, Rosemary." His face was white, his expression deadly. "Are you sitting there telling me you've been unfaithful? You've *cheated?*"

"No. Not exactly." Her lilting laughter rang out into the clear, dark blue sky of near-dark over Wyoming. "But I bet *you've* cheated."

"That's different. I'm a man."

"Oh, bull!" Rosemary got out of the car and walked home.

XVII

At the end of her first year at the university, Johnny asked Rosemary what she would say if someone asked her what 1961 meant to her. Her answer was prompt:

"Started college and fell in love. What has 1961 meant to you, Johnny?"

"Meeting you and learning how great it is to laugh with someone. It's no fun to look at a glorious sunset unless you have someone to share it with. Oh, well, it's enjoyable, of course. But more than twice as enjoyable when you know someone you care about is seeing it with you. I like that, but I like the way you laugh, the way you *appreciate* a well-turned phrase, a double meaning."

She enjoyed all those things about him, too. More than anything else, she appreciated his depth, which caused him to be concerned about areas too many others didn't think about, didn't know existed.

Much later, he turned to her in the bed and gave her a searching look.

"You love me, but you won't marry me. I don't understand that kind of thinking." He turned over on his back, put his hands behind his head, and looked at the bedroom ceiling.

"We're too young."

"I have one more year of college, then what?"

"I'm going to finish mine. After that, who knows?"

"You're putting me off, Rosemary."

"That's better than putting you down, Johnny. See, I don't want to make any commitments. Not yet. Maybe I won't want to make any for a long time. Maybe never." She frowned as she searched for words to describe how she felt. "I keep searching for something, looking for something important. Not another man, particularly, but a—an idea or a feeling or a—I don't know what it is."

"But you see other men."

"Sure, but I don't go to bed with anyone but you. You see other women, too. And you go to bed with them. I'm not so sure I like that, Johnny."

He smiled, lifting one eyebrow. "Does that mean if I stop seeing other women, you'll stop seeing other men?"

"I'm not sure," she said. "So don't give up anything that makes you happy."

"Jesus. You're elusive as a breeze. Oh, well. Nobody ever has anybody. All we have is ourselves, and that's temporary at best. I'm really great when it comes to philosophizing, but I have a hard time handling all the things I think others ought to accept."

She caressed his arm. "That's because you're human, Johnny."

"I don't want to go home to Columbus for the summer. I don't want you to go back to Cheyenne, either. I don't want to be away from you for three months, Rosemary."

Since she'd already told him she didn't think it was another man she was looking for, she saw no reason to repeat herself although she realized he probably meant he was afraid of losing her. "It's getting late. Hadn't we better get up and dress if we're going to meet Paula and Calvin for dinner?"

"Maybe I'll go to Las Vegas for the summer," he said as he got out of bed and headed for the bathroom. "You ever been there, sweet baby?"

"Huh-uh. Reno, but not Las Vegas. One of my brothers lives in Reno. What would you do in Las Vegas all summer long?"

"Find some work. My dad will be disappointed because he's got the whole summer planned for me. Six weeks in his law firm, the rest of the vacation in Florida. That's his idea of a vacation, mostly because he can get away from Rita when he's down there. She won't set foot across the Ohio River because to my stepmother, Kentucky is the beginning of the Deep South and her ex is down there."

"Why doesn't your dad get a divorce if he wants to be away from his wife?" Rosemary brushed her teeth while Johnny stepped into the shower.

"Because he likes to be married to her so he can bitch about her. He bitched about my mother until they were divorced. Then he wanted her back, but she married someone else. Then she was killed in the accident and Dad went around telling everyone she was going to leave her second husband and come back to him. She wasn't, though. Tell me something. Are your parents happily married?"

"I'm sure they are." She wasn't positive he heard her because of the sound of the shower. But she was sure her mother and father were happy with each other, and that was one reason why she didn't want to be married. If she ever did, she'd want it to work, and she wasn't sure it would work all that well with Johnny. They were too much alike.

Paula Merriweather and Calvin Knight lived together in the downstairs apartment beneath Rosemary's. Paula was married to a career Marine some fifteen years older, had a three-year-old daughter named Sheila, and a sweeping, all consuming drive to be ultra-rich and powerful. After she had her law degree and was established, she would divorce her husband. She spoke crisply of her future in which everything was mapped, timed, and ready to check off. Rosemary had seen the list. In June of 1971 she would divorce her husband. In June of 1972 she would buy a home.

Every night before she went to bed, Paula wrote her Marine husband a two page letter in which she swore undying faithfulness and eternal love. Then she signed the letter with a flourish, addressed the envelope, stamped it, and hopped into bed with Calvin. He was two years younger and in his first year at the university, a sweet, introspective young man with a taste for the exotic, including astrology and anything else that had to do with the unknown. Paula was viperish, arrogant, brilliant, and beautiful. She loved herself and her daughter, who was her image in looks, but was oddly angelic. Paula blamed Sheila's sweet disposition on Calvin's influence, and she obviously detested it. When Rosemary asked her why she continued a relationship with a man she didn't really care for, her answer was typical of her: "Because neither of us have enough money to live in separate apartments. Because he's good with Sheila, in spite of turning her into a sweet child—I *abhor* sweet children—and he takes the laundry to the

235

laundromat and brings it back all folded neatly. And because he's the best I ever had in bed. And don't get the idea that I'm conning him the way I am my husband. Calvin knows the way things are with me. I only lie to my husband."

She would end the affair at the end of the term.

Calvin Knight was an organic food freak, a flower-child, and devoted to anything different or mystical. He'd found the little restaurant on the second floor of an old, run-down building in San Francisco and went into lyrical praise of the cuisine, the atmosphere, and the far-out owner who sometimes sat down with her customers and gave them spiritual readings. They'd all agreed to go the night before Rosemary would drive back to Cheyenne for the summer.

The downstairs rooms of the ramshackle building were being renovated by several different owners. For years the building had been empty, a victim of progress and time, including rocks through the windows, siding that had been bashed in by automobiles, and damage by vandals. "It was a warehouse until about 1940," Calvin said as everyone climbed out of Johnny's Volkswagen. "Before then, it was a private residence. It still has the feel of once having been a house where people lived. Just stand back and look at it for a second, people. Can't you visualize a big family with twelve children running through the rooms? I love all that gingerbread, the long, narrow window, and the feeling of solidarity. Victorian is my bag."

Some of the downstairs rooms were already completed and open for business. Before the two couples went up the wide, sweeping staircase to the Peacock Feather Restaurant, Calvin wanted everyone to go through the downstairs part.

"You'd think it was his very own place," said

Paula. But she was agreeable to taking the tour, so they browsed. There was a candle shop that smelled heavenly. Two pretty girls in cut-offs and T-shirts ran it. They looked hopefully at the browsers, and Rosemary bought a confection of a candle that looked like a Victorian mansion. There was even a widow's walk, and the tiny windows looked like stained-glass. The next room was filled with small antiques, mostly jewelry. Rosemary was enchanted with the collection of mustache cups, but she didn't buy one. Paula purchased a green box with a lid. It was about the size of half a pack of cigarettes, and the young man was haughty as he explained the box was neither an antique nor a piece of jade. He turned in over and showed Paula the mark that showed it was made in Japan. He said, "We have to keep a few items for those who don't appreciate quality merchandise."

"Screw you, too," said Paula. But she paid for her purchase and wasn't at all perturbed.

"He's gay," she said loud enough to be heard a block away.

Embarrassed, Rosemary walked toward the exit. She wanted to tell Paula there was no reason for her to behave so arrogantly, but didn't want to spoil her last night with Johnny by creating a scene. Just then her eyes fell on the little glass case of earrings, one in particular. "I have to have those ruby earrings," she said.

The young man came quickly to turn the revolving case. "Exquisite," he said as she pointed to the ones she wanted. "Rubies are sensational." He looked at her, disappointed. "But your ears aren't pierced. These are for pierced ears." He rotated an identical display case, saying she'd find the ones for unpierced ears there.

"But I want those," she insisted. Then she turned

to Johnny. "You've been asking me to have my ears pierced, so now I'll do it."

Johnny smiled. "I wanted to get you a going-away present. This is great."

"But I wanted to buy them for myself."

"No, I want to get them for you. Rosemary, for God's sake! This is the first time I've ever seen you look at anything with desire in your eyes. You actually coveted those earrings!"

"They were made for someone who must have looked like your lady," said the young man. "They're over a hundred years old, but they're just right for a... woman of quality." He turned to Rosemary. "Let him give them to you, honey. A woman should accept a gift with as much grace as she gives one, and I'm sure you've given this fortunate dude plenty. You look like the loving and giving kind of lady." He looked wistful. "And I'm not gay. What's wrong with that broad, anyway?"

Quickly changing the subject, Rosemary said they were going upstairs to eat. "Is the food good?"

"Excellent. Tanya, who owns it, is the world's best cook. Not that she does all of it now that her place is making a profit, but she sees to it that her chef follows her directions."

Paula and Calvin had already left the shop. Rosemary thanked Johnny for the earrings, lifted her face for his kiss and smiled at the salesperson. "You're a groovy couple," he said approvingly. "Those earrings were hand wrought."

They decided not to go into any more shops because Paula was famished, and when Paula was famished she became more aggressive. As they mounted the steps, Rosemary wondered why she'd agreed to go out with another couple her last night in town, but realized it was because of Calvin. She liked

238

him. Paula, she could do without. Halfway up the steps she felt dizzy and broke out in a cold sweat. "I feel funny," she said as she staggered against the railing.

"You're starved to death," announced Calvin. "For quite some time I've felt that you have low blood sugar, Rosemary. You'll be all right."

She laughed and felt better even though she didn't believe she had low blood sugar. Calvin read everything he could get his hands on about medicine and food and proper diet. He'd tried to get everyone he knew on the low blood sugar diet, to embrace the theory that half the physical ills of the world could be traced to hypoglycemia.

The food was exotic, delicious, and perfectly cooked. Paula was pleasant throughout the meal, and when all the plates were taken away and Tanya came to sit at their table she made no snide remarks about only idiots falling for fortune-telling. Usually she ridiculed Calvin for his preoccupation with the occult.

Tanya was a plump little lady of undetermined age. She affected shawls with bangles, too much dark foundation makeup, and artificial eyelashes. But immediately explained why. "I'm the reincarnated spirit of an Assyrian princess. I have the gift of the true psychic." She took a crystal ball out of the voluminous pocket of her paisley skirt and placed it in the middle of the table. "While you dear young people are finishing your wine, I'll just tell you what I see."

Nodding, she squinted at the crystal ball and was quiet for a while. Then she informed them that all four of them were linked by Karma; that in a former life Calvin was an American Indian, and Paula his dear, tragic love. Smiling, she turned her friendly

239

eyes toward Calvin and said, "That's why she's submissive to you in all things in this life. You see, in your past life when you were a fine Brave and she was a beautiful little Indian maiden, she was the woe of the whole Navajo Nation because she turned away from her own true love and married a white man." Shaking her head and making little tsk-tsk sounds, the round little lady advised Paula not be to overly-submissive in this life, otherwise she would become a doormat. "And nobody likes a wishy-washy woman, you know," she added in her trilling voice.

"Now you," she said to Rosemary, "were the other lady's mother, and your young man was your brother during the time you lived before. Yes, indeed. I can see it all clearly. Oh, my! Oh, my! How broken-hearted you were when your headstrong young daughter left her own true love to marry a white man. But that was just the beginning of your trials and tribulations, poor dear. Her husband killed her. So sad, these past lives. Well, my dears, I hope I've given you some understanding into your inner selves." She stood, asked them to come back often, and moved on to another table.

Even Calvin was disappointed. "It's a good thing she doesn't charge anyone for her readings," he remarked. "Jesus! Can you imagine Paula being overly submissive?"

Rosemary wanted to leave. The wine was finished, she wasn't interested in coffee, she wanted only to get out of there. The cold sweat that drenched her when she was coming up the steps was back again and she was sick. Not physically, but emotionally; and even though she realized her state of morbid depression had nothing to do with the phony "reading", she connected her unusual state of

240

mind with the restaurant. "I don't feel very well. It's hot in here," she said. "Would anyone mind if we leave?"

Calvin stood up immediately, saying she would be all right, that she was just having a sugar rush because of the wine and the rich food. Johnny had to help her to her feet, and she felt ridiculous because she had to lean on him. She was as weak as a kitten and overcome with a feeling of fear.

It seemed to her that it took an endless amount of time for the men to pay the check, to navigate the stairs, and to wobble crazily through the downstairs part of the building to the outside, where she felt immediately better. "Something got to me in there," she said apologetically. "I think it's an allergy, although I've never been allergic to anything before that I know of."

"You're a prude at heart, Rosemary," said Paula. "You picked up the vibes of what the place was before."

Rosemary waited until Paula and Calvin had squeezed themselves into the back seat of the Volks, then Johnny saw to it that she was inside before he closed the door.

"It was a whorehouse once," said Paula. Her voice was strident. "If there's anything to the business of picking up bad vibes, that's what happened. Your good Christian upbringing would be offended in a whorehouse. Calvin, what did you say the name of it was when it was a house of ill repute?"

"Come off of it, Paula," said Calvin. "You don't believe in the occult in the first place. Rosemary doesn't feel well and you've no business needling her."

"What *was* the name of it when it was a house of prostitution, Calvin? I want to know and I'm okay now anyway," Rosemary said. And she did want to know.

"Sweet Bird of Paradise, or something like that."
Sweet Bird of China, maybe," he answered. "But I'm not sure if it ever was one. Tanya is a smart lady. It would be good business for her to make up a story like that.

"Sweet Bird of China," Rosemary whispered. She wondered why it sounded right, even though it sickened her.

It was good to be home. Strangely, she'd not noticed how her home town had shrunk until she had a chance to relax and drive around the streets. Her old high school had once looked enormous. The same change had taken place in the business section and the shopping malls. Books she'd read had mentioned the odd way time and living somewhere else tended to change one's perspective, but reading about it wasn't the same as experiencing it.

Sarah wanted to go to Boston. Frank was retired, and she saw no reason why they couldn't take a month and visit her birthplace, perhaps get a chance to see the house where she was born, and look up relatives from her father's side that she didn't know. She wanted to find her father's grave.

"How can you have any feelings for a man who has been dead for years and years, a man you don't remember anyway, Mother?"

"I could listen to the sounds of my heart," Sarah said defensively. "I don't know, I just want to look at the place where I came from, that's all. Why do you and your father find it so strange?"

"You adored your stepfather," Frank Poindexter reminded his wife. But he added that he wouldn't mind taking a trip if that was what she wanted.

Sarah said, "Sometimes I feel utterly rootless. Except for Aunt Nancy and her children, it's as if the Stevens side of my family didn't exist. And now since Aunt Nancy has passed away, we never see any of her children."

Rosemary wondered why her mother appeared restless. Since she'd come home she expended a lot of energy on nothing. She moved a vase from one table to another, opened and closed the draperies for no reason, and walked aimlessly about the house at odd hours. "I wouldn't mind going to Boston," she said.

"What about your young man, dear?" Sarah gave her a strange look. "You know, your daddy and I were looking forward to meeting him. We'd thought maybe you might bring him home with you, that you might be thinking of getting married."

"Johnny has gone to Las Vegas. I'm not going to get married for a while, though."

Her mother wanted to know what her young man was doing in Las Vegas. "Does he gamble?"

"No, at least I don't think so. He didn't say anything about it if he does. People go to Las Vegas for a number of reasons. To see the big name performers, to watch the people. Richard lives in Reno and you never worry about *him* gambling."

Sarah said she didn't mean anything special when she asked if Johnny gambled; it was a harmless question, just small talk. "But I should think a young man would want to spend all the time he can with his family, that's what I was thinking, dear. My, but you're picky. Jump down my throat at the slightest thing!"

"Oh, Mother!" Johnny doesn't get along well with his father. His parents were divorced, and his mother brought him up. Then she died and Johnny spent the last two years of high school with his dad and stepmother. He gets along fine with his stepmother, but his father and he don't see eye to eye. So he went to Las Vegas. He's going to be a lawyer, but he'd rather buy a big casino." She laughed. "Unfortunately, he can't afford to buy a casino and besides that, he knows he'll be a fine lawyer."

"Well, I would rather see you married to a lawyer than to a man who runs a casino. They say those gamblers are mixed up with the underworld."

It then occurred to Rosemary that one of the things that was upsetting her mother was her unmarried state. She had an idea Sarah suspected she slept with Johnny. She sensed that her mother worried about her getting pregnant, and wished she could set those fears to rest by stating that she was taking a birth control pill. Shortly after she entered college, she had a chance to become part of a control group, but the doctor assured her that even though the pills were still in the experimental stage they'd do her no harm and would insure freedom from fear. A couple of girls in her classes could tell their mothers about their love life, but she knew better than to mention anything along those lines to Sarah.

They left Cheyenne the fifth day of June and drove leisurely to Boston. Rosemary enjoyed every minute of the trip. Sarah had decided against visiting any of the Stevens relatives, but they drove past the mansion where she was born, then drove around the block and stopped in front of it, just to look at it in amazement.

"I knew the Stevenses were rich," Sarah said, "but I didn't know they were *that* rich."

Frank reminded her of the windfall of several thousand dollars that had come their way through the Stevens connection. Rosemary was going to

244

college on a part of that inheritance. Her brothers used theirs to buy homes or go into business. She didn't care for the Boston mansion, but liked the smaller two-story brick home in Middletown, Ohio that was once owned by her grandmother, Teresa d'Angelo Stevens Gerard. While they were sitting in their car outside on the street in front of the house, a young woman came out and smiled, then asked if they were looking for someone.

Rosemary was sitting in the driver's seat. She explained why they were there under the big maple tree at the side of the street. The girl said her grandparents had bought the house from Teresa Stevens and offered to let them come inside to look around.

Sarah said, "Oh, no, we wouldn't want to impose—" but anyone who was sensitive to expressions of voice and features could see she wanted to go in that house very much.

The young woman insisted and the Poindexters got out of their car and went inside. Laura McAlpin was interested in history, antiques, and her own family tree. She was alone that afternoon because her parents had gone to Cincinnati. "I love this house," she confided to Rosemary. "Mom and dad had six children, but I'm the only one still at home. And I'm getting married next week, so they're going to move into a small one-floor house. It's too big for two people, but I hate to see it go. It's expensive to keep up, though."

"It's so friendly," said Rosemary as she walked through the spacious rooms. "And so beautiful."

When they were back on the wide, shady front porch, Miss McAlpin said, "When I was a little girl, I found a picture in my room. The furnace broke down and the old radiators had to come out. Stuck

245

down between them was a picture. I wonder if it could be your grandmother." She said she'd only be a second, and Sarah spoke tenderly of her mother, wondering what it had been like growing up in Middletown, Ohio at the turn of the century. The girl came back and gave Sarah the miniature. "You can keep it."

"Oh, yes. I have one just like it," said Sarah. "It's in my album. You've seen it a hundred times, Rosemary. This was mother when she was about thirty, before she was married."

Rosemary remembered having seen the picture, but it had been a long time ago. She looked at it and recognized the pronounced resemblance she had to her grandmother for the first time. The girl noticed it, too. "You look almost exactly like her."

"People have been telling me I do for as long as I can remember," answered Rosemary. "But I never could see it until just now." She was pleased. The slight apprehension she'd had when her mother first mentioned the vacation was no longer with her. The feeling of having been there before, the feeling she'd known at the restaurant, had brought her down. She'd hated the place. Feared and loathed it enough to make herself sick. But there had been no weird dream-world in Boston or Middletown. Now she was ready to accept Johnny's explanation for her reaction to the Peacock Feather. He'd believed that the restaurant, the atmosphere, or the woman had reminded her of a bad experience she'd had when she was too young to remember. Either that, or she had had a bad dream of a setting that resembled the restaurant. Calvin swore she'd had an upsetting experience in that very same upstairs room when she'd lived before. Neither Johnny nor Rosemary believed in reincarnation, but they were not unkind, and Rosemary said she had an open mind. Sarah was light-hearted and no longer inclined to be nervous after they left Middletown. Knowing her mother as she did, Rosemary realized why she was back to normal. All that time she'd tried very hard not to worry her parents by being any different from the way she'd always been. But she'd not been able to shake the remembered fear, the terror that came over her in the restaurant. She'd been afraid there was something to the silly, faddish notion of reincarnation. Now she knew better, because the *déjà vu* hadn't come back to her during the trip. Although she'd not been interested enough in reincarnation to read anything about it, Calvin had assured her that nine times out of ten, the spirit died, then returned within the blood lines. She'd been in her grandmother's house and felt nothing. The house had originally belonged to Vivian, her *great* grandmother. In Boston, she'd been close enough to have felt *something*.

She sang as she drove away from the brick house on Main Street; the gloom of fear was gone. Rosemary laughed as they got out of the car at a Frisch's Big Boy. "Mother, you were afraid I was pregnant," she said in a low voice.

"How did you know that was what I was worried about, Rosemary?"

"I just knew. But I'm not, so you can stop worrying."

"You came home all withdrawn and quiet. That's why I—"

Frank, walking behind them, said jovially, "You girls include me in your conversation, or don't talk in those tones in front of me. I bet you're telling blue stories."

"We were just talking about a little surprise we

247

had in mind for you, honey," said Sarah. The next day was Frank's birthday, but mother and daughter already had his surprise planned, so everything was all right and Frank never knew what the quiet words and subsequent giggles were all about.

XVIII

When she went back to Berkeley, there was a distinct difference in the way Rosemary felt compared with the way she'd felt the year before. She now knew she could survive on her own, but there was more to her self-assurance than accepting the fact that she'd successfully cut the ties. A year ago she'd not had sense enough to know she was scared to death about leaving home and making all those adjustments. In 1962 she knew herself much better than she had before. She felt much older, too.

Johnny moved into his apartment the day after her arrival. She'd not written to him. He'd sent her a card from Las Vegas. They didn't talk about their lack of communication; they sat on the floor of her apartment surrounded by books, records, suitcases, clothes bags, and two brown paper sacks filled with groceries she'd just purchased. She put the perishables away and after three hours they told one another all about their respective summers. Then they stashed all the things she'd brought from home out of sight and went out to eat. When they came back to the apartment house, she helped him square away his scattered belongings, and they went to bed at her apartment because he'd forgotten to bring his sheets.

Rosemary occasionally went out with other men. Johnny saw other women. He fell into his old pattern of bedding one of the girls he saw now and then, but she slept with no one but Johnny. There was no particular reason for it, but she was comfortable with the way things were. She did not tell Johnny she was faithful to him and suspected he believed she slept around some. Why she didn't tell him she hadn't was one of those things she would think about someday in the future, when she had more time.

The term ended and Rosemary spent a month in Omaha. Then she went to Reno to visit her brother Richard and his family for three days. While there, she flew to Seattle to attend a wedding, leaving the car there to pick up after she'd returned.

On the return flight from Seattle to Reno, she talked to a woman who was in medical research. "It's a coincidence that we'd have seats together," Rosemary said. "I've spent two years as a Liberal Arts major, trying to make up my mind what I want to do with my life. In Seattle I talked to my friend's father about forensic medicine. It would be interesting, but I'm not sure I could deal with all those dead people. He encouraged me to give it a try, and I was tempted, but then I settled on medical research. Now I've met you."

She was Evelyn Caldiron, a woman in her fifties. She was happily married, the mother of a grown son, a doctor. She'd had no difficulty fitting a career into her marriage. At the moment she was going to visit her son, who had recently opened his medical practice in Reno. Then she would fly on to Mexico where she would combine a three months' vacation with a trek through desert, mountains, and jungles to gather herbs, plants, and flowers that had long been used by Mexican Indians for medicinal purposes. They left the plane together, laughing and talking. Rosemary was exuberant. At last she'd settled on something definite for her future.

Richard's wife, Joy, was waving and smiling. A number of people were waiting for the flight from Seattle, but Doctor Caldiron said she didn't see her son and asked Rosemary if she could pick out a tall dark-haired young man with a full beard. "I put my glasses in one of my suitcases," she explained.

"There are three young men who are tall, and have dark hair and beards," answered Rosemary. "And they're all waiting for someone to get off the plane. One has on gold-rimmed glasses and he's taller than the other two by several inches. He's wearing a suit and tie. One has on jeans and a T-shirt. The third one is meeting the woman with the three children who sat in front of us. A young doctor wouldn't wear jeans, so it must be the first one."

"Oh, Greg does. Today he doesn't go into the office. Will you point me in the right direction?"

"He's standing less than three feet from my brother's wife," Rosemary said. "So I'll take you to his side."

"Good. Greg is interested in psychiatry. He's thinking about devoting five years to the practice of medicine, then going back to school and studying psychiatry. I have a habit of leaving my glasses around. Now and then I lose a pair and Greg thinks it's because I'm vain, but since I only wear them when I want to see something at a distance, I just plain, old-fashioned, forget."

Joy and Rosemary embraced, and over her sister-in-law's shoulder, Rosemary watched the handsome young doctor put his arms around his mother and kiss her cheek. She heard him speaking fondly to her as they moved on down the corridor to claim Doctor Caldiron's luggage. Rosemary wondered why his voice sounded familiar. She'd never seen him before but felt as if she knew him and wished she did. When she picked up her bag, she looked up and met his eyes. He stood across from her and looked directly at her for a long, searching moment. He smiled. She smiled, feeling shaky and giddy and morbidly forlorn as Joy picked up her other bag and they began to walk toward the street.

"What in the devil is wrong with you, Rosemary?" Joy's hazel eyes were wide. "Were you airsick, or did something happen to the plane?"

"No, I—" She was standing on the pavement while Joy waited for her to put her weekender bag in the back of the station wagon. Her back was turned to the car because she was scanning the people who came spilling out of the airport, anxious to get another glimpse of young Doctor Greg Caldiron. "Greg," she said as she turned and looked at Joy. "I suppose his full name is Gregory."

"Who?"

"He's—Joy, do you believe in love at first sight?"

"I believe in it, but I wouldn't trust it," said her practical sister-in-law. "You're acting crazy as a tick. Richard will accuse you of smoking pot." Rosemary got in the car and closed the door while Joy settled herself behind the wheel, backed up, then drove toward the gate. After she'd paid the parking ticket, she asked if Greg was the name of a new man in Rosemary's life.

"No. Not exactly. I mean, no. Just plain old no." Even to her own ears, Rosemary's voice sounded hollow, her words confused. "He's a man I would very much like to have in my life, though."

"Did you meet him at the wedding?"

"I didn't meet him at all. But I wish I had. Strange. I've made up my mind what I'm going to do with my life. Now I've seen the one man I would like to be with . . . I think."

"But I thought you and Johnny Davis were serious about one another," said Joy.

"That's why I tacked on the 'I think.' Joy, maybe something's wrong with my head. I wouldn't want to lose Johnny. But on the other hand, if I had a chance to get to know that dude I caught a glimpse of in the airport, I think I would probably fall at his feet in a heap of adoration."

"My Lord, Rosemary! I'd better get you home and get a cup of coffee into you before Richard comes home. Did you have a few drinks on the plane?"

"Not a one, but I could use a few right now. Joy, let's go back to the airport. No, forget I said that. I know his name. His mother sat next to me on the plane and she's happily married, so they're bound to have the same last name. All I have to do is look him up in the telephone book and call him."

Joy gave her an incredulous look. "You wouldn't do anything like that, surely! Your mother would croak."

"Oh, but I would, Joy. I'm not going to ask him for a date, so get that look off your face. I have to know whether he's married. If he is, I'll probably kill myself. But if he isn't, well—I'll transfer to the

University of Nevada and hope for the best."

Before Joy brought the car to a complete stop, Rosemary opened the door, jumped out and ran toward the house. Richard and Joy's fourteen-year-old son opened the door for her and did a double-take as she raced for the telephone stand in the front hallway. "Go get my bags, Rick," she yelled as she turned to the yellow section. "Please! Your mother thinks I've lost my mind, and she'll carry in both bags. You know how she is—"

Rick grinned and slammed out the front door while Rosemary ran her finger down the list of Physicians in the yellow pages. "Duckworth," she muttered. "Rats." Then she went back to the beginning of the listing, through the A's, B's, and C's. "No Caldiron."

Rick came in. She gave him fifty cents out of the pocket of her slacks suit when he put on a begging act and said. "Oh, I know. He's just started. So naturally, he wouldn't be in there yet."

"Thanks," Rick said as he stood up. "*Who* wouldn't be in there yet?"

"Doctor Caldiron."

"Oh, sure he is." Rick took the telephone book, clutched the spine and shook it. "I pressed him between the pages. He'll fall out in a second if I shake it hard enough." He put the directory back on the stand and said, "Mother isn't the only one who thinks you've lost your mind, you know. You just gave me fifty cents for carrying in your bags. Not that I can't use the money, but last week I carried in four bags, and you only gave me a quarter."

Rosemary dialed information and asked for the new listing of Doctor Greg Caldiron.

Thirty seconds later, the operator informed her that she had no listing, new or old, for Doctor Greg

254

Caldiron. "Could the number be listed in another way?"

"G? Doctor G. Caldiron, maybe?"

Sounding weary or out of sorts, the operator said, "I don't know, ma'am, but I'll look under that listing."

When the metallic voice came back to report that she had no Caldiron listed, not G., Greg, or anything else, Rosemary said, "But he has to have a telephone. He's a doctor!"

Sounding even more out of sorts, the operator informed her she was very sorry, but if ma'am didn't have more information she could not be of assistance.

Richard came home at exactly six-thirty, and neither Joy nor Rick wasted any time telling him about Rosemary's insanity. He looked at her with a disapproving frown. "You're having a drink, a real drink with booze in it, and you're only ninetten years old." He lit a cigarette, leaned back with his own drink, and shook his head. "First thing you know, you'll be smoking cigarettes. And joints. And then it'll be the hard stuff. But before you turn into a junkie, how would you like to go see Jimmy Durante? He's playing at the Nugget in Sparks."

"I would love to," said Rosemary. She had always admired Jimmy Durante. But more important, she might accidentally run into Doctor Caldiron, unless she'd invented Doctor Caldiron, the interesting conversation she'd had on the plane, the fantastic airport scene, *and* the handsome, fascinating man who'd been there.

The enormous show room of John Ascuaga's Nugget was packed with dinner-theater patrons. The food was excellent and the show was terrific. During the time she was there, Rosemary tried to forget about the elusive, perhaps imaginary man she'd seen at the airport. She searched the hundreds of faces that sat entranced at the antics of Durante and the other entertainers. The only time she looked into the vast sea of clapping, shouting people was during the applause. The price for the dinner-theater tickets would have paid a month's rent on her Berkeley apartment. Not that a hundred dollars would put a dent in Richard's bank account, but it wasn't every day she had a chance to see big name entertainers. When she asked the other couple Richard and Joy had invited if they knew of a Doctor Greg Caldiron, she understood Richard's long-suffering glance. After the performance, when they were slowly making their way toward the exits, she saw a woman who looked very much like Doctor Evelyn Caldiron and stared at the back of her head. It wasn't until they were outside that she saw the woman's profile. It was definitely not the woman who had flown down with her from Seattle.

Before she went to bed, she sneaked the telephone book into the kitchen and looked at the white pages under the "C" listings. No Caldirons. The next morning, she awakened with the idea of inventing a physical ailment and making the rounds of every doctor in town. Richard had left for work, and Joy didn't fall for her sudden sore throat.

"You've always been so level-headed, Rosemary," said her sister-in-law. "What if this man is a pansy? Or what if he's married? Maybe he has a high-pitched, squeaky voice. People in real life don't see someone once and fall madly in love. That only happens in books."

"You're right. I guess I'll get ready and go on home," Rosemary said. She called her mother and said she was going to leave Reno in the morning, but that she'd call again and let her know if she could make it to drive straight through. After she hung up, it occurred to her that the woman she'd met on the plane might have been married more than once. Her son could have a different last name. She hadn't said so, but it was possible. Another look in the telephone book gave her hope. Several doctors were listed under their initials and last names. The initials of three of them were "G." When Joy went to the beauty shop and Rick went swimming, she called all three of them. Doctor G. T. Newman specialized in Eyes, Ears, Nose, and Throat. Doctor G. G. Harris was a neurologist. Doctor G. T. Lamb was a G.P., but she could check Lamb off the list of possibilities. The receptionist said, "Doctor Lamb is out of town. She isn't expected back in the office until next Thursday. Would you like to make an appointment for Friday at 2:15? That's the only opening on her appointment book."

"Thank you very much," Rosemary answered. "I'll call later."

No such happy fluke occurred when she talked with the receptionists of Doctors Harris and Newman. The office nurse gave no information about sex. She couldn't get an appointment with the neurologist until the following month, and not only that, she had to be referred by Miss Poindexter's family physician.

"But I'm not a resident of Reno," wailed Rosemary. "And I simply must see a neurologist right away. You see, I've been having fainting spells every time I get on a plane. I'm afraid to drive back to Wyoming, and my sister is at the point of death."

"I can squeeze you in tomorrow," said the receptionist.

Rosemary made the appointment, hung up, and

made another appointment with Doctor Newman for the following Tuesday. A week later, she called her mother from the motel where she was staying, afraid to go out because of the possibility of meeting her brother or his family, and swore that this time, for sure, she was coming home. "I know I said I was coming home last week, but I ran into this friend from college, Mother, and she's all upset because she's getting a divorce. So I felt like I had to stay here and sort of—console her."

Sarah said, "I called Richard and he said you left a *week* ago."

"I know, Mother, but see, this girl is In really bad shape and I didn't want to bring her problems to Richard's house, so I just sort of—"

"Richard said you were behaving strangely."

"Oh, Mother! Richard thinks everyone behaves strangely." She hung up, paid her bill, put her luggage in the trunk, and drove away from the motel. The neurologist set her back fifty dollars to find out her fictitious fainting spells were brought on by smoking, although she didn't smoke and never had. Or, said the grey-haired doctor, there were other serious possibilities, and he would learn more about them after he'd put her in the hospital for a series of tests.

Doctor G. T. Newman was portly and middle-aged. He found nothing wrong with her throat and charged her ten dollars for the examination. The motel bill and eating in restaurants for a week had almost depleted her finances, unless she called her mother and asked her to wire money. She didn't want to do that because she'd be forced to tell more lies, which she didn't like to do in the first place. "There's no doubt about it," she screamed as she drove under the arch that told her she was now leaving Reno, "I'm crazy!"

Every time she stopped to get gas or eat or go to the restroom, she told herself she was out of her mind, but she knew she really wasn't. Finally she figured out a reason why she'd believed she was in love with a man she had seen but once.

When she was a little girl, she'd gone to an auction with her mother and father. A scrap book, along with several other items of interest to a nine-year-old girl, had gone on the block. Rosemary wanted the scrap book because she liked the picture of Judy Garland on the cover. Her father told her to bid a quarter on it. Boldly she'd raised her hand and shrieked, "Twenty-five cents!" Suddenly she owned the scrap book.

Inside the scrap book were pictures of movie stars of the thirties, forties, and fifties. Some were cut out of movie magazines, others were eight-by-ten glossies. Rosemary remembered how she'd developed a crush on the picture of a dark-haired, dark-eyed star whose name she couldn't recall. For months she'd slept with his picture under her pillow, and sometimes she kissed it. Once she'd even drawn a bright red lipsticked mouth on her little-girl lips, and put a great big red kiss on the actor's pictured ones. But she'd forgotten to take off the lipstick she'd borrowed from her mother's dresser, so Sarah threw a fit when she found bright red stains on Rosemary's pillow case. Then her mother found the picture and did not take too kindly to the lipsticked outline of her nine-year-old daughter's mouth on that, either. A faintly reddish smear on the carpet at the side of her bed where she'd stepped on the picture and ground the lipstick into the pale beige carpeting remained for years.

By the time she arrived on the outskirts of Cheyenne, Rosemary Poindexter was all back together again.

XIX

There was never enough time for Rosemary to get everything finished. She kept her grades high, took part in the demonstrations against the rising threat of war in Viet Nam, and committed herself to writing a weekly column for an underground newspaper, a pursuit that she didn't mention in her infrequent letters to Wyoming.

After the end of the term in 1963, she gave in to her mother's pleas and brought Johnny Davis home. He spent three days in the house and captivated her parents. He also slept alone in the bedroom where Richard had slept when he was a young man. It wasn't what he preferred, but Rosemary couldn't bring herself to cross the hall to sleep with him in her parents' home. Even though the situation wasn't completely to his liking, he took in stride the way things were, revealing a part of his personality that she'd always admired and sometimes envied. He said things that put her mother and father at ease, but not by design. He liked them both and said so openly and honestly. Instead of helping the situation at home, though, Johnny's visit created an even greater strain on Rosemary's and Sarah's relationship.

"He's just exactly the kind of boy I would pick for you if the choice were mine," Sarah stated after he left.

Frank reminded his wife that the choice was not hers, it was Rosemary's, but his own thoughts on the subject were painfully clear. He, too, could see no reason why Rosemary shouldn't jump at the chance to marry a fine, upstanding young man like Johnny Davis. Johnny was going to amount to something. A lawyer. Rosemary could do a lot worse. Sarah said it flatly while Frank looked baffled and said very little.

"He has a beard," Rosemary said half-teasingly to her mother.

"So did Abraham Lincoln and Jesus Christ," answered Sarah.

"I said those very same words to you a year ago, Mother, and you said that that was all right in the past, but not for today."

Sarah threw her hands up. "Well, lands sake! So I'm learning. So what do you think about that? Nobody gets too old to learn a thing or two, Rosemary."

"How about his views on peace and war, then? You know very well how you and Daddy feel about young men who say they won't bear arms for the country."

Sarah had an answer for that one, too. "Oh, he'll get over those notions if we actually get in this war in the Middle East."

Rosemary wanted to tell her mother that Johnny had only mentioned marriage once, at the beginning of their relationship. Her answer was ambiguous, which was probably why he'd never brought the subject up again. She would marry him if she were pregnant, but it was the only reason she could think of that would drive her to commit herself to living with someone forever. In the back of her mind was the memory of the young doctor.

"When you were born, I was thirty-eight years old and it almost killed me," Sarah said one morning when they were breakfasting on fresh strawberries.

"But you said you had an easy time having babies," answered Rosemary.

"With your brothers, but not with you. There were thirteen years between you and Richard. I was too old to have a baby. When you were in grade school, I used to watch your face when I came to school to bring cookies. Then you'd look at those younger mothers and I could tell you wished I looked more like those other women with their youthful figures and their pretty faces."

"Mother, you've always been beautiful. You still are. I never wanted a younger mother, and didn't even realize you were older than the others. When you came to school, I was the proudest little girl in the whole wide world." She pushed aside the bowl of strawberries and cream. "Mother, why in the devil have you felt insecure all your life?"

"Because I was so little and stunted, I suppose. And because I had buck teeth and everyone called me 'Bucky,' and 'Shorty,' and 'Runt.'"

Rosemary went into the downstairs bathroom and grabbed a mirror. "Tell me what kind of face you see in there, Mother," she demanded as she held the mirror in front of Sarah's face.

"I see a woman with greying hair and a worried look."

"Your smile is absolutely radiant. You grew into

262

your teeth and your eyes are big and expressive. Every feature reflects a serene woman of extraordinary looks."

Sarah looked at her hands. "I wanted to be tall and graceful. To look like my mother and have her talents. I've never loved any man except your father. Maybe I loved him because he loved me first; I felt so insignificant that I *needed* someone to love me. Mother tried to make me feel worthwhile and she loved me; but I'll carry a memory from my early childhood with me to my death. My father came into my bedroom once—my real father, not Daddy David. He stood over my bed and looked at me with contempt and said I was the ugliest little brat he'd ever seen. I felt awful lying there with the lamp light shining on my face. He said I was deformed, that he was ashamed of me. Now I'm going to tell you something, Rosemary. I never forgave my father for saying those monstrous things to me, and when I wanted to go to Boston it was because I felt the need to go to his grave and try to forgive him."

"Wasn't your mother around thirty-seven when you were born?"

"Yes. And I was her first, of course."

"Were you ashamed because she was older than the average mother?"

"What a terrible question for you to ask me! Of *course* not! When my mother walked into a room, everything took on a special glow."

"That's the way you made me feel, Mother."

Sarah looked doubtful, but Rosemary was speaking the truth, and her gaze was unwavering as she looked into her mother's eyes.

"There's one thing I want to know," said Sarah Poindexter. "I have a feeling that you don't really want to get married, that you don't really want children. To me, that would be a dreadful waste. A woman isn't complete until she has a child."

"You brought me up, Mother. You gave me the security to be at ease with myself. I feel complete and whole without being a mother or having a husband, and you're the one who did it. Oh, sure, Daddy helped bring me up, but you were with me more than he was. So what I am, you've made. I think I'm . . . all right. Someday I might want to marry and have a baby or two—not any more than two, because the world is already overcrowded. I want my children to be able to breathe fresh air.

"Richard and Joy have that one little boy. The rest of my sons had two children each. Mother had three, but I had nine. Maybe I shouldn't have."

"You didn't know how things were going to be, Mother."

"I wasn't thinking about the ecology or any of the other words that weren't used when I was young. I was thinking about losing three sons. When your young man spoke of the war as being evil, he made a lot of sense. Not that I agree with him one hundred percent, but he did show me a side that I never thought about. Are you really and truly going to go on that Poor People's March, Rosemary?"

"Yes."

"But you're not poor."

"No, but I'm a good public speaker. I can also work in the center where food and clothing will be distributed."

"But why do you feel you must get excited about these things?"

"Because we're a rich country, Mother, and too many people in the United States go to bed hungry every night."

"But burning brassieres and carrying on like that. What does it accomplish?"

"Nobody's going to burn any bras on the Poor People's March, Mother."

Sarah stood up and went to the sink to do the dishes. "You know what I mean, Rosemary. It's so silly. So useless. What's the Poor People's March on Washington going to accomplish? What good does it do for a bunch of radical women to stand on the street and burn up their underwear?"

Rosemary took the lettuce and radishes to the vegetable sink, ran cold water on them, and said she doubted if it accomplished much. "It's symbolic. Some people have to do daring things in order to get the attention of those who are filled with apathy. If a bunch of radical women hadn't carried banners, worn bloomers, and made speeches, women wouldn't be voting in our elections today. If those radical pilgrims hadn't hopped aboard the Mayflower and come to the New World, we wouldn't have a country. They carved it out with their sweat and guts and blood, but if we don't keep on battling to make a better world, we're going to lose it."

"Oh, dear. Well, I guess I never looked at it that way. But there's one thing I'm going to ask you to never, never do, Rosemary. Please don't smoke marijuana. I wouldn't like it if you smoked cigarettes or drank, but that's not nearly as bad as taking dope. Now wait, I know you take a glass of wine now and then, and maybe a highball. But marijuana makes people crazy. They kill at the drop of a hat when they're on that stuff."

"I promise, Mother," said Rosemary. But she didn't add that Johnny Davis had rolled a couple of joints and smoked them on the front porch. It wasn't

265

hard to make the promise to her mother. She'd never wanted to take a chance on messing up her mind, anyway. When her friends told her grass was harmless, she didn't argue, but she said she didn't need it.

She felt good about the morning. For the first time in a long time, she'd talked to her mother in a straightforward manner. And for the first time in a long time, she felt they understood one another. There were a number of things she would have preferred to say—that alcohol was a narcotic, and that people who smoked grass were more gentle than frantic, kill-crazy maniacs—but she'd save them for another time.

On the tenth of August Rosemary and Johnny arrived in Washington, D.C. to work in the warehouse where they distributed clothes, found restaurants to provide food at half price, and helped find sleeping quarters for the influx of marchers who would rally on the 28th for the massive Civil Rights demonstration. August in Washington D.C. was hot and humid. The air-conditioned motel where she and Johnny had a room made her feel guilty because others were sleeping outside under the stars. Some had tents, but there was no running water in Resurrection City, and no bathing facilities, nothing but the portable toilets that the marchers referred to as honey tanks. Johnny told her not to feel guilty. She said she couldn't help it. He said she could stop feeling that way if she wanted to, it wasn't her fault the politicians were so rotten, that they'd been rotten for generations. She was doing all she could to help recitify the wrongs.

"Have you ever been to New Orleans, Johnny?" she asked, lying down.

"Yeah, my dad and I went down once for the Mardi Gras. It was all right."

"I ache when I hear the name," she said dreamily. "New Orleans. It's like feeling homesick, but that's not possible because I was never there."

"Maybe you were in one of your past lives."

She laughed. "You don't believe in that. At least you didn't." She stopped laughing. "But you do now. I can tell because you aren't looking at me, and you aren't saying anything. What happened? Why do you believe in reincarnation, Johnny Davis?"

"Nothing happened." He smiled at her. "Well, maybe a little something. But I'm sweaty and stinking and tired. We'll talk about it some other time. Let's take a bath together and go to bed. We'll save time."

They barely made it back to the coast in time for Rosemary to start school on opening date for classes. Johnny eventually went on to Las Vegas, where he had bought half an interest in a small casino/bar. He told her about the bar. They talked almost continuously as they drove back across the country, with the top down, their hair blowing in the breeze.

Johnny burst into laughter sometimes for no reason at all. "My dad was upset. Said he didn't send me to college to take pre-law so I could go to Las Vegas and be a bartender. Said he didn't like me getting mixed up in these hippie protests; he was sending me to school to get an education. I tried to tell him I wanted to do something else before I put on a shirt and tie and act like a lawyer. But my dad talked to me about virtue and integrity and Playing the Game. So I said, yeah, my stepmother played the game and had plenty of integrity. So did my mother. I didn't tell you my stepmother is getting a divorce. She's in Reno right now. She walked into his office, and he had a girl in there on his white leather sofa. Why would a man forget his wife was coming to have lunch with him and let that happen? My stepmother didn't take too kindly to seeing her husband, my virtuous, truthful father, mind you, making love to another woman. Anyway, that's why I'm laughing. Because he said my stepmother *and* my mother lacked the milk of human kindness."

"Johnny, you're putting me on."

"No, I'm not."

She believed him. Johnny rarely skirted the truth, and even then he did it in order to keep from hurting another's feelings. He said he wished to God he'd been lucky enough to have her parents instead of his own. His mother was great, but she died, and his father was a phony.

"Your mother is remarkable," he said. "I don't know of another person her age who can listen as well as she can to ideas that are new and different. She has such depth, and compared with many people who are much younger, she has the ability not only to accept change, but to even look for it!"

"What are you talking about? Of course I realize my mother is something special, but just what *did* the two of you talk about that afternoon?"

"The threat of war, the bomb, and religion. We talked about the possibility of reincarnation. But you don't want to talk about it. Every time I bring the subject up, you change the subject."

"It's stupid."

"You're afraid of the possibility that there's something to it."

"Maybe. But I don't want to talk about it."

September and October in Berkeley were hectic. She had taken on too many extra-curricular activities, when there wasn't enough time in one day for her to get everything done. November was worse. Sometimes Rosemary felt as if she were a part of a gigantic avalanche heading hell-bent for destruction. The beginning of the third week in November she stepped on the scales and realized she'd lost eight pounds. It was time to call a halt to all those feverish activities and concentrate on her grades and on her health.

On the twenty-second of November she felt rested and refreshed as she began her classes. She'd regained her perspective along with two pounds, so the guilt she'd felt when she dropped out of some of the obligations was worth it.

About ten minutes after one of her classes began, the announcement came over the loudspeaker that President Kennedy had been assassinated.

"Oh, no!" Her reaction was instinctive, and it blended in with all the other exclamations that came to the lips of her fellow sutdents. She listened intently as the voice over the loudspeaker gave the solemn details.

Rosemary left the classroom. She had no memory of doing so, but once she was outside on the campus she realized she wasn't the only one who had to get away from the confining walls of a room, away from others. Some sought companionship. They gathered together on the sidewalk to speak of the tragedy, to weep and to cry out in anger. Others took refuge inside soda shops, restaurants, hamburger joints, or bars. Still others walked around aimlessly, even mindlessly, sometimes in twos and threes, sometimes alone. Rosemary could not bear to speak of the horror to anyone else. Stiffly, she nodded to acquaintances when she met them on the street. After a while she stopped nodding, because she no longer saw anyone she knew. Nor did she hear anything but the thundering, baffling words that were inside her head.

She heard her own voice as she walked along the gloomy streets. "President Lincoln is dead." It was her voice, and she knew she had spoken the words out loud and was frightened. Only crazy people walked along the streets carrying on a conversation with themselves. Anyway, it wasn't President Lincoln who was dead, it was President Kennedy. She passed a furniture store and was reassured at her reflection in the window, which looked perfectly normal. That morning she'd worn a pale beige dress because it was raining and cold. The dress had long sleeves and a pleated skirt that came to just above her knees. Over it, she'd worn her raincoat, but she wasn't wearing the raincoat as she walked numbly along the streets, so she supposed she'd left it at school. But it was all right; the rain had stopped and the sun was out. A damp breeze riffled her long, straight hair and it was chilly, but not cold. There was no doubt in her mind that the reflection she saw in the window was her own because she recognized her tall, slender figure, her long, shapely legs, and her familiar posture. Even so, she could feel no relationship to the reflection except to know it was hers.

Another thing kept inserting itself into her thoughts. The mind-blowing inability to separate the two selves was only a part of it, and she tried desperately to do so. It was better when she could see her image, but she couldn't bring herself to stand forever in front of the furniture store. People would notice there was something wrong with her. *She* knew there was, and halfway realized what was taking place. But she didn't want anyone else to know. So she crossed the street with the light, walked quickly, and looked down at the sidewalk, because there were no store windows to cling to for the comfort of the reflection of her over-the-shoulder bag, and her 1963 clothes and hair style. There was nothing but a service station. When she reached the Good Will store, she looked again at her reflection and confidence grew. If she could continue to walk along where store windows abounded, she would be all right, and there were several blocks of them ahead. It was when she looked down at the sidewalk or away from the store-windows that she lost herself, and knew she was looking backward into the dim recesses of a memory she could not possibly have.

For a long time, she was all right because of the windowed store fronts. But then she was not all right, because the store fronts gave way to used-car lots, fast-food stands, boarded-up buildings, a warehouse, and other buildings that had few or no windows. It was something like looking inward at a little screen inside her brain. Just as she was now walking the streets of a city, she walked then, but it was not the same city. Nor was it the same time of year. It was early spring and the streets were wet, the boardwalks slushy from a recent snow. She wore a long, full-skirted dress that was wet around the hem, over which was a full-length fur cape with a hood. Her boots were wet. They were black leather, with little round pearl-like buttons, and when she walked her dress flipped and swirled enough to reveal a flash of red silk stockings.

The detail was exquisite, but painful to her inner eyes because there was such a glare and because she was afraid, especially when she felt the heartbreak of another time, another era, when she'd mourned the death of a President—the tragic, sudden death of a President—which she suspected had brought her to the brink of mental disaster. Walking and trying to keep the part of herself that remained Rosemary intact, she knew she must hang onto the present with all of her strength. If she didn't, she would be sucked into the past and lost forever.

She felt relieved as she crossed the street at a run in order to walk along the side of a many-windowed building, an elementary school. Standing in front of the windows where school children had pasted up pictures of turkey gobblers and Pilgrims, she stared unabashedly at her reflection, hanging on to the present. Even the recent past was a welcome relief, because it was far safer to think about than the confusing far-away past.

Oh, yes. Those ruby earrings. That hoked-up Tanya who had pretended to look into the past, who said Paula was submissive. Her laugh was tinged with hysteria. They'd gone home and she'd wanted Johnny to pierce her ears right then. Insisted. He didn't want to, but she pleaded. He gave in and went to the drugstore to get some things he would need. Then he came back and sterilized a needle, stuck the eye-end into a potato, and she sat in a kitchen chair while he froze her ear with ice cubes. She remembered how she'd felt no pain. What she did feel was disappointment when he handed her the mirror after he'd pierced her right ear. Instead of a red ruby earring, he'd put in a little gold button. "But that's not what I want," she'd cried.

"You can't put those dangly earrings in your ears right after they've been pierced," he'd told her. Funny she could remember his exact words and the

272

way he'd looked. "You have to wear fourteen karat gold posts. When I went to the drug store I bought these!" It was six weeks before she could take out the gold posts and put in the rubies.

A cab rattled along the street. It had no passenger, but she'd not seen it in time to call out. The streets were quiet. Not at all the usual hustle-bustle of San Francisco. Looking around, she wondered if earlier, long-ago Rosemary had walked the April streets of San Francisco the day Lincoln was killed.

Another cab went by, then another. She hailed the fourth one and directed the driver to the old building that had once been a warehouse but was now a house of boutiques. "Do you know if the restaurant is still there on the second floor?"

"Sure, lady. I guess you heard about the President. God Almighty."

Yes, she'd heard about the President. Both of them. First hand, too. No, not heard. But knew the shattering pain of both assassinations.

"I've changed my mind," she said to the driver when he stopped in front of the building. "I want to go to Berkeley."

"Whatever you say, Miss." He turned around in the middle of the street and she closed her eyes against the churning in her stomach. Sweat drenched her forehad and ran down her face into her eyes. It was a mistake to even think about going back to the Peacock Feather. She'd been afraid to go back again after the other time. It occurred to her that she was afraid of a number of things, but she'd never allowed herself to dwell on any of them.

"If you can't swim," she said to the driver, "it's best to not go in the water."

He looked at her suspiciously. "Are you high on something?"

"No." She was offended.

He said something that sounded like, "Goddam college kids," but she let it pass. After careful consideration, she concluded that she had no business making that stupid statement about swimming.

But it was true. She was afraid to look too deeply into herself. Afraid to go back to the restaurant, although Johnny, among others, had wanted her to. Afraid to go to New Orleans, although she wanted to. When she told Johnny she ached for it, she was truthful, but when she told her father she wanted to go down there and he offered to send her with Sarah, she'd changed her mind. But if she didn't look the truth in the face—if it was the truth—she would never know. She was reacting like someone who feared she had cancer but wouldn't see a doctor.

"I think I want to go back to that restaurant," she said resolutely.

"Sister, I'm not taking you back to any goddam restaurant. You gave me an address in Berkeley, and that's where I'm taking you. Understand?"

"Yes, sir." At least she tried, she thought to herself, feeling relieved that he had refused.

It would be good to talk to Johnny, anyway. She would call him as soon as she got to the apartment. Sitting rigidly, staring straight ahead, she yearned for the long taxi ride to end so she could put the call through to Las Vegas, so she could talk to Johnny, who would bring back her sanity. He'd not think anything of it if she called him because she was upset. The entire nation was mourning the death of the President, so it was only natural for friends or lovers to want to talk to each other on the telephone.

The cab driver accepted her money, gave her change, and she tipped him well. He assumed a fatherly role. "Look, kid, take my advice and stay off of whatever it is you're on. You look like a decent kid—you don't want to screw up your mind with acid or dope or whatever. Go get yourself a good drink of whiskey when you feel low, okay?"

"Thanks," she said.

"Listen, kid, I got a daughter about your age. If I find out she's taking dope, I'll beat her head in. But the wife and I have got no money to send our kids to college. Maybe it's a good thing, hey? Where you from kid?"

"Wyoming."

"Damn. For two cents, I'd made you give me your old man's telephone number. If he was any man at all, he'd come out here and get your young ass back home so fast it'd make your head swim. Your eyes are glassy. You can hardly stand up."

"I'm all right. Let me go, please."

He took his hand away from her arm and stood there on the sidewalk until she was inside the building. She knew, because when she turned back to look and wave, he was still where she'd left him.

Johnny's bartender said he wasn't there.

"Do you think he's at the apartment?" She'd talked to the bartender twice before, and Johnny had told her he would almost always know how to get in touch with him.

"I dunno, honey. He left about an hour ago and said he'd be back at three. It's almost three."

She tried the number at his apartment and let it ring seventeen times, but at least the picture inside her head was gone. She wondered if she would have to stay inside her apartment for the rest of her life if that thing, whatever it was, was going to get to her when she went out. She had a terrible feeling that it would. She'd been out when it happened, so in her frame of mind it seemed reasonable to believe that outside was where the danger was. But that was ridiculous, she decided after a while. When the letter came from Joy she'd not been outside on the street any more than she'd been outside when she first experienced the same pull backwards into the past. No, she'd been inside the Peacock Feather Restaurant for the first time. Going up the steps when the invisible curtains came down on her and she was enveloped in a memory of something she couldn't remember because it hadn't happened to her. Then the fearful thing returned after they'd had dinner, and Tanya the fortune-telller regaled them with all that nonsense.

The letter came from Joy after she'd behaved so ridiculously over a young man named Greg. She'd been at home in Cheyenne when it came. Joy said she'd learned from a friend that a Doctor Keith G. Bennett had recently opened an office in the Medical Building. He would not be listed in the telephone directory until the new one was out. Joy was merely passing along the information that the new doctor was tall, dark, and handsome.

Cassie's husband is also in general practice (Joy wrote). *I've met Doctor Bennett. Richard went to San Diego and couldn't play last Saturday, so Cassie's husband brought along Doctor Bennett so we had a foursome. His middle name is Gregory, his mother is Doctor Evelyn Caldiron, who lives in Seattle, and is now in Mexico. So you can put your mind at ease. You didn't dream up the whole scene, Rosemary. He explained the whole thing to me. The telephone company has him listed as Doctor Keith Bennett, but it's their mistake and when the new book comes out they'll correct the error. He prefers his middle name.*

Now get this! When we were talking, I happened to mention that my husband's sister had come down from Seattle, on the same plane with his mother. He gave me a really freaky.look and told me he'd tried to find you for weeks and weeks, that he couldn't get over the feeling that he'd seen you someplace before. Incidentally, he grew very animated when he spoke about you, describing the whole scene at the airport that day, including beautiful, beautiful you! So I promised to get the two of you together when you come back to visit. Richard will have a fit, so we'll not say anything about our little scheme to him. When are you coming to see us again?

When she wrote back to Joy, she thanked her for the information, but said she doubted if she would be there for quite some time. She'd wanted to say she would never set foot in Reno again, but she couldn't make such a statement without a reason, which had something to do with the feeling that came over her when she read the letter from Joy. The name, Keith Gregory Bennett, meant nothing to her. She should have been grateful for Joy's letter, which proved she'd not undergone a flight of fancy concerning Doctor Evelyn Caldiron and her son. And she was. But at the same time, she felt afraid for a little while after she had read Joy's letter. She knew deep sadness and profound grief and she kept telling herself that she couldn't allow herself to love him again, then lose him. For several minutes, she could do nothing but sit in the chair in her room and weep copiously for the love she had lost—but could *not* have lost.

Eventually, she'd told Johnny about it. Not

entirely, but she'd touched on the incident and implied that it was a puzzling incident that had happened to a friend. He was very quiet after she told him. Then he said, "I know this girl who thought she was pregnant. And she went to a doctor and told him she had a friend who thought she was pregnant. And I know this dude who was afraid he had the clap, but he told me he had a friend who was afraid he had the clap and asked me if I could tell him where he could find a good doctor. Rosemary, honey, why don't you let me—"

But she'd not let him finish the sentence. He was going to offer to help her, and she didn't want to hear it, so she'd left the apartment and gone out on the street to take a walk. Like the subject of marriage, this subject was one which Johnny never brought up again.

She looked at the telephone and sighed. Then she called the casino/bar again. The bartender said he wasn't there. She hung up, but the doorbell rang. Johnny was there.

XX

"As soon as I heard the newscast about Kennedy's death, I had to come," he said. She remembered the way Johnny had spoken of sharing a sunset and felt he'd come to Berkeley because he needed to share the shock of his grief.

"Well, Jesus," he said as he stood up, twisted the end of his mustache, and looked out the window. "We're not the only ones who are holding a private wake. But we can't let ourselves wallow around in sorrow for the rest of our lives, either, which means we have to take the first steps toward getting ourselves back together again. Maybe we ought to eat."

"Would you mind letting me cook for us?" I realize I'm not a gourmet cook, but you can suffer through a steak and a salad."

"You look beat," he said as his eyes swept her from head to toe. "And you've lost weight. You're too thin. What have you been doing?"

She went to the kitchen and he followed her. He

took the steaks and prepared them for the broiler while she removed the green vegetables from the crisper for a salad. "I've been going crazy," she said solemnly. Anyone else would have paid little or no attention to an everyday statement that was made often but didn't usually mean what it said, but Johnny was a man who listened.

"What's the trouble, Rosemary?"

"I can't run away from it any longer, Johnny. The past, I mean."

He understood. "Tell me about it, baby."

From beginning to end, she told him, leaving out no incidents, sliding over no rough spots. When she finished, the steaks were done and the salad was made. As she seated herself across from him at the table, she said, "I'm afraid of it, but I know it's there and it's very, very real."

"It fits in with something I know about," he said as he trimmed away the fat from his steak. Then his blue eyes met hers and he said, "President Lincoln was killed in April of 1865. You were living in Virginia City, Nevada, at the time."

If he'd been anyone but Johnny, she'd have forced a laugh out of him.

"Your mother showed me a snapshot album and your baby book." he chuckled. "Then she told me about a stage you went through when you said you were Juliette. I didn't think anything of it at the time, and when she said you spoke French in your sleep, I sort of—well, doubted it."

She remembered a bottle of wine he'd brought the last time, and went to get it from the cabinet above the sink.

"Great," he said, looking at the bottle. Then he grinned. "Remember when you told me about your friend who saw a dude at an airport and did nutty things because she fell for him? We should have talked about it then, but you closed me out. Like you closed me out when I wanted to marry you. You're the kind of girl who lets a man know whether she wants to talk about something, or get married, or make love. I'm not a weakling—I don't care particularly to be dominated—but I don't like to push, either. All right?"

"All right." She'd never thought of him as weak.

"But I'm not going about this thing in chronological order." He shrugged. "Doesn't matter. Okay, you know my stepmother went to Reno for her divorce. I went along to sort of help her over the rough places. I care very much for Rita, you know. While we were there, I decided to look up your brother, Richard. He was out of town, but Joy and Rick were there, so we talked."

"I had forgotten that you knew them." They'd come to San Francisco when she was in her freshman year, and had dinner together at Fisherman's Wharf.

"Joy told me about you and the good doctor," he said.

"Joy has a big mouth."

"She was concerned about you, Rosemary."

"Forget I said that. But really, it was an idiotic thing for me to do. I guess I'm not too pleased with my stupid behavior." She was blushing.

"You're leaving me again, Rosemary. You're trying to talk about the incident as some kind of spur of the moment behavior instead of letting yourself listen to what I'm saying. A few seconds ago you said you can't run away from it any longer. Either you mean it, or you don't."

"All right. I mean it. After this morning, I know I must have help. A psychiatrist or a psychologist or . . . but you're going to help me, Johnny."

He reached across the table and took her hand. "I hope so," he said quietly. Then he said, "When I left your sister-in-law, I drove around for a while, then I went to Rita's hotel, and she wanted to go to Virginia City before I left. She flew out from Columbus. I drove up from Las Vegas and met her. It's strange the way things work out. She could just as well have gone to Las Vegas for her divorce, but she went to Reno instead, so I drove her to Virginia City, and there on the wall of a saloon I saw a full-length, oil portrait of a woman who looked so much like you that I stood there and stared at it for a good five minutes. It blew my mind. Rita was wandering in the saloon. We'd ordered a beer but there were so many interesting things to see. The saloon has numerous artifacts from the days when it was a booming silver mining town. Rita came and stood at my side. She'd seen your picture. And she said, "My God, Johnny! If she wore her hair in that particular style, that could be your girl friend."

"Who *was* the woman in the picture?" Rosemary asked.

"Her last name was Bernard, and she was a Virginia City prostitute during the Comstock days. Does the name *Julia Bernard* mean anything to you?

"No."

"How about the name *Tom Spencer?*"

"Means nothing."

"Tom Spencer was tall and dark and quick as a leopard. I went back, Rosemary. I went to Julia's grave. Didn't ask a soul where it was, but I knew where it was, and it's still there. She's a legend. Her grave is well kept, even today."

"How do you know what Tom Spencer looked like, Johnny?"

"There's a description of him in a little booklet I found in a museum. He loved her, Rosemary, and I kind of think she loved him, too."

"Do prostitutes love?"

"How the hell do I know? But I don't see why they wouldn't."

"What about the doctor? Doctor Greg Bennett?"

"Maybe he's the man who did her in. She was murdered. I went to see the picture of him, too, and I don't like the son of a bitch. Her murderer was John Millain. They hanged him, but the good and virtuous ladies of Virginia City did everything they could to keep him from the gallows. From their point of view, he deserved a medal."

"*John* Millain?" She smiled.

"John is a fairly common name," he said a little crossly. "You picked up on something pretty awful that night at the Peacock Feather restaurant. Maybe the fair Julia had a bad experience there when the place was a whorehouse."

"But nobody knows for sure that it was."

He looked triumphant. "But it was. I did a little research. It was owned by a beautiful Chinese woman named Sweet Bird of China, before Julia Bernard came to Virginia City." Let's go there. I'll show you."

"I'm afraid."

"Let's go anyway. Have you ever been there?"

"No, every time Richard and Joy planned to take me when I visited them, something came up to prevent it." She'd developed a bad headache once, she recalled with a start. Another time, she decided to leave early, which cancelled their plans. "I think maybe I—had a feeling I wouldn't like it. Johnny, was Julia Bernard married? I mean, was she ever married?"

"Not according to the little pamphlet. Why?"

"I just wondered."

"Let's go."

"All right," she said reluctantly.

"Throw some things into a suitcase and I'll do the dishes, love."

They left within a half hour. Most of the time they spoke of the tragedy that had struck the country. It wasn't until they were inside the room of the motel that Rosemary brought up the subject of Julia Bernard.

"You sure you want to go through with all this?" he asked.

She replied nervously. "Yep. I told the friendly taxi driver to stay out of the water if you can't swim. No wonder he thought I was wasted. Then I wanted to go back to the building with the boutique shops and the restaurant on the second floor because I wanted to face it. I *have* to face it, Johnny. If I don't, I'll spend the rest of my life wondering about it, and staying away from places that scare me just because of the sound of their names."

"You know, of course, we'll be put in a padded cell if we let anyone know what we're doing, what we're talking about."

She laughed, took his hand, and held it as she walked toward the saloon with him. "Let's hope we're locked in together.

He held the saloon door open for her and said in a barely audible voice that a different barkeep was on duty.

She sparkled as she looked around, took a seat at a table, and ordered wine. Then she gave him a blazingly beautiful smile and said, "You're Tom. I don't care if your hair is blond. You're Tom and you're my lover. At least you *were* Tom. And I love you."

"Jesus. You wait until a time like this to tell me you love me. How come?" His hands were shaking.

"Because I didn't know I did. I know where the painting is. As soon as the bartender brings the wine, let's go in the other room. You have to go down a step. Maybe two steps. And there I am, on the wall where—" She frowned, her tongue stumbling over a name she had a hard time with. "Ethan? No, not Ethan. Something like it, though. Evan. Evan Willoughby was the artist. He signed the painting in the bottom left-hand corner. Julia knew him well. And Sam Clemens. He was the editor of the *Territorial Enterprise*."

The bartender brought the wine and overheard her last few words. "The *Enterprise* is open if you want to go over. You can get a front page of the newspaper if you want it. Fifty cents, with a choice of headlines, you know? Like Mary Doe Wins Fifty Million At Craps." He added that they were welcome to look around. "We've got all sorts of relics from the silver-boom days."

Rosemary was even more excited, but not at all surprised when she went into the room where Julia's picture hung on the wall. It was just as she had expected it to be. She knew where Julia's house was, and wanted to go there. Johnny objected. He'd already been there, and in spite of her admirers' tendency to call it a palace, he said it was just a house.

They walked down the street after they left the bar. She stopped in front of the house where Julia Bernard once lived.

"No. I can't go in there!" She had a feeling that if she did, she would live through the moments of terror when Julia had fought for her life and lost. "Let's go somewhere else, Johnny."

He was relieved. "Where do you want to go?"

"Anywhere. Back to Berkeley. To Las Vegas. Reno."

"What about the handsome doctor. Do you want to see him?"

"No. Not now. He was Henri, my husband."

"But Julia was never married."

"Yes she was. Someday, Johnny, I want to see him, and talk to him. Maybe I'll fall in love with him. But if I do, you'll understand, won't you?"

"Yes, darling. I'll understand."

He put her in the car and closed the door. She was quiet for a long, long time. It wasn't until they were in Reno that she spoke again.

She vaguely remembered the thick notebook that was one of her mother's most prized possessions. "My mother has a loose-leaf notebook of our family history. The first entries were recorded by Vivian, who was allegedly my great-great-grandmother. Her daughter, Teresa, did considerable research, but she was never able to tie certain ancestors together. My mother brought the records up to date, but she's always been puzzled about an area in the past that can't be verified. It has to do with an Italian connection." She laughed. "Now I can understand why the Italian connection has never been proven. It didn't exist." She shrugged. "Oh, well . . . in order to save the family reputation, I'm sure a number of people have always tampered with records. But this insight into the past of mine is not something I'll mention to my mother. I've come to terms with my past; now we can live in the present."

The wedding invitations went out in May. Rosemary and John were married soon after.

SEND TO: BELMONT TOWER BOOKS
P.O. Box 270
Norwalk, Connecticut 06852

Please send me the following titles:

Quantity	Book Number	Price
_____	_____	_____
_____	_____	_____
_____	_____	_____
_____	_____	_____
_____	_____	_____

In the event we are out of stock on any of your selections, please list alternate titles below.

_____	_____	_____
_____	_____	_____
_____	_____	_____
_____	_____	_____

Postage/Handling _____

I enclose . . . . . . _____

FOR U.S. ORDERS, add 35¢ per book to cover cost of postage and handling. Buy five or more copies and we will pay for shipping. Sorry no C.O.D.'s.

FOR ORDERS SENT OUTSIDE THE U.S.A.
Add $1.00 for the first book and 25¢ for each additional book. PAY BY foreign draft or money order drawn on a U.S. bank, payable in U.S. ($) dollars.

☐ Please send me a free catalog.

NAME_____
(Please print)

ADDRESS_____

CITY _____ STATE _____ ZIP _____
Allow Four Weeks for Delivery